The Lesbian Cow and other stories

Indu Menon

Translated from the Malayalam by
Nandakumar K.

eka

eka

First published in English as *The Lesbian Cow and Other Stories* in 2021 by Eka, an imprint of Westland Publications Private Limited

Published in 2023 by Eka, an imprint of Westland Books, a division of Nasadiya Technologies Private Limited

No. 269/2B, First Floor, 'Irai Arul', Vimalraj Street, Nethaji Nagar, Allappakkam Main Road, Maduravoyal, Chennai 600095

ISBN: 9789395767972

10 9 8 7 6 5 4 3 2 1

This is a work of fiction. Names, characters, organisations, places, events and incidents are either products of the author's imagination or used fictitiously.

Typeset by Jojy Philip, New Delhi 110 015

Printed at Nutech Print Services - India, Faridabad

The Lesbian Cow

Indu Menon, hailed as one of the Best Young Writers by *India Today* in 2015, works as a Lecturer in Anthropology/Sociology at the Kerala Institute for Research Training and Development Studies of SCs and STs (KIRTADS) in Kozhikode. She is the author of six short story collections, a memoir, a book of poems and two novels in Malayalam, all bestsellers. Winner of over ten awards, including the Kendra Sahitya Akademi Award for young writers, she has also co-written screenplays with her husband, Rupesh Paul. She holds a doctorate in Sociology and is currently doing a PhD in shamanic discourses of the tribes of Kerala.

Nandakumar K. started his career as a sub-editor at *Financial Express*, after obtaining a master's degree in Economics. Following a career in international marketing and general management, which has taken him to about fifty countries in the world, he now works for a shipping line in Dubai. He is an empanelled copy editor with Indian publishers and IIM Ahmedabad. He has co-translated from the Malayalam M. Mukundan's novel *Delhi: A Soliloquy*, the autobiography of Prof T.J. Joseph (*A Thousand Cuts*, to be published in late 2021); and has retold a selection of stories from *Kathasaritsagara* in English (due in 2021). Nandakumar is the grandson of Mahakavi Vallathol Narayana Menon.

Contents

RETRIBUTION AS REDEMPTION

Nandakumar K.

Indu Menon's stories are not for the fainthearted. At the centre of all the blood, gore and broken bones lies the inveterate, indomitable spirit of wronged women, who refuse to go down without a fight. In Indu's stories, the preservers and cohorts of patriarchy or garden-variety chauvinism and abusive or philandering partners get their comeuppance in myriad ways. Her stories live unabashed, unvarnished life truths. With the imagination of a poet, in lyrical and inventive prose, her narratives startle the reader by refusing to draw the line between lived and imagined terrains; the reader can seldom make out where lived-life ends and imagination takes over and vice versa.

Many consider Indu Menon a successor to Kamala Das—having inherited the same insouciance and open, liberal, progressive outlook; the same acknowledgement that sex isn't only what happens between sheets in darkened rooms, to be spoken of in hushed tones, if at all; the same jousting at patriarchy; the same identification with aggrieved women and their unfulfilled desires. But where she parts ways is how—perhaps in keeping with a bolder social milieu than Kamala Das lived in—she uses raw images, bolder language that verges on the shocking, and the way an avenging spirit in her characters are developed to let no one have an easy pass—neither the perpetrators nor the reader who wants to stay disengaged but gets pulled into the vortex eventually, kicking and screaming. Sex in her works is dirty enough, as it should be, and full of passion; they are no more genteel, missionary acts done with eyes tightly shut. Sex is sometimes tender and caring and at other times a device of mind-numbing domination.

Indu writes with empathy and compassion about the marginalised, subaltern sections of the society. She writes about their stark, unleavened lives visited by gratuitous violence and oppression, that make them lash out with all their—often insufficient—might, despite their paternal and protective nature.

The brutes and angels of death in her stories use more refined ways to inflict mayhem, both physical and emotional. Only to be taken on by women who trump over them in the end. Her stories tread paths that no Malayali author, and perhaps no Indian woman author, has ever ventured into. Her female protagonists have survived horrifying adversities in Vietnam; escaped from eye-watering brutality in Sri Lanka; silently suffered the depredations of their men, for long, before getting even. Her women know that no avenging angel will be there for them, nor any fairy godmothers. They can only rely on themselves.

Indu hit the Malayalam short story scene (she has written only two novels so far) with great panache and attracted wide readership among the young, who were themselves chafing under the hypocrisy of the patriarchal and restrictive, social mores. The title of her first collection itself was a shocker (*The Lesbian Cow*) that announced the arrival of a fresh, bold voice, giving vent to the aspirations for a freer society and lesser moralising.

Her stories provide an unmatched appeal, with their young, rebellious, honest, and raw expression of desire, seeking validation wrought through a unique imagination allowed to run riot through our staid and placidly pretentious lives. Their reach moves beyond the domestic and into larger issues of gender politics and rights of the individual.

I started the translation of these stories in early 2016. I was taken in by their 'terrible beauty'; I have striven to reproduce her style and verve as much as a translation permits, without any attempt at transcreation.

I am happy that Eka/Westland have decided to bring this brilliantly talented young author to the non-Malayali audience. I would like to record my gratitude to Dr Fathima E.V. for recommending me to Indu, and to Indu,who declared that, if her stories are to be published in English, then the translator would be me and no one else. No compromises, as in her stories!

I am fortunate to have Minakshi Thakur as my editor who has polished my prose, wielded the scalpel on my prolixity, and instinctively caught my errors. A big thank you!

The Creature

1. The Hunt

It wasn't a human being—its entire body was covered in dark hair, like that of a bear or an ape. A strange creature. A wild animal.

The hair on its head was curly, matted with mud and blood, and in a tangle. The lips, reddened like crushed guava, were bloodied and swollen. The right eye's edge was bloodshot from a kick it had received; the light had gone out of it. The left eyelid was half closed from the clotted blood and excessive swelling in the rheum-filled veins. The nose was a bloodied tomato, resembling an old-style circus clown's red bulbous prop. Two incisors had already been knocked out by the first punch. Its laboured breathing made the molars sway like drunks. The thick blood spread on either side of its cheeks gave it the appearance of Nagoba Devi, propitiated by blood offerings. Like a creature partially evolved, it continued to moan even in a semi-conscious state.

'Shut up, you mongrel! Don't whine!'

Amorinderjeet swung his booted leg and landed a kick on its navel. Motilal, Parekh and Nana cheered their boss on. The horseshoe-shaped metal piece on the heel of

Amorinderjeet's shoe made an imprint on the flesh around the navel.

Scratching his ass, Rattan shouted, 'Shut up, shut the fuck up!'

That was enough to stop the creature's cry abruptly while on its way to becoming a shriek.

'Boss, is this a human being or an ape?' Rattan spoke in Hindi, striking the creature's face with his foot.

'This is a human being … an ape-man, or a man-ape,' Nana said, as he tore off a ganja-blended lick of tobacco stored in a khaini packet and slipped it into his mouth.

Rattan's eyes narrowed with greedy anticipation. Motilal laughed uproariously.

'Who *is* this guy?' Crawling on his knees, Rattan approached the creature. He dipped his head towards its near naked body. 'It's like dark hardwood!' Rattan sat down, inhaling deeply the smell that the body of the creature was exuding.

'Oh, incredible … the intoxicating smell of wild wood!'

'Hey, Rattan, leave him alone,' his boss warned him in a threatening voice, indicating to him with his eyes to move away.

'Rattan, it cannot happen in here. We men can't stand it …'

Rattan let out a primal growl, like a famished wolf.

'Shameful, you worthless fellow … keep quiet. Like a bitch on heat … horrible!' The boss averted his face in revulsion.

Leering and running his tongue over his lips, Rattan sat down in one corner. He was the only queer in the gang. And a thug among homosexuals.

Rattan had arrived from Odisha in Mumbai as a thirteen-year-old. He had been contracted to make bhelpuri on an annual salary of fifteen thousand rupees. He, like his mother, dished up very tasty food. When his finger touched the bhel, it throbbed as if touched by a female finger. The puris ballooned as if they had smelt a feminine odour. The crowds queued up in front of his vending cart.

Many of the customers latched on to his weaknesses. Blushing like a coy lady was the simplest and most obvious of those. In the sultry air of March and the vending cart's lantern light, he looked bashful; even the bell of the paan-seller's cart set off a blush. The sight of the bronzed muscles of the Marwari youth slavering for his bhel, and even the unintended brushing of fingers as the pleasantly warm bhel dish was handed over, were enough for him to dissolve in a bout of effeminate shyness.

Rattan's effeminateness was not confined to his mind. Within his muscled, masculine and energetic body, a girl giggled, her bangles tinkled … Squeezing her hand through the narrow chink in Rattan's soul, she beseeched, 'Give me that tulsi flower, give it to me …'

It was the Punjabi drug peddler Gurbeer—lifting Rattan onto his shoulders saying, 'O, my tulsi'—who liberated the intense, loving man inside Rattan for the first time. Rattan, overcome by a feminine anxiety and surprise, lay there gazing into the marble-like eyes of Gurbeer through his own half-closed eyes, brimming with the love of a lifetime. His heart became weightless like the seed of a fireweed; it soared into the sky. Love rendered his hair follicles into tiny lotus buds. Inside a tiny room in the alley, in the blue light created by an atmosphere of torrid love, Rattan discovered himself for the first time. The thought that he needed another man's body to bring out and feel the pleasure resident inside him made him smile shyly.

'Who is this, boss, who is this animal?' Nana wrapped the potent and warm cannabis granules in the tobacco and rolled a joint. He set it alight with great deliberation. A mouthful of the cannabis smoke made him close his eyes.

'Huh?' Amorinderjeet was peering at the new photograph that had appeared in his smartphone. 'This is Big Bro's goods. He told me a guy would be coming. A dangerous guy.'

'Holy shit, is this that guy?' Nana laughed aloud. With each of his guffaws, the smoke escaped from his mouth in whorls and dissolved in the air. The room filled up with the sweet smell of cannabis.

'Nana,' Amorinderjeet said, scratching his head. 'Big Bro had said that thirty guys will be coming in the truck … *Sheesh*! I had a lot of expectations …' As the message's erotic part got truncated, the boss slapped the mobile phone on his thigh in frustration. 'I had expected a crack team like in *Sholay*. I had thought they would pop like the corn of Bastar. And here we have only wailing and whining. Fucking dog, son of a whore!' Amorinderjeet kicked the prostrate form again, unable to contain his anger.

'Tell me, you mongrel, who are you?'

'I … I … I …' *Plop*. He vomited blood from the severity of the kick, and lost consciousness.

'Huh, looks like this piece of shit is dead.' Lost in cannabis's hazy mists, Nana probed with his leg.

'Parekh, fetch some water. Who is this, Nana?' asked Amorinderjeet.

'Him?' Nana started to laugh uncontrollably. His bloodshot eyes kept blinking.

'This is not a human being. This is a monkey …' he chortled. Nana could not control his mirth. His cheeks felt fatigued from the laughing, and tears streamed down from his eyes.

'Ho-ho … he's not fully formed. His life is standing dumbstruck between human and animal on the evolutionary path. Ha-ha-ha …'

Parekh taunted him, 'Don't unload your old Naxal claptrap here, Nana.'

'There is no water, boss. What should I do?' Motilal asked.

'There must be some in the room inside. Go and fetch it.'

Holding a cut-off mineral water bottle upside down, Motilal went straight into the toilet in the inner room. Using one hand to pinch his nose, he opened the lid of the commode with the other. A swarm of flies rose from within with a *whoosh* sound. Without flinching, he dipped the bottle and scooped up the yellow, shit-laced water.

'Is this enough, boss?'

'Oh, it stinks like hell. If that is all there is, use it. Splash it on his face.' Amorinderjeet was wiggling his pinkie inside his nostril.

'*Gvaaa … hvaaa …*' Gagging, the body on the floor sprung up with a loud retch. Though it had been moaning from the time it was bundled into the sack, it was a low whine in a semi-conscious state. The creature now started to shriek in terror seeing the strangers around.

'Damn … shut up! Shove something into its mouth.'

As if he was waiting for such an order, Rattan leapt up from the corner. He unzipped, pulled down his trousers and removed his underpants. As the creature stood bewildered by Rattan's nakedness, Rattan shoved the underpants into its mouth. When it tried to shake him off, Rattan was furious.

'Stand still, you prick.' Rattan caught hold of its testicles and started to squeeze them.

'Rattan, leave it be … it'll die … Don't be an ass. Leave him.' Nana tried to stop Rattan. Rattan continued to squeeze its genitals with a malicious delight.

Someone was heard knocking on the door. Then, the doorbell rang.

2. Porn Flick

'Bhaisaab!' Boss jumped up from his seat. His mien showed deference and servility.

Big Bro was standing outside. A tall, lanky guy. Smooth pate which glistened like glass. His clean-shaven face betrayed a eunuch's indeterminate sexuality. His teeth were long like a wolf's, but paan-stained and had lost their sheen. Since he was suffering from hyperhidrosis, his clothes had maps sketched in dried salt on them from excessive sweating. The armpits of the jacket held bundled in his hand had apple-shaped damp patches. His protruding belly reminded one of a well-rounded pot.

'Oh yes, Bashundhara, come, come, come in.' A seventeen-year-old girl with a brownish complexion stepped into the house. If one did not account for her inordinately long tresses and full breasts, her face was innocent like a doll's. A mole shining on her left cheek added to the effect, enhancing her childlike looks. Her eyes were wide and dark, like the flowers of the wood apple tree. Her lips had a melancholic reddish hue.

'How are you doing, Parekh?' Big Bro lowered himself weightily onto the old sofa. On his cheeks, ruddy and distended from beer consumption, black zits shone like tiny sweat-filled pits.

'Where is he?'

'Inside.'

'How's he?'

'We have given him some tough love, Big Bro.'

'Hey, Amor … is he still alive?'

Amorinderjeet bowed his head, chastened.

'I have merely caressed him, Big Bro.'

'Okay, okay, I will directly come to the point. I want to shoot a movie. Can you do it, Amor?'

'Big Bro!' Amorinderjeet's lips trembled with gratitude. His eyes lit up.

Amorinderjeet Gupta was the youngest child in a middle-class family. One who ran away from home, mad after the movies.

'Big Bro, haven't I told you? I studied at the Film Institute. Just tell me—what kind of movie do you want?'

'A somewhat different film.'

'You mean an art film?'

'No art and other fucks. A porn movie. To begin with, you shoot a porn film. Then we can move on to other films.'

Amorinder's face fell. Seeing that, Parekh and Motilal winked at each other.

'There, she is the lead actress, Bashundhara. And that guy there—that's your hero. It should look like an original, as if it has been shot in a hotel room or someplace like that, using a hidden camera.'

Big Bro's face appeared to be burning with hatred. He was the CEO of a corporate giant—one which had bought adivasi land in Bastar for mining.

'This … this fucking dog has spoiled everything. And now, he was going to testify against me in the Supreme Court. Cunt!'

'Oh yeah? He is *that* guy?'

'Wild dogs! What do they need land for? I was ready to pay millions. Still, these guys didn't want any. Fuck them! He set out with a group of Gond tribals. With the press and some RTI activists ready to lick his ass …' Big Bro undid the top button of his sweat-drenched shirt. 'If this clip appears to be an original, I am saved. I will scatter thousands of copies of the flick. To the press … to the courts … Oh yeah, he will stink like shit. I will ensure he does. Watch me!'

3. Room No. 106, Queen's Palace Lodge

It didn't take them long to make the arrangements. White bed sheets normally seen in hotels. Pure white pillow covers. A half-empty mineral water bottle. When the blue-tinted made-in-China bulb was switched on, light descended and lay upon the bed invitingly. Bathed in an attractive blue, the whole room had the semblance of a very romantic first night setting. An old basket of plastic flowers stood in one corner with a patina of dust on it. The dark tones of the room made the fake flowers look more beautiful than real ones.

They dragged the naked creature onto that bed.

'Why the fuck is the hero drooping like this? Keep him upright, let me plan a super opening shot,' Amorinder played gently with the digital dials and buttons of the Panasonic P2 camera.

'Boss, he cannot sit upright. I had given him the *treatment,* hadn't I?' Parekh confessed shamefacedly.

'Why the fuck are you mucking about? What did you do?'

'I had hit him in the chest. I suspect he's broken some ribs.'

'Oh!' Amorinder shifted the camera and looked at Parekh. Parekh was a butcher in an abattoir near the Delhi Masjid. One who, ever immersed in the warm smell and the scarlet stickiness of blood and gore, used to kill and consume animals. In his free time, he used to hold kid goats on his lap and, clasping a pair of legs in each hand, twist and break their backs. The spine would be heard cracking with a *tuk* sound. That sickening sound, the loud plaintive, pain-filled bleating of the dying kids, and their writhing in their death throes thrilled and energised him. He thought it was fun.

'Damn! Is this a kid goat to have fun with by breaking its spine … Will he die?'

'I can guarantee you two hours, boss. I have broken three lower ribs on the left side; it's a trifle. He won't die. Let your movie get over. We should then capture breaking his spine too.'

'Bashundhara, come here. You have changed your costume, haven't you?' Bashundhara stood playing with her dress, showing reluctance.

The artificial light in the room had turned her skin tone a pale yellow, the colour of a maturing wheat field. Her long tresses lay like soft silk over her ample breasts.

'I can't do all this. You didn't tell me at the beginning,' she spoke sharply.

'You bitch …' Amorinderjeet jumped up, caught her by her hair, and pushed her roughly onto the bed.

'Lie down there and do what I tell you!' He returned to his spot behind the camera and zoomed in on her.

'Action!'

Motilal switched on a cheap video light; Parekh used a thermocol sheet to reflect that light onto Bashundhara's body. The initial disorientation over, Bashundhara squatted over the creature.

'Let the actress start the action. It needn't be a typical Indian style one.' Amorinderjeet declared that he was planning a grand opening shot with a kissing scene like in foreign movies, with the actress hovering over the actor.

'You should lower yourself over him tenderly, like falling coral jasmine flowers,' the director in Amorinder was bubbling over.

'*Gvaaa* …' Bashundhara retched. 'What's this? Stinks like shit!'

'He will stink, you slut. He had shit for breakfast today,' Rattan guffawed.

'Don't mind all this. You lie with even lepers if you get money. What the heck, then? I will give you an extra five hundred for this scene. Enough?' Amorinder rolled his eyes at her.

Nana emerged from the white mists of the cannabis fumes like a zombie. His lips were trembling in an unprovoked fury.

'You bitch, every day you walk out of here with our money after spreading your legs and having fun. At least today you earn the money, work for it.'

Bashundhara's face blanched and twisted with shame.

'Hell, look at her attitude, and her put-on chastity,' Motilal chose ridicule.

'Enough … that's enough, take off your dress. We'll sizzle up things now.'

With an agonised shriek echoing inside her, Bashundhara undid the hooks of her dress.

'The legs, too.' Amorinder set the camera at a low angle.

'Boss, why is her bra like this?' Parekh was staring at her chest.

'Damn! If the virgin appears in the frame wearing a nursing bra, the viewers will catcall me.' Amorinder smacked his own forehead.

'Take it off, you …'

As Motital rushed to her and touched her breast, Bashundhara glared at him like a nursing tigress. 'Get yours hands off me!'

Her face was flushed with anger and indignation; it took on the colour of the red banana. The next moment, she undid the buckle and took off the bra. When her hand touched the dampness of her breast milk on the bra, she was reminded of the tender, unsoiled feet of her two-and-a-half-month-old baby girl. The baby who smelled of her womb, of her breast milk and cheap baby powder. The breastmilk-like smell of the bra brought tears to her eyes.

'Wow, what a fucking figure she has …' Parekh's eyes pawed her beautiful curves and her glowing skin.

'She is toned despite having had a baby. What a piece!'

'Let's finish up here … then we'll give her first to you. Hey you, Bashundhara, hug him nicely … yeah, yeah … that way, in a clinch … hard … let him wake up.'

Bashundhara pressed lightly on the body of the creature. It lay there, cold like a corpse.

'Is this man dead?' Bashundhara kept her finger under his nose.

'It's Parekh's mischief. He broke the creature's ribs. Once the spine is broken, even the mightiest is a mere corpse.' Nana was swaying gently where he stood, like the tender leaf of a marijuana plant in a breeze. Feeling weightless, he stretched his arms to balance himself, like a fireweed seed spreading its pappus.

'This Parekh should have been a cop,' Nana simpered.

'Oh, get up, sir, get up.' Bashundhara slapped the creature lightly on its cheek.

'What the hell is this!' She was losing patience. 'Do one thing. You all leave the room. I will shoot this movie for you. Just switch on the camera and leave it on the table. He may wake up after half an hour.'

'Shut the fuck up,' Rattan screamed at her. 'Are you overruling the director? Shut up and do what you're told.'

'It's all right, Rattan. Spare her. What she said is the proper thing to do. Let's give her half an hour. You know what she's capable of.' Amorinder pulled the teapoy over and placed the camera atop the TV placed on it. 'A porn flick has only one angle. We needlessly …' Amorinder grimaced in self-deprecation and left the room.

4. Double-headed serpent

In her own lifetime, Bashundhara hadn't seen anyone so fatigued. If he wasn't naked, she would have assumed he was a wild animal or a black creature from the Ape family. If he lay motionless for so long in the proximity of a naked, nubile girl like her, there must be something seriously wrong with him.

'Oye …' She opened the small pouch inside her hand bag. 'Get up, come on, get up.'

She took out a long, slim cigarette and lit it.

'Arrey ji …' She kneeled beside him and blew smoke into his face. Bending over mischievously, she rubbed her nose on his own. He only shifted and moaned a little.

'I shall have to give him a bath.' Bashundhara dragged him by his feet to the bathroom. 'So damn heavy!' Cursing him, she turned on the shower. Rust-coloured water rushed out in a spray. Terrorised, he managed to pry open his eyes.

'Are you satisfied?' Bashundhara dragged him over the mosaic floor back into the room.

'If we finish the work quickly, we can split early … Out there, I charge by the hour, you know that?' She tapped the ash off the cigarette with the tip of her index finger. 'Look here, buddy, try to do their bidding without getting knocked around. Don't you know this much?' She hid half her face, as if she were self-conscious. 'I am capable of doing everything. If you can't do it yourself, let me know. I'll take over.'

With a surprising litheness, Bashundhara bounded and landed on top of him. He broke down the next moment and started crying uncontrollably.

'Please leave me, behen. For God's sake, have mercy, please leave me alone.' He begged with folded hands, calling her 'sister'.

'Hell! What now?' Bashundhara climbed off him and started to light another cigarette.

'Mother … Ma … My mother …'

'Ma, ma … who's this mother of yours? Who will come? No mother is going to come.' Furious, she looked at him. 'He's wailing without doing his work—animal!'

'Ma, Nagoba …'

'Nagoba?' Startled, Bashundhara dropped the cigarette. 'Nagoba?'

She went up to him and peered into his face.

'Are you a Gond?' Her voice trembled.

Yes, he nodded.

'Are you from Bastar?'

'Yes.'

'Are you a Maoist?'

'No.'

'My God! How did you end up in the hands of these evil men? Who are you? What is your name?' Bashundhara felt as if she was choking. Countless questions leaped around on her tongue.

'Bannuram Bhed.'

'God … Oh my God,' Bashundhara wanted to scream out.

'Bannuram? Bannuram of Inderveli Mandal?'

Yes, he nodded again.

Bashundhara felt like crying.

The image of narrow ridges resembling a green vine snake twisting through fields of bountiful soya and corn swaying in the wind … the dark Bannuram running along the ridges … in his hand, a spinning fan made from the fronds of palmyra palm …

Bannuram, who used to run around and cavort at the southern edge of the shrine of Nagoba …

Sounds of the mini drums … The Serpent Goddess, propitiated by her worshipful serpents and in rapturous repose to the accompaniment of the pipes … Gonds and Murias with ash-smeared torsos and peacock feather crowns performing the Gusadi dance during the festival in Kheslapur …

'My village …' Bashundhara sobbed.

The khot tribal shops of Inderveli Mandal. Bannuram wearing a turban on his head. As the dance steps quicken, the ring worn on his ear comes loose. The tempo of the drums increases. Ten-year-old Bashundhara … When she plays the pipe, the peacocks dance ... They spread their wings and tail feathers like fans and prance around.

'Bannu ... do you remember? Bannu, look at me! I am Bashundhara.'

She knelt beside him, like a forlorn penitent. 'You?!' Bannuram rubbed his eyes in disbelief. 'No!' The fifteen-year-old Bashundhara on whom he had laid eyes for the last time on the night the Gondi river was in spate.

'No, it can't be you.' He turned away in great turmoil. The cool breeze of January from the Satpura range rustled her loose green dhoti. A chungidi dupatta glided over it like a soaring kite. A wild forest honey-coloured topaz sparkled on her copper nose ring. The golden mermaid who didn't know how to swim had slipped off the rock into the rushing waters.

'Bannu ...' she was shrieking.

The churning, muddy waters were carrying her away.

'No ...' he screamed through his clenched teeth. 'She is dead. Perished and gone. She left for the akashmandir of Nagobadevi.'

'No, Bannu, it really is me. Your Bashundhara. I am not dead, Bannu. They ran ahead and saved me.' Bashundhara broke down. 'The mining company's men.' She was trembling like a sheaf of wheat stalks caught in the rain.

'I would have been better off if I had drowned,' her voice quavered. 'My family, my clan, they have been shamed and stigmatised because of me ...'

'*Aaah* ...' As Bannuram moved, the wound on his chest started bleeding.

'Bannu, how did you land up in Delhi? How did these guys ...?'

'I came to appear in court, Bashundhara. To give witness against the mining company. My God ...' he broke down.

'Please don't cry, Bannu,' Bashundhara sat down near him. She wretchedly ran her fingers over his bloodied torso in anguish.

Her lips, like a magical healing stone, acted like poultice on his wounds. Her long tresses, resembling strong vines and infused with the aroma of Nagobadevi's benediction as well as that of Bastar's soil, flowed down and spread over his body. They sang the 'song of sowing' of the Murias in their wailing voices. The sounds of the dholaks and ankle bells filled the room.

Nagoba has arrived astride the tigress at the foreground of the shrine. The tigress is pawing the ground, its claws digging into the soil. It lets out a deep roar, proud that it is the deity's vehicle. The breeze suffused with toasted corn's and soya flowers' fragrance is blowing. Nagoba's waist-belt tinkles as she laughs. Turmeric powder and saffron have rendered her swollen incarnadine breasts ruddier. Will the spatter from the sowing season's rain wet the deity's jamun nipples? The double-headed serpent is spreading its hoods. The hoods loom over Nagoba as canopies.

5. Deity of the Clan

You, the presiding deity
of another clan
A forest maiden who blooms

in mist, rain, and sunshine;
The family deity of
blood and fire
And the crystal necklace of tears.
One who has donned the holy anklets of laughter.[1]

Even when the action on the screen was over, Amorinder could not rid himself of the consternation he was feeling inside. The blue he saw in Bashundhara's eyes had by now covered him like a death shroud—as if the blue fog coming down the Satpura mountains had suddenly enveloped and tautened over his body. Her every glance ... like fingers caressing every single pore of his skin.

An experience of a lifetime: the shock of seeing for the first time, a man and woman engaged in lovemaking so pristine and unaffected. The digital screen of the TV encompassed the radiance of a whole universe. He was shaken by the sight of love transforming lust into something pure and holy as a hymn. The holiness of the lips on which the hymns were muttered put him in an agony, which a gang boss like him should never ever undergo. He had slept with Bashundhara countless times prior to this day; but today, he stood transfixed, looking avariciously at the sight of love wiping the look of a sinner off her face, which was a constant whenever she was with him.

It was a strange sight. Like the blooming of bright flowers among the dark leaves on the branch of an ominous, wild tree in springtime. A strong and enchantingly fragrant breeze

---

[1] *Hambirighatile Chilangkakal* (*Ankle bells of Hambirighat*), by K. Jayakumar.

was blowing, while two serpents lay on the silky green bed at the tips of the leaves. Why are they coiling and uncoiling in such frenzy? Why? Why are they lunging at each other with their hoods raised and biting with such passion? Why do they embrace till their bones begin to crack?

'Fuck me!' Rattan screamed, looking at the screen.

'Super.' With his eyes bulging, Motilal stood staring at the screen, having forgotten to blink. Nana and Parekh stood in shock, aflame and tumescent, as if struck by meteorites. They had never seen a porn flick like this one before. They would never see one like it thereafter. They were amazed by the strange chemistry of this man and woman.

6. The Hero who underwent Penectomy

Bashundhara sat back on the sofa, smoking a cigarette. Her face had lit up. A golden-hued shyness, seen normally only on the faces of new brides, made her cheeks radiant. On the verge of spilling over, the red-hot eroticism on her lips sizzled with each inhalation.

Amorinder was sitting on the floor at her feet, his legs tucked under him, with the servility and timidity of a street dog. Unbridled lust and amorousness had transformed him into another man, albeit temporarily. Like a hopeless lover, he kept kissing her dainty feet.

'Bashundhara, just once, only once ...'

The alluring feet of Bashundhara. Those shapely soles, fashioned by the red earth of Bastar; the tiny, pink toes that reminded one of the summertime red dates hanging from the palms on the ridges of the corn fields.

'Once … like I saw on the monitor … just once,' he grovelled.

He lovingly gathered both her legs in his hands. They were like tender lotus buds. He pressed his face on them. Their softness, their coolness, their fragrance of wild flowers and the pleasurable pulsation of blood flowing through them made him break out in goose pimples.

With the bewilderment and anxiety of a lover touching his beloved for the first time, Amorinder kissed probingly her rose apple-like navel. Amorinder felt as if this minor girl, with her diamond eyes and pearly teeth, was blooming in front of him, spreading her heady scent. As she touched him, he could feel the pale blue poison of love spreading inside him. His fingers were sliding over her sweaty skin.

'Bashundhara,' he panted with passion, looking into her eyes.

'How many girls have you destroyed, Amorinder?' There was a bluish glow in Bashundhara's eyes. 'A hundred? A thousand? Ha-ha-ha,' she laughed wildly. The next moment, with the skill only a prostitute can command, she tightened her internal muscles. Amorinder felt as if a giant crab had caught his penis in its claws and was choking it. He shrieked in pain. He pulled away from her in panic and ran off, still screaming. Blood was dripping from the sliced penis stub.

Bashundhara let out an evil laugh and squatted. She inserted two fingers inside her vagina and extricated two halves of a safety razor blade, which she had placed within her muscles like the shears of a scissor. The bloodied edges of the halves shone with an alluring sharpness.

The earth shook under the weak dance steps of the Gonds and Murias; the red soil floated up.

The hacked penis' blood dripped from the two halves of the blade onto Bashundhara's fingers, and thence to the floor, like Nagoba's scarlet vermillion bindi. In the bloodbath, the room appeared to have turned increasingly lurid. The hacked male penis, a propitiatory offering to Nagoba, wiggled for a brief time like a billion-year-old primordial snake and sank to the bottom of the water closet.

7. Waterborne/Alcohol-filled

Nana was the one who had rescued Bashundhara from the torrents of the Gondi river. The red soil of Bastar, which smelled of iron, mixed with the waters of the great river, and surged like monsoon's blood in the cloudburst-induced landslide. Bashundhara was like a log in the clutches of the river. A wild teak log, completely soaked and decaying. She was being carried away swiftly like a corpse by the current.

'That's a girl,' Nana said, and jumped into the water. He had come to Bastar to deal with the adivasis who were raising slogans against the mining company.

Those on the shore teased him, 'Greedy pig! Nana, you will drown.'

He got a grip on the corn-coloured skirt and the muddy, bronze-coloured hair. Challenging the big waves of the Gondi river, with great effort he swam like a giant river fish and hauled her to the shore. In her semi-conscious state, she was shivering with chills.

'This is mine,' Bashundhara heard Nana's voice. 'Mine alone.'

'Did you bait and catch it, Nana?'

'Whatever you may say. Whether she is alive or dead, it's me first.' As she heard him unzip his jeans, Bashundhara trembled.

'This one's a kitten.' Nana opened his palm and touched her stomach. Bloated with the water she had swallowed, it was bulging like an earthen pot. Her navel resembled a small cap on top. He ripped her pyjamas with a knife. Then, pressing both his palms on her stomach, he started to pump the water out.

'Is she at least ten, man?'

'Looking at the size of her breasts, she looks like fourteen.'

'See if she is alive. I am not into necrophilia,' Amorinderjeet spoke up. 'Even if she's not alive, I want her. Nana, resuscitate her.' Alcohol was slurring his words.

Nana's dark, dead lips, smelling of cannabis, breathed life into her. How succulent the lips of Bashundhara, lying inert like a wild fruit of unknown provenance! A mouthful of life's breath out of the narcotic-laced air from Nana's lungs was blown into hers.

A fifteen-year-old girl. A gamine body, redolent with the smell of earth, having been sanctified by myriad forest streams, rain-filled muddy canals and fresh springs bursting forth from aquifers under the iron ore-laden red soil. A little girl's body, which had not yet matured into even a half-woman.

The memories made Bashundhara retch again. His senses addled by the cannabis, Nana lay supine in the room, laughing vacuously. Soon he started to snore like a snorting bull. She used her shawl to tie up his hands and legs. Using the sharp heels of her shoes, she kicked viciously at his face. His lips cut open and became tattered like rags. His face was washed in blood, and his yellowed teeth were exposed. Even in his drug-induced stupor, he cried out and squirmed in agony.

'What the hell did you think, you dog?' She spat on his face. This wasn't mere revenge for raping her while she lay semi-conscious. She wanted to tear apart his body. She took off her shoe and beat his face repeatedly. Then she opened a brandy bottle. She sunk her knee into Nana's throat, clamped his mouth with one hand, and poured the brandy through his nostrils. His lungs filled with alcohol.

8. Silencer, 2 kg

A rusted, muddied iron silencer. Its weight, a mere two kilos. It reminded her of the loudspeaker of an old gramophone or a bugle. She stood behind the door, surreptitiously, like a paramour. Motilal entered after taking a pee. *Wham* ... a heavy swing with lots of follow-through ... Can two kilos crush the skull? What's on his face? What's that scattered with the blood—the pristine white chhota halkusa flowers? Could it be *that*? The grains that cannot be eaten—grains of a smashed brain.

She laughed heartily and whispered, 'Brain-dead!' With a beatific smile, Bashundhara threw away the silencer.

9. Screwdriver

Bashundhara had planned a hole each as gifts for Rattan and Parekh. On so many nights they had penetrated her, sometimes flinging a hundred rupee note at her and sometimes, not. Deeper than any screwdriver can go.

She sited the hole on the small bump behind the left ear for Parekh and for Rattan on the index finger-thick artery on the right side of the neck. The quantity of blood was little—only as much a broken hymen would have served up. How can the tresses be anointed with such a meagre amount? She had to let go of her desire unfulfilled.

10. Arise, the Forest Deity tattooed on the Bhil's Arm[2]

The creature lay in a foetal position in the room. Nagoba—his family deity and serpent goddess—revealed herself to him in this room, even though she hadn't turned up for the harvest festivals of Bastar, or during the designated days of propitiations and worship, or when the mining company had slaughtered the people of Bastar.

'Ma … Mother …' he cried out with folded hands.

She is the Raktadurga, bearing the Satpura mountains' tempest in her blood-bathed tresses. Blood stains on her red tongue and cheeks, resembling the scarlet beams of the setting sun. Lightning bolts streak from her piercing, diamond-bright eyes. In the blood that flows from her

---

[2] *Oru Maddhyenthan Vilapam* (A Central India Lament from *Ente Priya Kavikalkku Nandi*), Sachidanandan. These two poems were the inspiration for this story.

lips—the roiling reddish waters of the Gondi river. Human flesh between her teeth and under her nails.

'My Mother … Ma … Save me. Please save me and my clan, my Ma.'

With a heart rending cry, he fell at Bashundhara's feet in full prostration.

He saw Nagoba getting out into the street, bearing the short sword still dripping with blood. He also saw a thousand peacock dancers in array for the Gusadi dance, and sensed the tinkling of their ankle bells. He dreamt of the ranks of the mining company's earth-movers frozen in their tracks, their giant excavators falling silent, their transportation trucks, which used to raise dust from the red tracks, standing parked, and Nagoba, tattooed on the chests of Gonds and Murias of Inderveli Mandal, waking up and throwing down corn seeds onto the mined earth's red torso.

Chaklian

The smell of slaughter hung heavy in the air in the Chaklians' street. The red hide strips hung on the lines bled afresh with the rain falling on them. The wind smashed its face against these cowhide strips, turning them into the matted locks of a deranged woman. The blood-soaked paths turned incarnadine like exposed flesh. The discarded eyes of the slaughtered animals floated in the gutters like squashed water bubbles.

The street was deserted. No one strolled in it toting black umbrellas; unclad, snot-nosed children weren't playing tip-cat with their sticks; Chaklian women, with their cast-iron torsos, scorching hot armpits and faces sprinkled with silver beads of sweat, weren't walking around with avaram senna flowers in their hair, wet blouses stuck to their chests and sarees pulled up and tucked above their thighs, exposing their seductive knees and shiny ankles bathed in blood. Only Chaklian was seen walking unsteadily, like a weak raindrop on its way down from the heavens. The rain fell on his face. His grey navel was soaked, and the desiccated brown skin on his face, seared from years of exposure to the sun, was crumpled in the dampness, as if with old age wrinkles.

The sun was beating down on him all the way from the police station till there. The boiling bitumen blanket of the road scalded his soles. On the right was the stormy Arabian Sea, growling piercingly with manic energy. In the police station, he had felt humiliated and disgraced, like a slaughtered and flayed ox. The insulting laughter of the Writer of the station kept echoing in his ears like an old bell tolling.

'What kind of father are you, man? Pandering your girl to make money!'

It was mortifying to recall it; it was as humiliating as being gelded. At that moment, his younger daughter Arati touched him. Her cheeks, wet with tears and rain, had slap marks on them. Chaklian's body convulsed. Arati staggered and nearly fell.

'Don't touch me!' he screamed terrifyingly, as if from the depths of a bottomless pit. He glanced at his daughter once more before stepping into their hut. He could see the repressed lament trapped between her purple lips.

He gathered up the dirty laundry before the rain stopped. His two daughters' underwear were also in them. Then he started washing the clothes with his turmeric-stained hands.

As Arati looked out through the window, she saw her old black brief fluttering on the clothesline like the dried hide of a cow. She froze.

'Appa …' She ran out and fell at her father's feet and clutched at them frantically. Her tears washed his feet. 'Don't foist this sin too on my head, Appa.' She bowed and kissed his dark feet. His purple, sharp toe nails hurt her lips.

'I didn't do anything. I swear.' Chaklian gazed at her with contempt. Arati was in her white school uniform. The skirt that he had so painstakingly ironed, using the charcoal-fired brass iron-box to give it sharp pleats, was now damp and crumpled. The red-and-purple welts made by the police batons on her thighs reawakened his parental love, his loathing notwithstanding. He sat on his haunches and gathered her hands in his own, which smelt of soap and washing soda.

'Why … why my daughter?' A wail caught in his throat interrupted his words. 'Why this unbearable betrayal?'

Memories of his wife Arundhati assailed him. Her droopy eyes were like the half-open flowers of a wood apple tree. When provoked, sparks would fly from them. Her slim, firm body had alluring, sculpted curves and swells. The colour of a fawn, her soft and gleaming skin. A black mole above the lip, as if a drop of kohl had dripped on it. Like a honey bun, she always excited him—even in her pregnancy.

It was a Christmas night. In the back of a truck coming from Tamil Nadu, Chaklian, Arundhati and their older daughter Jyothi lay looking up at the sky which resembled a black silk skirt with its pleats open and studded with little diamonds. It flung at them occasional spikes of chill. Arundhati's pregnant belly bulged like a conch. She kept clutching at it every now and then. There was an ocean inside it, and it was heaving. As the waves rose at the rush of the tide, Arundhati's pain became apparent.

'Ammaaa …' She pressed against her stomach.

'What is it?' Chaklian sat up.

'It's paining.' Tears welled up in her eyes.

'Isn't this just the eighth month—what's the problem, then?'

'I don't know.'

She delivered as soon as she had said that. Chaklian was rattled. A big fish squirming in the white amniotic fluid—a baby girl. His Arati—his Arati baby.

Church bells were tolling. The wind carried over the sound of Christmas carols to them. Chaklian sat perplexed for a while. In the light of the red Christmas star hung on the truck, he pulled out a wide-blade chisel from his tool bag. With it, he sliced the pink umbilical cord which stretched between Arundhati and Arati like a taut violin string. A drop of placental blood shone like a ruby on the edge of the chisel blade. He was the one who pressed the baby to his chest first. Before Arundhati had laid a hand on her, he hugged her close to him. Baby Arati shivered in the chill of the December night. With her tender, still bloody lips, she licked Chaklian's chest, searching for the source of milk.

Chaklian squatted in front of his hut. Rain was peppering his front yard, baying like a rabid dog. While dancing its manic dance among the young coconut trees, mango orchards, jackfruit clumps and the lagoon in the vicinity, the rain created small ponds in his small front yard. Drying tears had shrivelled up his face. His wet shirt stuck to his bony chest with a dejected weariness. The phlegm collected inside his chest gurgled. At the end of the street, he saw strangers carrying umbrellas. Every rainy evening, he and his daughters used to take the same route. Two girls under a bleached, old umbrella. Two wraiths, two shadows. Two swarthy Chaklian girls sketched by the dark signs using darkness.

Chaklian remembered that it rained every time a calamity befell him. The warm summer evening when Arundhati had left him and their daughters, he had smelt the odour of betrayal—and he got the same smell today.

That day, he was in his workshop. He was beating the hide with the mallet to soften it. Since the morning, when he had come to know that his wife was in love with someone else, he had confined himself to the workshop, stitching sandals. In the evening, she came to the front of the shop, carrying the infant on her hip. When seen from a low angle, Arundhati was a slim, tall woman. Her arms were slim and long, like vines. He raised his eyes. She wore red and black horn bangles on her arms. Her nails were long. He imagined the bottu mangalsutra round her neck—that he had given her for their wedding—choking her. Arati smiled at him from her perch. Arundhati's discomfiture had turned her face red. There were beads of sweat over her upper lip. He understood everything.

'Where is Appa's daughter going?' He looked at Arundhati's eyes.

'Nowhere.' Seeing the bewilderment spreading in her eyes, he felt amused.

'Here, just till there. To see the Goddess.' She pointed towards the Arundhatiamman temple. Her silver nose stud glinted briefly with defiance.

'Keep this.' He took the flower garland from the photograph of Arundhatiamman and proffered it to her. There was a small catch in his throat and his hands trembled.

'Give me my kid.' Chaklian extended his hands. Arundhati hesitated. 'GIVE,' his voice deepened. Arundhati bent over and mechanically handed the child to Chaklian. Chaklian could smell champak flowers. He suppressed the wails quivering inside him.

'Go. Go quickly.'

Arundhati tarried for a moment. He thought he saw her eyes shining, as if filled with tears.

He never set eyes on her after that. Never. Two girls. Two girls who had lost their mother. He stayed alive by loving and indulging them. All the lonely nights, and with the knowledge that love is a responsibility, he slept holding them close. Every night after the children slept off, stuffing his limp wrist in his mouth, he wept silently. On many of those nights, everything could have ended in a small bottle of Furadan. Like a contemptible responsibility, his love for his children made him helpless and voiceless.

On those evenings, when he would be sitting in the workshop, some of the slim and tall, brown-complexioned women who got off the bus and walked with her gait, deceived him. When it was clear that none of them was Arundhati, and that Arundhati was never coming back, his fragile heart, throbbing to welcome her back, reconciled itself to ministering to the soiled footwear of those strangers. On other days, when he saw the legs of young men who approached wearing brown shoes, clicking their heels, he lost it completely. Those sun-shrivelled shoes, polished and shining ... their shine reminded him of Arundhati's paramour hiding in their bedroom.

Today, unable to face the dirty looks the assistant sub-inspector was giving him, when he lowered his gaze and saw the ASI's shoes, they reminded him of his wretchedness of many years ago. They had the look of roasted flesh. They had the arrogance of a paramour's shoes.

He bowed his head in shame and smashed his fist on the cow-dung floor. He pulled at his hair like a mad man. Then he lay down on the floor of the patio, which had received and sent off thousands of footwear, and bawled his heart out.

Chaklian fell asleep; he dreamt. Of a Christmas night, fourteen years ago. The baby girl, smelling of the blood from the amniotic fluid, crying non-stop. The red train speeding in front of Chaklian and the baby. Near the train's door, he saw many legs wearing tattered leather footwear. A train without an end. The wailing, too, without an end. It was his daughter Arati.

'Baby ...' He sprung up and out of the nightmarish memory. The intoxicating midnight moonlight seemed to have inebriated the street and put it to sleep. He could no longer hear his daughter's weeping. He went inside and called out loudly: 'Baby.' Her bed was empty. Its sheet, crumpled up from human contact, made him feel helpless.

'Baby.' A great dread rose inside him. His fingers trembled. His throat burning, he called out to his daughter again.

'Baby.' He searched for her in the darkness of the room. He heard a glass bowl shatter in the kitchen.

'Baby ...' Filled with anxiety, he ran to the kitchen.

'Appa's baby.' His daughter stood facing the window. Her wet hair was being blown by the sea breeze in the drizzling rain. The heart-shaped zircon ear studs he had bought her flashed briefly. An overwhelming fondness enveloped him.

'Let it be, my daughter, I understand everything.' His voice was tremulous. 'Even if no one else understands, your Appa does.'

Chaklian reached out and touched Arati. Lightning flashed briefly in that moment. Chaklian was stunned. Unanchored, Arati's body swung gently.

'Baby …' He tried to scream. Lightning flashed again. Though blinded by the flash, he saw it clearly—the flesh-coloured plastic rope, connecting his daughter's neck to the ceiling.

'Baaabbbyyy,' he bellowed.

'I didn't do anything, Appa … Am I not your daughter? Nothing … I promise.'

He heard her voice. He held her in a tight embrace. He felt the faint warmth of her body that had left its life on a noose only a few moments ago. The silent wails of her heart, which had stopped its pulsation, smashed on his chest. Like the most helpless person in the world, Chaklian kept bawling.

He sat on the floor. He saw her in his own soul—his Arati in a dress with red buckles. Her feet with thick, blue veins and tiny nails turned cold and violet.

'Baby.'

Broken-hearted, he saw the tiny feet he had kissed with so much love and wonderment before anyone else had. Toes which reminded him of petals, heels which smelled of the sea. He bent his face towards them and, with his wizened lips, he kissed them hard. His saliva and the cry which didn't escape him burnt her cold feet.

He got up and gazed at the street through the kitchen window. In the shadowy light, the wretched street appeared to be a beggar woman who had lazily wrapped the blanket of darkness around her. The strips of hide, soaked in the rain, were like sentries. At one end, on the country road, he saw a darling girl skipping along, holding her father's finger. She was laughing. Her lips had honey drools from the lollipops she had sucked on.

'Appa …'

'Uh-huh, what's it, baby?'

'I need Cinderella's shoes.'

'Ha-ha.' Chaklian laughed aloud.

'I need them, Appa … the prince has to come, no? Will you make them for me?'

'I will. But for that, we need a queen fawn. We'll need its hide for that. How can we take the skin off her? It would hurt her …'

'Where is the queen fawn?' She looked all around.

'Here,' Chaklian touched her cheek, 'Appa's *queen*.'

Chaklian rubbed his rheumy eyes hard. 'My queen fawn,' he said, touching Arati's cheek. He thought of the magical shoes she wanted to wear as a child. He went inside his workshop and fetched the wide-blade chisel used for cutting leather. It was that old chisel—the one he had used on a Christmas night to cut the umbilical cord and bring his child into this world. That day, there were blood drops on its edge. He swiped his right hand softly on the blade. A drop of blood fell on it. Using the chisel, he cut the umbilical cord-like plastic rope from which his daughter lay suspended. Her body fell to the floor with a loud thud. It lay prone in a kneeling position, with its head touching his feet.

'My daughter, my baby …' His face contorted with sorrow. 'Forgive your father, my baby.' His cries were lost in the rain.

Like a wicked sorcerer, he bent down and used the chisel to cut away Arati's clothes. Her oily back was exposed. He placed the chisel below the neck and made an incision on the skin. Her still-warm blood formed red, shiny bubbles.

'My queen fawn.' He rubbed his eyes once more. Then, without spilling even a drop of blood, he started skinning her from the neck down.

He sat there like a demented old man with the smell of clotted blood around him. Then, after sharpening his tools, slowly, ever so slowly, he started to make the magical shoes using human skin.

D

Robert-François Damiens Born: 9 January 1715 Birthplace: La Thieuloye, France Died: 28 March 1757 Location of Death: Paris, France Cause of Death: Execution Gender: Male Religion: Roman Catholic Race or Ethnicity: White Occupation: Assassin Nationality: French Executive Summary: Attacked Louis XV of France
Chella Durai Dipakaran Born: 9 January 1970 Birthplace: Valvettithurai, Sri Lanka Died: 28 March 2010 Location of Death: Kankesanthurai, Sri Lanka Cause of Death: Execution Gender: Male Religion: Hindu Race or Ethnicity: Mogaya Occupation: Leader Nationality: Sri Lankan Executive Summary: Killed Major Parijat Malhotra

Pasu Malai Dipakaran
Born: 13 June 1980
Birthplace: Kankesanthurai, Sri Lanka
Died: 28 March 2014
Location of Death: Chennai, India
Cause of Death: Execution
Gender: Female
Religion: Hindu
Race or Ethnicity: Vala Araya
Occupation: Leader
Nationality: Sri Lankan
Executive Summary: Killed the Indian Prime Minister

That was what really threw Pashumala. What Dipakaran used to, from the time of his birth till his death, call 'perdition', that 'Tamil perdition'—as the culmination of a series of events beginning with the dwarf Kandasamy—after being exiled from India—discovering a cannabis plantation in the Nandikadal lagoon where the sea had jettisoned him and allowing it to flourish from circa 1960 onwards; later moving on to become a plantation slave; morphing into a swarthy muscleman; eloping with Ujjar, the half Dutch Sidappa's daughter with pure Dutch features, in a breathless flight all the way to Kilinochi; their love blooming red like cannabis flowers during the sojourn in the old boathouse on blazing hot days redolent with the smells of the provenance of their clan; their life amidst the Tamil hordes that congregated inside it; their hunger, songs and eccentricities; and eventually Dipakaran being born in their midst as their son.

After being born in Sri Lanka as one in a pig-litter-like brood, after having forgotten the damp, earthy birth-smell of one's hoary Tamil ancestry; after fleeing from Lanka as a child, debilitated by rickets, emaciated by chronic diarrhoea, and with hunger stuck to his desiccated bones like his fleshless skin; after having found sanctuary in the refugee camp in Dhanushkodi and getting baked in its hot sands in adolescence; and, later in his youth, when stuffing strips from the torn saree of Pashumala into the cracks in his arsehole caused by the bombs thrown by the soldier-dogs, and walking long, painful kilometres, spread-legged, holding his entrails in his right hand; and finally, when the bullets of treachery, propelled by rabid gunpowder, punctured holes precisely in his heart and his forehead, being drained of the last of his vital fluids and giving up his ghost and falling dead; then, getting torn into two halves, dumped for the mass burial in the swampy pits of the city of the dead, only to commingle with the air as a nauseating stench, only to be obliterated over and over again—the final destiny of Dipakaran, the dark, cataclysmic perdition—the primary destiny of every Sri Lankan Tamil …

That this fate came in search of her, too, crossing the sea to arrive at the Chennai court, as if it was something commonplace, surprised Pashumala no end.

For Pashumala, too, as a fitting finale to her astonishment, the end came in the form of a noose at the end of a hangman's rope on the gallows placed somewhere in the court premises, the only difference being—if in the case of Dipakaran, it was the sticky black sea mud on his face—it was the roughness of the black cotton hangman's hood for her. The death of a Tamilian which is very ordinary … The so very ordinary death of a Tamilian woman. Pashumala laughed aloud with her usual mischievousness.

The silence that pervaded the court shattered in its own helplessness. The Tamil-speaking roosting doves that had made its roof their cote, shuddered, flapped their wings and flew away. The judge was ill at ease and sweating profusely. His fingers kept grazing the judgement books on his desk.

Pashumala's lawyer looked at his colleagues, seeking their validation for his argument that she was of unsound mind.

'Do you have anything to say? Say it now and be done with it,' the judge's shaky voice echoed, as if from the innards of an old church's antechamber.

'For myself? Uh-uh.'

With the innocence so characteristic of Tamilian women, Pashumala laughed again as if it were a sign of negation. The scorched muscles in her face tautened. The healed and dried-up wounds opened again. Her tongue snaked out from between her teeth to places which had no cheek shielding them. Tamil words became menacing, like the guttural growls of a hungry tigress.

'All perdition is me … every perdition is because of me … Only me … I am assuming responsibility, with pride, for all and any crimes committed by anyone for the glory of this Tamilian land.'

The judgement ran into 345 pages. When the judge pronounced the death sentence at the end of the reading, his voice splintered and was caught in an asthmatic wheeze out of shame. The court was suffused with the hallowed smell of gunpowder that starched, well-groomed Tamil words made when they split and fused. The public was stunned. The sea of sweat on the court announcer's bald pate lapped on his forehead as waves and spread like slippery oil. The Tamil odour blew in, and in its heat, the secret conspiracy split into smithereens. Only Pashumala could see it burn up the man from inside.

As always, the Tamil breeze, with its usual acidic, stinging fumes, blew inside the court as a covert and relentless defence. With the rebellion's vengeance and hostility, it squeezed and strangled the judge's lungs.

'With pride ...' Pashumala spoke serenely. Yet, her voice hung above the British-built court's silence, its intensity reverberating off the lofty wooden ceiling and rafters. Bats and barn owls flew out in droves. The wind blew its conch, deafening the judge. He closed the judgement register. The court adjourned in the usual manner after the pronouncement of the death sentence.

The city looked pale in the grey light. The smell of wilted flowers emanated from the black, silk-wrapped coffins. With the bells on their necks jangling fearfully, tall horses drew the hearses to the catacombs. The bones gathered from the grave clicked with the vanity of those lusting for life. The priests and padres did not look up from the holy books. Monsieur Le Breton took off his black headgear. Wielded like a weapon between his fingers, the sharpened point of the quill for writing the judgement was poised in the air. Wiping the sweat away from his brow, he looked at Damiens and laughed irrationally.

'Do you have anything to say?' Monsieur Le Breton asked in a timid voice unsuitable for a judge. His voice broke when he looked at the soldiers.

Damiens's sharp aquiline nose resembled the curved beak of old birds of prey. His lips kept repeating '*la journée sera rude*' with the cold calmness of a maniac.

A small bomb that could be fixed to a belt. Vedika pressed the buckle of the thin leather belt below the bulge of her pregnant belly rather forcefully.

La journée sera rude. The day is going to be hard.

Balasingham's full-term child inside Vedika kept kicking below her navel in protest.

When the bomb exploded, Vedika got splattered all over the place like rainwater. The child was blown up too; she too disintegrated. The police guards scattered as well. The public fled in all directions, screaming.

Pashumala listened intently. The girls' giggles, mingled with the tinkling of bangles, wafted over from the thatched huts on the seashore. Twenty-five thousand types of giggles. Giggles that sounded like pearls falling, like the anklets of the waves clinking. The girls happily showed up their palms that had been crushed under the boots of the peacekeeping force. The pain-killing peacock oil applied on them gleamed in the sun. The sea repeatedly crashed against their nipples which had lost all sensation. Flowering mangrove shoots emerged from their navels. The orphaned children, who used to cry with the discipline and order inherited from Indian soldiers, also bellowed with laughter.

Their scorched and blackened corpses reminded one of a seer fish left unturned on the pan while being roasted. Pashumala laughed in honour of the blown-up Vedika.

A closed-circuit camera gave Pashumala away. She got stuck on the lens of its all-seeing eyes like a cloudy cataract. For unknown reasons, the rest of the field went out of focus. The stitches on the wound—caused by the butt of a rifle—on her plump left cheek detracted from the eternal grace of her face and the sleepy look of love in her eyes, and sewed on the cruel look of a hundred-year-old witch. The crowd scattered when the explosion took place. Shrieking and screaming, they ran for their lives. Only Pashumala went forward with her gentle steps, careful not to hurt the earth, to end up in the vision of the CCTV camera.

The sight of her face horrified the people. Women fainted seeing the fissure resembling a millipede's nesting hole where her left nostril had been ripped away. Flesh was missing from the top of her jawbone till her lower lip. Her teeth stood fiendishly exposed as broken stubs in the split gums. Her days in unrelenting sea breeze had caused her gums to turn a virulent blue, as if snake venom had spread in them.

But the right side of her face remained elegantly beautiful. The reflection from her coral-coloured saree made her look younger than her thirty-four years. The smaller three stones of her five-stone nose stud glittered like tiny stars, as if to make up for the dullness of the acid-tarnished bigger two.

Looking at Pashumala's right profile, no one could imagine that the left half of her face was so disfigured that it resembled a piece of burnt charcoal. Her divine figure, wrought from the proverbial beauty of Tamilian women, and her honey-tone complexion, often compared to unhulled sesame seeds, had earned her quite a reputation back in the day.

Television channels ran in a loop the visuals of her walking hand in hand with Vedika, of taking off, wiping and putting back Vedika's thick-lensed spectacles on her nose, of the long, hard kiss on her forehead, as if wishing her victory in battle, and of her abruptly pulling back her hand from Vedika's belly when she felt the palpable kick of the baby.

When the bomb exploded, Pashumala thought in a detached way that it didn't sound as powerful as the mortars which used to be set off during the dog days of the Sreemariyamman equinox festival. Nevertheless, everything within a radius of seven metres was wasted totally. A lightning-like flash; a thunder-like boom, like an accompanist's percussion piece; then, the rain—a small spray of the amniotic fluid from the exploding womb of Vedika.

Pashumala turned towards the site, unperturbed. Vedika's right thumb, with the thick ring on it still intact, flew and smashed against Pashumala's forehead—the same digit Vedika used for the thumbs-up sign whenever she conveyed 'success' to her. It convulsed a few times like the autotomous tail of a startled lizard, and then became still. When she got over the initial shock, Pashumala bent down and picked up the thumb with the copper ring on it. The embossed capital letter 'D' on it—Dipakaran's initial—shone with a bloodied, vengeful smile.

On the sixteenth page of the judgement, there was a reference to the telephone call made by Pashumala after the incident. Since they couldn't trace to whom it had been made or why it had been made, they wrote up their conjectures and labelled them as the truth. They reported that it was a VoIP call to Colonel Thambirasa Pottuamman, who had succeeded Captain Chella Durai Dipakaran after his death. If not that, then it must have been the secret instructions to Colonel Theeppan Manushyaputhran, who was leading the fight at Valvettithurai. The third option: it could have been a call made to convey felicitations to Dipakaran's Trincomalee Ponnallae Tamil FM radio station. Pashumala found these conjectures ludicrous.

That call had been made to Pulendran Balasingham. Balasingham was Vedika's husband and Pashumala's brother Pulendran's son—the timid Balasingham, who had faithfully inherited his mother Jayakkodi's pusillanimity, her limpid affectionate nature, her docile demeanour, and an amazing facial resemblance to Pulendran.

The folks in Valvettithurai were amazed at the sight of Balasingham. Pulendran had been killed in a police commando operation at Trincomalee. The Tamil's corpse was picked at by crows, then taken apart by marine life, and, as ever, swept away by the sea like a rotting ship. The government confirmed the death and his photograph was published in the newspapers. Balasingham was born three years after that, out of the commando operation six policemen had conducted on Jayakkodi. Ironically, P. Balasingham grew up with the same nose, fiery eyes and the sloping gait of Pulendran, who used to favour his left side.

P. Balasingham had met Vedika in the same Dhanushkodi camp where Pulendran had found Jayakkodi. Likewise, he lived in Pondicherry and went to France to start a rice business. Pulendran's paths; Pulendran's style. At twenty-one, he married Vedika and left India with her and Jayakkodi.

However, unlike Pulendran, he never returned. He didn't hear the beckoning call of his Tamil roots. Even if he had heard the call, living up to the ineradicable heritage from the craven young policeman who had ravished Jayakkodi—all the time checking if she was alive, with his finger below her nostrils—Balasingham chose to stay away.

'For all your rites-shites and all those matters, this will do, no?'

Balasingham's silence punctuated his conversation with Pashumala when she called to inform him of the finger.

'Aththaye … Aththaye … what are you saying? Have you gone mad …?'

Pashumala could hear him scream as he sat in his Parisian rice store.

'*Ayyyo* … *ayyaayyyoo* … what kind of atrocity is this! My darling … my Vedika … Aththaye, can you please give the phone to her once?'

'*Cheee* … *cheee* … shut your mouth …' Pashumala snarled at him, as if slapping him across his face with her sandals.

'She is my girl. My baby. Why should I lie to you? She is dead. Suicide. She herself set the bomb off. Go, watch the TV.' Pashumala softened: 'Bala, what I have told you is the truth. It was a vow we took for the Tamils. You tell me, do you need Vedika's finger? Shall I courier it?' Since it was a call through the internet, her undulating voice echoed back to her, as if from inside a cave.

Balasingham was wailing away. As she listened to his howls, she felt she too would break down. Pashumala switched off the phone, broke the SIM card into two, and threw it into a bonfire made from chairs.

The television was showing, intermittently, the scorched face of Pashumala and the blackened, shorn-of-clothes, prone body of the prime minister.

On the twenty-first page was Pashumala's statement on the lady, gleaned from her memory. Pashumala was thirteen, and studying in class five, when that lady had become the prime minister of India for the first time. She had stacked her class books in the aluminium school box. It was while she was searching for a ribbon to tie her hair, anointed with mustard oil and tightly plaited in two, that she had heard the news on Radio Ceylon. She had heard her two grandmothers say that women in India would face no problems from then on, and laughing about it.

Pashumala was the one who had stuck the lady's photo on the school notice board and read out the three-minute bulletin about her in the school assembly. When she read out that the lady's aim was the welfare of the nation's girls, there was a lot of cheering in that girls-only school.

Pashumala felt the lady's bobbed hair, cropped at the ears, was throbbing with life in the sea breeze. An elegant streak of grey hair above her temple shone like polished silver. Like the carrion-seeking beak of a vulture, cruelty clung to the tip of her aquiline nose. In her eyes, a benevolence so extraordinary that it looked affected. And on her lips, like dew, glistened a loving, innocent smile.

All the Tamils in Kankesanthurai were in a celebratory mood. Hope for justice in the land of their birth had kindled. If not that, at least a return from exile, a transplanting from the refugee camp in Dhanushkodi town to the Tamil *eelam*.

While listening to her addressing them over Radio Ceylon in Hindi as 'My Tamil children, my Tamil brethren', Pashumala was ready to rip out her beloved Lanka from her own being as a snake moults to stay alive.

'All these are lies. Every administration, every government is the same. My Tamil brethren, we didn't fight to become refugees. We fought to win our rights.'

Pashumala scowled at Dipakaran's image on the TV. Looking closely at his face, she thought that it wasn't a cruel face; it was only the small scar of a stitched-up cut on his face that lent him a cruel look.

It was during one of those blistering hot days, when blazing shoots of fire were being planted in the body politic, that a policeman called Alagiri had gifted Dipakaran that mark on his cheek. All the innocent features on his face—the always-pink, plump lower lip that seemed to hanker after milk-filled breasts; brown, helpless eyes that looked like the bubbles on an elephant's caparison; the orphaned curve of his unibrow; the shy smile—everything was smashed into a mess that day. The deep gash made by the rusted metal strip on the rifle butt became septic. The scar left by the medical student who had stitched him up on the third day of the incident remained near his lip as a permanent testimony to the botched first-aid.

When they were going to kiss for the first time, and Dipakaran looked into her eyes, shyness made Pashumala avert her eyes. She used to often stand looking anxiously at the scar, the only feature on his face which made him look cruel. Every time she looked at it, she would be aware of the lust rising in her to consume the man in him. When she looked at him, covering the scar with her mind, she could perceive an adorable child hiding behind Dipakaran's face, a boy starved of love. The scar was an enigmatic feature that transformed the child in him to someone ruthless as a pirate. An endearing feature which lent energy to the hand like the tip of a sword. When she touched it with her finger, she felt a prick, as if being nicked. When she was kissing him, the invisible rustiness on the sword scored her lips and gave her tetanus fever. But she happily conceded that there was no other feature which worked him into a tiger-like wild frenzy, and every time she showered him with kisses in a geometric progression.

What Dipakaran had stated on the television was the truth. At the end of the first month, they arrived with their hollow, white lies. The people on the coast could see the white froth rising far out in the sea.

The peacekeeping force was landing without peace from the ship, flying a white flag on its mast. The festering yellow of the day was rising in the sunshine. Like the sparks from a smithy's furnace, the shore bubbled in the stifling, boiling heat. The heat caught in the metal studs of the army boots rose through the leather soles as blisters. The army entered the villages in a hasty march, like wild animals with burning feet. They barged into the Tamil houses in hordes to satiate their ostensibly military, but in reality, base biological needs, much like usurping food immorally when hungry, and like diving dishonourably and head-long into a water-body when thirsty. Those who opposed them, they tied up, tortured, killed.

Pashumala sent a missive to Dipakaran at the secret address found scribbled in Pulendran's diary. Her neat handwriting had an equal admixture of blood and tears. She began with the women being fed up of living like bitches in the huts frequented by the peacekeeping force. She had been raped eight times in the previous month alone. She had undergone one abortion. She wrote heartrendingly of how she didn't know what the soldiers might do next, and how many times in the coming months. She also added that after seeking refuge in the church, she had found some relief, but the condition of other girls was deplorable and getting worse day by day.

It was in those days—after the arrival of the peacekeeping force shredding their peace and happiness—that Pashumala saw Dipakaran for the first time. The call from Dipakaran came to the phone in the Thyagarajar Thiru Hrudaya Church. Pashumala had not imagined that the letter would reach him or that he would call on the old phone in the church. It was only a desperate attempt like launching an SOS message inside a bottle when marooned at sea. Exactly as promised, targeted attacks on the peacekeeping force's camp took place within a week. Thirteen bombs exploded simultaneously. Twenty soldiers were shot dead. That evening, Dipakaran came to see Pashumala.

He came wearing a camouflage uniform like that of the Indian soldiers, all five-feet-eight-inches of him, with a permanent angry scowl on his face. Leaning on the compound wall of the graveyard, he spoke to Pashumala. She felt like crying. She complained to him that Pulendran's body may have been boiled and eaten by the policemen.

Dusk had fallen. It had started drizzling on the bottoms of the upturned fishing boats on the Kankesanthurai beach. Pashumala had a litany of complaints. Showing unabashedly the cigarette stub marks on her breasts and thighs, she kept up the jeremiad. The rain became denser and her tears more copious.

'Hellfire for that bastard! He will die and rot, and worms will eat the brute ...' she continued her weeping and imprecations.

'What did you say his name was?'

'I don't know his name. He's a major. But his eyes—they look like crystal marbles. I will kill him for sure.'

'Is this him?'

Dipakaran took out a doll-like head from a yellow cloth bag with LG Asafoetida branding on it.

Pashumala was stunned. It was the head of that guy. Major Malhotra! His light eyes were open. His tongue hung out. It had deep gashes from biting down while being attacked.

After her initial shock, Pashumala willed all her strength into her hand. She swung hard at the face of the major. She took his head from Dipakaran's hands and, holding it by the hair, slammed her own head on its forehead. Then she rubbed the major's face in the grainy sand on the ground.

Tears streamed down her cheeks with a wild vengeance.

The events of that day—when her cheeks were slashed by the shards of crab shells and the abrasive outer part of cuttlefish, and she was left to writhe in the sand on the beach after being wounded and abused—had bored into her soul and brutally torn up her insides.

The sand that had been pushed into her through her vagina and up her fallopian tubes, right into her uterus, had been removed by the doctor in the medical college after six days through a D&C without using anaesthesia.

'It was done because the condition was so critical … otherwise I would have lost my uterus in another surgery.' Her shoulders dropped at the memory.

'It was all done by this dog. This bastard!'

When she had cried in sheer agony at Kankesanthurai, the major had pressed her face into the sand. Her mouth had filled with sand. In memory of that, she buried his head in the sand.

'*Phthoo,*' she spat on the head.

Even Dipakaran was taken aback. 'Woman, what kind of debasement is this? Leave it.' 'He killed my brother, too. You know that, don't you?'

'Drop it,' he caught and squeezed her hand, making her drop the major's head.

Pashumala gave Dipakaran the feint and savagely kicked the major's head with the ease of kicking a football. It sailed high like a ball, trailing the sand, and fell into the sea. Pashumala hugged Dipakaran, pressed her face against his chest, and kept on crying.

That cut-off head—the gift of love from Dipakaran. That was the beginning of Pashumala's return to the *eelam*. Holding Dipakaran's hand, calloused from handling guns, she dove into the endless happiness of the *eelam*, also its repressions and its sorrows. Paul Anthony, Vedika and Thiruchelvi came into their lives at an interval of two to two-and-a-half years each. Feeding on Pashumala's breast milk, the 'tiger' cubs grew. She imbued their tongues with the grit of the Tamil Tigers' life-breath. They had guns as toys and bombs to play throw-and-catch with and to blow up.

Paul Anthony met the same fate as Pulendran. High on Tamil ambrosia, while invoking Tamil culture shouting, 'Let's fight the battle, let's fight, Tamil is the elixir', his bullet-riddled body fell to the ground carpeted with wilted gloriosa flowers—the official emblem of the *eelam*. His raised right fist, the symbol of the *eelam*, remained unlowered. Thus fell Paul Anthony to the bullets.

'My son, my son …' Pashumala was inconsolable.

'I have to see him. I must see him once.' She clung desperately to Dipakaran's uniform.

'It can't happen. It definitely won't happen. There in Kankesanthurai, is his resting place. Tamil women must not cry like this.'

'No, no, no … I have to see him one way or the other. I am beseeching you.'

Pashumala clung to Dipakaran's legs. 'Please dear, any which way. Please …' His feet were washed with her tears.

That was how Paul Anthony came home. Pashumala's prince. On a boat. Like the carelessly dried hide of a tiger steeped under dried fish.

When the boat reached, Pashumala gripped Dipakaran firmly. The soles and sharks which had been salted and dried for months in Kankesanthurai had deathly thin fins, resembling butterfly wings. The violet-hued broken shells of the molluscs grinned widely at her. After removing the stacks of sharks one by one, the workers pulled out Paul Anthony's body from beneath. He lay there, coated with salt like a dried fish, among other dried fish.

Dipakaran had warned Pashumala that his body would arrive only after ten or fifteen days or even a month, that too buried under dried fish. He'd said it would be better to bury him in Kankesanthurai itself.

She dug in her heels. 'I can't allow that. I can't. I have to see him.' She stopped eating. She had to see him, no matter how he was brought, salted, sheathed or put on ice. However, the moment she saw his body, she wished she hadn't. She cursed her own obstinacy.

His body reminded her of sharks. Like Karna, born with the divine body armour and earrings, Paul Anthony was born, his hands full with Pashumala's breasts. Holding her breasts in both hands, he slid around on her chest like the young calf of a shark frolicking in the waves of Vellamullivekkal. It's him ... *it's him.* Pashumala squatted beside him. His body seemed to have grown into a large, fleshy shark among the myriad salted fish corpses. The salt stuck to his dark face like an undertaker's talcum powder. The golden sands of Kankesanthurai, embedded in the sticky, dried blood which had oozed out of his nose, glittered. The coconut-oil-filled bullet hole in his forehead had turned the colour of a half-fried shark heart. When she leaned over and kissed his forehead, she caught the smell of burnt gunpowder on a desiccated fish, which overshadowed the odour of a thirteen-day-old corpse.

The blue evening light played hide-and-seek between dusk and night. The shadows of bare, leafless trees lay above the vaulted columns and bas reliefs. Louis XV descended to the ground below, where the trees' shadows drew ghostly images. The white horse of his waiting gilded carriage neighed like a herald of death. Though the ornate Italian marble steps lay in darkness, his shoes glistened.

Beyond the parapet wall, he saw a glint like the bluish smile of the moon's crescent. It was a well-forged, double-edged pen-knife.

'Dauphin.'

Like a dog that had smelt danger, the king shrank back and summoned the bodyguard. Undaunted, Damiens approached, pleasant-faced. It looked as if the serenity of that January evening and the amiability of that Wednesday had all leached into him. The green tint of the unfulfilled promise of a dense beard lay beneath his clean-shaven cheeks.

In a show of deference, a smiling Damiens doffed his cap and bowed as if wishing the king. A strong breeze blew in, bringing along the typical January chill of Versailles. Damiens thrust the knife with all his strength into the right flank of the king, aiming for the lower vertebrae. The king felt as if the invisible chilly hands of the breeze had walloped him. He felt the spot with his hand; it had gone damp. Blood flowed like a river of red wine. A small deluge. The king fell in a faint, as if touched by the cold hands of Death. The blood ate into the white marble floor, as would royal blood-fortified aqua regia. Each drop shook the earth. Paris quaked.

Major Sundararama Iyengar and Major P.J. Malhotra, the twin brother of the deceased Major Malhotra, were no ordinary army officers. Dipakaran told Pashumala that they were the moles and guard dogs of the government. Those pimps who pandered to the government were worse than a starving wild beast; every government servant was more virulent than the AIDS virus. They were capable of finishing off the human race by subjugating, usurping and annihilating. Justice and the rights of a citizen would be trampled under their boots, pierced by the nails in their soles, and mutilated and crushed by the sharpened edges of their metal heels. These men would make us beasts of burden with their brand of the law of the jungle, with the tender mercies of the savage …

'I don't want war. My people don't want war. All I ask for is peace … I live for that alone. We need justice, we need righteousness, we want peace.'

The public listened to Dipakaran's words over Radio Trincomalee. Sundararama Iyengar heard it. Malhotra the Second heard it. The government expressed readiness for an accord, forsaking their savage ways.

The peacekeeping force deputed Major Sundararama for peace talks. Dipakaran had agreed to the accord only for the sake of peace. It was not out of the unconscious ennui which affects men who have been fighting day in and day out. He wanted to wake to at least one morning without the smell of blood and raw flesh, without seeing fragmented humans—bodies which had to be scraped off the ground—and without the shroud of hatred's acrid smoke smothering him.

Damiens also wished for only that. Limpid thoughts, and a bright morning, resplendent in the rays of the rising sun. The merciful, healing touch of Jesus Christ without categorisation as Jansenist or Calvinist. Peace-filled baptism and last rites. Confessions and unconditional absolutions. The Confirmation sacrament like a full moon rising on the extended tongue. A lasting, sublime peace.

He thought that if he killed the king responsible for his ex-communication, he would find that peace. The regicide of an autocrat is not as easy or peaceful as squashing a mosquito, or an ant, or a winged termite. It is as good or bad as cutting off one's head and presenting it to one's enemy. He was determined that he would not let his weak flesh be interred without being absolved of the venial sins caused by errant thoughts, or without exculpation, or without receiving his last rites. He started to have dreams of pulling out a knife from the heart of the king. He had visions of the king's venomous blood, made fetid by unbridled power, dissolving into peace. Damiens had decided on the path to terminate a dominion.

The government was a cunning, conniving fox. Treacherous and vengeful, it kept creating opportunities to generate and keep regurgitating hatred. The peace offering was only a subterfuge, an elaborate drama. A planned release of the smoke of peace into Dipakaran's lair to smoke him out. The smoke of deception was to be used for the army to find, isolate and kill him.

Only three people, blindfolded, were brought into the top-secret hideout for the rendezvous. Major

Sundararamaswamy Iyengar and the representatives of the two countries. They, the peacemakers, reached by eight o'clock in the night. Though they were blindfolded and brought through circuitous routes and by changing vehicles in between, three thousand more came, surreptitiously, shadowing the deception of those three. Like ants following the trail of other ants' spoor. The dogs of war followed the sickening scent trail of their superiors, sniffing their way through. One after the other they set fire to the houses on the shore where people were sleeping. They wiped out life on the shore by eviscerating those who survived the fire with their bayonets and by shooting the rest with machine guns. The fully scorched bodies were flung into the sea. The half-burnt bodies were flung back into the fire. The piteous wails of women and children lost their way on the beach.

The *eelam's* war strategy dictated that if Dipakaran were to be captured, Pashumala should escape. And likewise, Tamilchelvi, Colonel Anton Kulasingham and Captain Guhasantha Vettri. A strategy made without emotion and with dispassionate Tamil logic. If it looked as if the battle was being lost, they should stop fighting and flee. They must stay alive for the *eelam*. Fight back only when the circumstances turned in their favour.

Defeat is like that. It wipes away all humiliations and makes us indifferent. We stand with our heads bowed. It flays the skin of arrogance. Louis XV lay on the royal bed inside the palace, vanquished, waiting for Death to arrive. The priest who had come for the last sacraments said special prayers for him. Weak-hearted, the king looked at the queen.

'You shall forgive all my sins and transgressions.' Forgetting her royal bearing, the queen wept openly. Cold-eyed, the king declared that after his death, the dauphin should become the ruler temporarily, and that he was at peace and was returning to the hands of God.

All this time, Damiens was waiting on the steps, as if waiting for his own death. He stood there, confused, holding the knife with its blade stained slightly. He didn't try to escape or flee. As if becalmed by a tug o' war between the youth and the elderliness of his ambivalent forty-two years, he stood there, insensate and with an inert heart. The superficial wound on the king's body was an animal of prey. Damiens was prey to it and was waiting. The man who had assailed authority and physically attacked it wouldn't be pardoned; his own punishment would be inexorable. Authority squelches people like boulders unleashed by a landslide, crushing them with its massive weight. Damiens stood there with the knife till the famished hunting lion of authority caged him.

It was a small hut. Water was still dripping from the nets hung up by those who had returned from the sea. The drops created antlion pits in the sand. The small fish, still caught in the suspended nets, struggled to get oxygen by opening and closing their gill covers. The sea breeze and the darkness made their eyes burn.

Pashumala was bewildered when she heard the death-whistle, a signal that Dipakaran's life was in danger. Not able to imagine what could have happened when there were thirty guards to protect him, she started to run instinctively.

The entire shore was lit up. Every hut was aflame. In the fire, their rights degenerated from orange plasma, to smoke, to ashes, to soot. The shrieks of those dying in their sleep were more terrifying than the growls of the ocean. People ran in all directions, like human torches or scorched and blackened, like scurrying ants. Some of them jumped into the sea. Some of them rolled in the sand. Others became one with the fire and melted in it. Since most of the men were still at sea, the majority of the victims were women and children.

Only the hut in which Tamilchelvi was hiding was enveloped in a deathly but dreadful stillness. Armed soldiers had surrounded it. Pashumala stood panting, hidden in the shadows of the slippery, precipitous rocks near the hut. She realised that, like Pulendran and Anthony, Chelvi too was irretrievably lost to her. A man resembling the deceased Major Malhotra went inside. The last shining star on the firmament also burnt up and fell to the earth. The earth and sky were dark now, like the black visage of heinous authority. Pashumala stifled her wails by covering her mouth with her hands.

Malhotra the Second sat inside the hut, accompanied by a rottweiler as big as a human being. A kick from the major made a startled Chelvi scramble up, awake now to the panting of the dog.

'No. 263 … Make sure it is her.'

A man was dragged in, hauled through the sand.

'Tell, you fucking dog,' commanded No. 263, the army officer called Arputha Amudan, pulling him up by his hair. 'Is this her? That Dipakaran's daughter?'

The man swallowed hard and looked at Tamilchelvi, fearing for his life. She was trembling like a tree caught in high wind.

'Yes.' Coated in saliva and blood, two teeth fell to the floor from the man's mouth.

Malhotra laughed like a pervert. His sharp canine teeth shone like spearheads. Vengefulness formed a film over his spectacles.

'Your mother and father together killed my brother. *Sernnthu … sernnthu*,' he said, trying to mimic the Tamil word. 'Isn't it so, 236? Tell this kid,' he continued, rolling a cheroot, filling it with Van Gogh tobacco, and lighting it.

'There is a gift for killing his brother. A small surprise. Sir has come to give it to you,' quipped No. 236.

Major Malhotra laughed aloud.

'That's good … that's good. Surprise … that's brilliant.' He bent down and held Chelvi by her chin.

'How old are you?' he asked in Tamil.

'Fourteen.' Her voice was shaking.

'Good age. But not for me, this age … 263, will she suit you?' He winked at Arputha Amudan.

Then he looked at Kulwinder: 'Or you?'

'320, would you do it?'

He walked around Chelvi. Every soldier was wise enough to turn down his offer.

'Then who's going to do it? Huh?' His cheroot glowed spitefully.

'What if it is No. 100?' He arched his eyebrow dramatically.

Getting over their initial shock, the soldiers clapped hesitantly.

'First class, sir, super first class.' Amudan became emotional and bit his lower lip. 'Superb, sir. What an idea! I have never seen something like this before.'

Anxious, Tamilchelvi tried to read the number plates of all the soldiers. She could not see the number 100 on any of them. She became alert once she sensed the severity of the danger.

'Number 100!' Malhotra clapped his hands.

With the conceit and arrogance of power, No. 100 came and stood in front of Tamilchelvi. When she read the figure 100 on it, she shrieked with fear. It was the major's dog. Panting with its teeth exposed and drooling copiously, the creature stood in front of her.

The major clapped his hands again. The dog trainer appeared and poured whisky into the mouth of No. 100. Then he opened another bottle and sprinkled Tamilchelvi with a chemical which mimicked the smell of a bitch in heat.

'Go, 100, go!'

What followed was a horrendous scene. Tamilchelvi bolted through the door. Showing signs of a dog in heat, the Rottweiler was in hot pursuit. It had been trained specially to copulate with women. Its organ was exposed and erect, like the raised spectre of authority. The soldiers cheered it on, turned on by the novelty of the perversion. The trainer cracked the whip, which flashed through the air. The dog brought down Chelvi, turned her over, and started attacking her from the back with its beastly agility.

'My God!' Pashumala jumped out from among the rocks.

'My baby, Chellam … Chelvi …' She started racing towards her, beating her breasts. Strong arms of a soldier grabbed her from behind. The cold steel of a gun barrel tickled her temple.

'Correct timing … come, come … you come with me.' He dragged Pashumala through the sand, towards the darkness of the mangroves.

Death was in the process of welcoming Dipakaran.

'Drawing and quartering … it's very painful, amma … Death by torture. The body is tied to four horses which are driven in four directions …'

Holding on to the pillar, when she tried to raise her head, Pashumala remembered the reference to Damiens's death in Vedika's letter.

Death was in the process of welcoming Damiens. Four horses, their manes etched in black by Death. He wished for darkness all around and in his eyes. He prayed for a quick end, without wriggling like a reptile for hours on end. Death should be with him before sunset, whatever happens. The executioner, Samson, sharpened again the glowing, hot pincers he was holding.

'They are called red-hot pincers. They are akin to the pliers used by the dentists in our place. Amma, what else could be used for that type of torture? It was fiendishly cruel.'

From the time he was sentenced for attempting to assassinate the king, Damiens was kept in the torture chamber. Suffering the weight of chains, the tightness of manacles and the torture of boots, he fancied that he would have to embrace death lying flat on his back. He was wearing only a thin chemise to hide his nakedness.

He felt a chill when he heard the jubilant crowd. His arms were fatigued from holding up a two-pound candle in each hand. The molten wax dripped on his hands and scalded him, skin and wax melding together. Samson dug the pincers into his hands, pressed and pulled out his flesh. Samson felt that Damiens's flesh was soft like ripe apples. He tightened his grip on the pincers. Damiens's thin skin peeled off like the petals of a hibiscus flower, and his flesh clung to the tip of the pincers. Damiens screamed and pulled back. He bit his lips till they bled. He roared like a wild beast. The pain gave him goose pimples.

His nipples were like fresh rose buds, yet untouched by sunlight. Samson applied the pincer on his left nipple, which his lover used to kiss with her withered lips and nibble painlessly during their lovemaking. Samson's beak-like pincers plucked out flesh from his supple thighs, the muscles of his chest and the dimples on his abdomen. A second knife was brought out and the wounds were deepened with it. Damiens stood with his head unbowed. Skin and flesh were torn off in many places, like colour-paper patches. Damiens lamented like a vampire's donor. He shrieked in pain.

'My God, my God, please forgive me.'

'Tamil is the elixir. Tamil means Mother.'

Unable to lift her broken neck, Pashumala writhed in agony. In the peacekeeping force's camp, the only outsiders were the three of them: Dipakaran, Tamilchelvi and herself.

Chelvi lay there like a heap of tattered clothes under a swarm of flies. There wasn't a spot on her body unmarked by the dog's teeth or claws. Looking at a sizable, burrow-like deep wound on the left side of her neck, Pashumala wanted to scream. Noticing that her windpipe wasn't moving, she realised that Chelvi was dead. Pashumala calculated that the time was close to dawn.

Major Sundararamaswamy Iyengar, Major Malhotra the Second and other soldiers continued to torture Dipakaran.

'Amma, in the museum here, there is a ring with D inscribed on it. It's like the ring that Appa has. When I imagine Damiens's torture, I am reminded of Appa. Amma, you aren't in trouble, are you? I am afraid.' Through her eyes full of tears, and with her vision blocked by her hair, Pashumala saw Damiens instead of Dipakaran.

The hot fumes of sulphur were burning his right hand. They kept haranguing him, asking—hadn't he used that hand to stab the king?

'Didn't you … didn't you use this hand to decapitate my brother?'

Samson scooped up the molten black lead like he would ladle out soup. He poured it over Damiens's wounds. He kept pouring the molten lead and wax into each of the wounds, as if it were a medicinal concoction.

Pashumala closed her eyes tightly. It was his life which was being yanked out. His life was coming out in pieces through the flesh plucked out by the pincers. They were his life's wounds that were being opened up, and molten tar, sufficient to vaporise blood, was being poured into them. Boiling lead was being plated.

'My God, my God, Jesus … forgive me … grant me absolution …' Pashumala also cried with Damiens.

'Tamil is the elixir. Tamil means Mother.'

The vigour in Dipakaran's voice shocked Pashumala.

The sulphur spread through him. It set Damiens's pubic hair aflame like a wildfire. He had an erection, as if a woman had fondled him. Samson knocked it with the sharp knob of the iron ring on this finger, mocking him. His testicles had the slight warmth of an egg being hatched by the mother bird. Samson squashed the bird's eggs with extreme savagery. Damiens's scrotal sac broke with an explosive sound.

'What kind of damnation is this?' Samson wiped his hands, sticky with blood, on his upper garment.

'Damn!' He pressed his boot above the bloodied sac. With the ease of grinding tender petals, he squashed Damiens's penis under his boot on the floor.

'My God … my God …' Pashumala also wailed along with Damiens and Dipakaran.

'Tamil is the elixir. Tamil means Mother.'

Dipakaran's voice was dying out. The crowd was cheering. 'Do it, do it … *ahhhhhh*,' they screamed in their intoxication.

The writhing form of Damiens energised them. They kept bellowing their encouragement and appreciation for what was on show.

'Kill him … kill him …' They pointed at the victim.

Pashumala crawled on her belly to reach Dipakaran. She kissed and embraced him, crying miserably. The fire embraced her in return.

'Kill him, kill him …' she howled, looking at the soldiers.

Authority is not greedy. Authority is never taken by surprise. It kills a citizen slowly. First his rights, then his justice. Only after that is he physically killed. Authority will stand by with patience and without any desire to indulge when the public in their frenzy will toy with a man for their amusement, knocking him about as would a cat its prey. Then Authority moves in politely when the time is ripe. Authority's leering grin is veiled by a sweet smile.

A horse was tied to each of Damiens's limbs. Four white, strong, tall, proud-looking stallions. The whip was cracked. They pulled apart in four directions. Quartering, tearing him into four pieces. The sounds of the bones getting displaced were lost in the hysterics of the crowd.

The ululations of the crowd became louder.

'Kill … kill … kill …' they clapped their hands faster and faster, and egged the executioner on.

With a cracking sound, Damiens's both arms came off their sockets.

'Amma, his legs never got torn off. They added one more horse at each limb and tried. It didn't work. They had to finally chop them off with an axe. Yet he didn't die. His still-live, limbless torso was impaled on a stake. Then they set fire to it. His ashes were scattered all over Paris. What gross savagery is this, Amma?'

Pashumala understood why Vedika had wailed while writing the letter. She also understood what she could have been afraid of.

With an evil smile, Major Sundararamaswamy Iyengar ordered Dipakaran's legs to be chained to the tow hooks of the military jeeps, leaving enough slack. The jeeps were parked on the path, back to back. An improvisation on quartering. Unlike a division into four, a tearing into two.

Pashumala felt her life-breath leave her.

'God Almighty, my God ...' She covered her face with her hands. The two jeeps to which Dipakaran was tethered kept moving slowly in opposite directions. Blood got splattered on the back of her hands. Split into two halves, Dipakaran went away from her. One half went to India, the other half to Lanka. His ring flew off his finger and landed in front of her.

They will still impale this Tamil brave's half-alive body on the whetted stake. He will be burnt for the minuscule life left in him. With festivities, his ashes will be scattered in the sea for kicks. He will be dissolved in the sea. The remnants of his ashes will be sent into the ether with a smack of their palms. It will float over the soul of Lanka, redolent of the *eelam*. Dipakaran will fill every Tamil's lungs with fire and spirit.

Pashumala closed her eyes. Her head was unbowed.

'Tamil is the elixir. Tamil means Mother,' she shouted in Dipakaran's voice. She requested the court that she be cremated in the public cemetery in the Dhanushkodi refugee camp.

She requested Balasingham that her ashes be split into three parts and scattered in Lanka, Tamil Nadu and Paris. 'A man of peace will emerge for the *eelam*. You should give this ring to him.' She touched Balasingham tenderly through the bars of her cell.

Then she got decked up like a Tamil bride, with vermillion on her forehead, flowers in her pleated hair, an eighteen-yard *chela*, bangles, *vellacheetu* and the nose stud. A black hood was placed over her head. The hangman's noose was placed around her neck like the mangalsutra.

'Tamil is the elixir. Tamil means Mother.' She mocked the Tamilian righteousness of the hangman.

The hangman pulled the lever for a remuneration of five hundred rupees. A lifeless Tamil letter was left hanging from the noose.

Balasingham was waiting outside for her corpse. That letter shone like a tender light for eternity on his ring finger. It was the letter D.

Author's Note: *My gratitude to Michel Foucault. Also, to him, now demised, whom I have never seen, and who has never seen me. To Prabha.*

This story or the characters therein have no resemblance or relation to anyone living or dead. I am not responsible for any such perceptions.

The Bloodthirsty Kali

Kamala paused. Wrapped carelessly in a blood-red sari, her eyes gleaming with vengeance, the pollen-like vermillion smeared on her forehead, lips aglow with red lipstick, her hair flying in the breeze, Kamala stood near the freshly dug pit in the graveyard. She laughed. He was lying in the grave. The husband who had tied a mangalsutra on her neck the day before yesterday.

Her husband had died yesterday, the day after their wedding. His body was covered in transparent, saliva-bubble-like boils, his plump lips that had throbbed to kiss her now purple beneath the hairs of his moustache, and there was pale, white, shellac-like dry gound at the corners of his eyes. Kamala couldn't stop herself from laughing as she watched him lie indifferently in the chill of the mobile mortuary, his stubbly cheeks withered, and with a frown on his forehead. Chicken pox had affected his brain. It was swollen, suppurating and throbbing. Death came quickly. A low-grade fever following the wedding ceremony. An itchy, sore throat. A runny nose. He was wiping it using a handkerchief with flowers embroidered on it in white.

He had looked very disturbed. It was a hasty wedding. The bride was eighteen only on paper. Her family had declared non-cooperation. He was a lecturer in the Government Law College and Kamala, his student. She was unlike any other girl he was acquainted with. A face suffused with dignity and pride. Eyes that flashed with a kind of intense hatred. A black mole adorning the tip of her aquiline nose, like a blue diamond nose-stud. Enraged hibiscus lips. Her face was chocolate-complexioned, like people tanned by long hours in the midday sun. A slim, short girl. Yet he felt there was something extraordinary about her. A face once seen and forgotten, a resemblance to someone from his past. Though the forgotten one always wore a vermillion bindi, this girl's forehead was lined with tiny creases as if from some mysterious melancholia. Clad in the white saree and black blouse of her college uniform, her body looked shapely, like a carefully carved statue. Her cascading curly black hair that swirled about in the breeze of the ceiling fan caused him disquiet in the class. Though he had always raised his eyes to look at her, he had never thought she had noticed him.

He was a lady killer, and had bedded every girl he desired, easily taking them to his Godrej steel-framed bed in his rented room at least once. He gathered from every woman the most she had to offer. After every love-making session, stroking the hair of the worn-out beauties resting on his hairy chest, he used to hide, without their knowledge, some piece of their underwear—whether a flesh-coloured brassiere, or briefs with doughty menstrual blood stains which any number of washes couldn't remove, or blouses that were as tender as a newborn child. Of the three adamantine girls who didn't yield to him, he had succeeded in raping two all by himself and one with the aid of his friends.

Yet when Kamala walked past him on the verandah, holding law textbooks pressed against her chest, trailing behind her the tinkling of her anklets and the smell of vibhuti, he felt his body go weak and come under an unexplained chill. His heart rate went up and he felt cold. His throat was parched and cracked. As he stood there, clammy with sweat and agitated, she swept past him hurriedly.

The heady smell of calomel muriate filled the air. The tinkling of mercury-alloy beads resonated in his ears. He realised that love was growing by the hour inside him, like agglomerating clouds. She was constantly in his sight as he hid himself along her route, or sat unnoticed on the benches she had occupied, or camouflaged himself behind the trees under which she sat chatting with her friends. Eventually, the day her first year examinations ended, as she emerged from the examination hall after submitting her answer sheet, he somehow managed to stutter, 'Kamala, wait a minute. I've to tell you something.'

Kamala stopped. The alluring smell of calomel muriate spread. The clashing of the tiny bells on her anklets ceased. Only the gold cage-shaped earrings kept swinging from her ears with their bells chiming.

'I must see you ... just for a minute, please.' His voice was tremulous, as if it was a plea.

She turned her face ever so slightly. Her cheeks gleamed in the sunrays falling on them through the small window. A smile spread in her eyes.

'I shall go to the hostel and come back.' He could hear her recede, her clothes brushing against her as she walked. A red single-petal flower slipped from her dark hair and fell down.

As he saw her waiting for him beneath the ancient mahogany tree in the college yard, clad in a red silk skirt and blouse, an irrational fear rose in him. The seeds of the mahogany tree fell to the ground with thuds like mini coconuts. The colour of her dress reflected in the nose-stud mole, turning it into red. It had started to drizzle. Droplets fell on the puffed sleeves of her blouse and rolled around like mercury beads. Even in that cool air, he felt warm and sweaty.

When she heard his declaration of love, she laughed aloud. A look of disdain appeared on either side of her lips that showcased her jasmine teeth. He remained perplexed till she finished laughing.

After three months, when he entered the newly-rented flat along with Kamala—returning from the old registrar's office in front of Rajendra Maidan in Ernakulam—he had that uneasy feeling yet again. He sneezed occasionally and wiped his watery eyes with the handkerchief. He stood with his congested head inclined to one side.

'Are you feverish?' Kamala touched his forehead. He recoiled as if touched by a flaming brand. Her hand was so hot.

'I will have a bath.'

Kamala nodded her head in acquiescence. She looked at the maidan through the window. Her eyes became bloodshot.

A straying sea breeze, reeking of bilge and mud, swept into the room. The same smell. The crackling sound of mustard seeds being sautéed. The murmuring lips of the crowd. Kamala felt as if her body was on fire. Rajendra Maidan. The same Rajendra Maidan. Where her sister lay dead. The same maidan where her sister lay, cold, gang-raped and killed.

Kamala gripped the window bars hard. She remembered it was a clear afternoon with bright sunlight. The sea, not far from the maidan, was boiling hot and frothing. Three hours later, her sister was dead. The sound of her skull being hacked, like the sound of a ripe coconut cracked open, the hiss of blood spurting from a vein in the head like coconut water from a tender coconut. Kamala's sister heard those sounds over the unbearable agony of her other wounds. Her eyes bulged, and two teardrops covered them like a patina of crystal. The bright blood from her split head, flowing along the channel of her parted hair, imbued the start of her hairline with vermillion—the marker of a married woman. Before she could see her killer, she fell into the sea, spread-eagled. The toy fans made from sliced-up discarded mineral bottles spun around in the maidan, creating a noisy racket.

Kamala reached three hours after the incident. She had walked back slowly from the law college gate on her tired legs after waiting for her sister the whole afternoon. The public commented among themselves on the impropriety of bringing a tenth-standard student for identifying the dead person. Yet she was led to the maidan.

As it was May, the trees were swaying, tickled by the red wild flowers that had sprouted on them. Kamala could smell the flowers' strong fragrance along with the strange scent of the salty sea on the steady breeze. Her palms were clammy with sweat. Her heart, within the constraints of her tight uniform, fluttered like a sparrow. As blood drained from them, her lips became dry as paper. Nevertheless, when she saw the sodden corpse of her sister, she didn't blanch or scream in fear. Her sister's male classmate, who had accompanied Kamala, fell into a faint.

Kamala suddenly recalled the pet name that her father used endearingly and also to make fun of her sister—Kalakutty, meaning bull calf. Her lips, ripe with sorrow, kept murmuring 'Kali, Kali'. Perhaps after she had fallen into the water, with her right hand, her sister had prised out the machete lodged in the back of her skull. A plastic cover in which molluscs had built their home hung from the front of her sari like a belled waist-belt. Her soft-as-cotton-candy tongue, which in her death throes she had bit into, hung down from her mangled lips, hideously bloodied and swollen. The capillaries in the whites of her eyes resembled angry, gnarled roots of an old tree. Her eyelashes, seeped in saline water, stood out as if coated with mascara. The bluish-black mole on her right nostril, prominent like a nose-stud much like Kamala's, shone in the setting sun's rays like a glowing ember. Her golden anklet, coppery in the twilight, tinkled. Her crimson silk sari, lying loose around her waist, billowed like flags fluttering wildly in the wind. Seaweeds lay on her belly, embellishing the soft, downy sagittal going down her navel. Only on her forehead, and only there, glistened a spot of blood—like the Evening Star. Kamala remembered the ember-like vermillion bindi of Bhadrakali.

With the honeylike smoothness of a young mahogany tree, her sister's dark, firm breast thrust out through the torn blouse. Kamala was reminded of the black chest of Bhadrakali and her black nipples, which rivalled the colour and sheen of black moles. Losing strength in her limbs, she sat down. Darkness entered her eyes. She heard the ankle bells and the drone of the bead-filled, hollow bracelets of Bhadrakali and the raspiness of her raucous laughter. She slipped into unconsciousness.

Kamala got back her speech only three days after her sister's funeral.

'I was murdered, *Nallachcho*,[3] I was murdered.' A murmur appeared on her lips along with a spreading blackness.

'*Eeeeh, eeeeh aaaaah aaaah aaeeeh* ...' A terrifying scream emanated from her lips. Her hair, usually tied up in a neat ponytail, came loose and cascaded down. Incarnadine became the bluish-black mole inherited by her and her sister. It sparkled like a single-stone blood-red nose stud.

'I was killed, *Nallachcho*. I am in pain ... my head is splitting, ayyo ...' Kamala's body stiffened and twitched as if electrocuted. Her head jerked from side to side.

'My baby, Kamala ...' her mother wailed, beating her breast. Relatives stopped their conversations and started murmuring under their breath. Kamala thrust out her crimson tongue and screamed: 'I am Shri Bhadrakali.' She bellowed in a quavering voice, 'Blood was spilled in her death. I must have blood, and nothing else. I am so thirsty.'

---

[3] Lord Shiva

Her eyes rolled around in the sockets like marbles. She pressed her index fingers against her canine teeth and blood spurted.

'*Eeeyyaaah* … *Nallachcho* … the goddess is hungry and thirsty. Serve me blood, *Nallachcho*.'

Her gleaming incisors were by now covered in blood. Blood was dripping from her fingers too. Kamala started to suck the blood from her fingers.

'*Nallachcho* … *Nallachcho* …' Kamala's fiery eyes widened.

'We must go to Kodungallur, *Nallachcho*, *eeeh eahhaha* …'

Her tongue turned red. Kamala's mother fell into a faint. Her father stood immobile; his eyes bulged like a purblind person. He understood she had been possessed by Kali. A wail got stuck in his throat. His ears rang with chenda beats.

Kamala went into the yard. She sat on her haunches on the cow dung-coated parapet in the temple, a seat which Goddess Kali used to occupy.

'Bring on the oxen,' she commanded the people who stood by.

'*Ayyo* … dear Goddess, have you let down this daughter of mine too?' Her father's throat found liberation through that wail.

He recalled the Bharani[4] day in the month of Meenam.[5] Mallika and Kamala were on his either side. They were looking at the cows cavorting in the temple yard. Two white milch cows with milk oozing from their udders.

---

[4] One of the twenty-eight stars of the Malayalam calendar. Also, the day of the famous Kodungallur temple festival.

[5] Corresponds to Gregorian March-April.

Their eyes were crystalline blue. When they stood on their stilt-like legs, ears pointed and tails curled, they looked like cute calves. The tender coconut-leaf festoons hanging from their bellies rustled and crinkled in the gentle breeze.

'Achcha, who's that?' Baby Kamala had a doubt.

'It is the Goddess Bhagawathy, baby. You worship her. Worship her devoutly.' Kamala's father joined his hands in prayer.

'Where's Bhagawathy headed, Achcha?'

'To the south mana in Kodungallur. The house into which the Goddess was married is there.'

'Now what tale's that, Achcha?' Mallika asked, laughing.

'Mmmm ... the story of our Goddess's wedding. Do you know what her dowry was? But then, how'll *you* know?' He stroked her head indulgently.

'Seven-and-a-half baskets of variola seeds.'

Kamala's father wiped his eyes. He went towards Kamala.

'My baby ... your Achcha's darling baby ... come to me,' he wearily held out his arms.

'Give me my *shankoozhi*, *malli* and *molom*[6] seeds *Nallachcho*.'

Kamala's shrieks struck the night and echoed back from all directions. The public holding burning brands fashioned out of dried hay stood guard at the temple grounds.

'Karuna, grab her and take her with you.' An elderly man pushed her father towards the temple yard.

'Come, my darling, let's go ...' Her father blinked back his tears and grabbed her hand.

---

[6] Contents of the seven-and-a-half baskets of variola seeds of Lord Shiva.

In that instant, flames flew out of Kamala's eyes. Her lips contorted grotesquely. She took out the finger she was sucking blood from out of her mouth and spat viciously. 'Edeee ...'

Kamala's father slapped her hard. Her eyes rolled back and she staggered; her leg slipped on a tiny pool of collected rainwater. Kamala turned into Goddess Kali, ready to cross the river. Her saree touched the water. Kamala felt as if she was inside a boat floating on chilly waters, with the bells on her waist-belt tinkling.

In the middle of the river, Kamala turned into Goddess Kali who had flung variola seeds at the Muslim boy. As the seeds fell on him, Kamala heard a sound. Bubbles, white as rice, rose up like flowers made of crystal and burst. Kamala saw watery cloaks, stitched with the silvery threads of the sun's rays, float and settle over them. Intermittently, the watery scenes from the beach beyond the Rajendra Maidan lapped at her memory weakly. She looked daggers at her father. She recognised him as her father and called out to him in agony, 'Achchachchi ...'

In the next instant, she heard the tinkling of the ankle bells lying discarded in the temple yard. She recalled her sister dressed up as Kali for a fancy dress competition. She recalled her lying dead. She was bewitched by the flame-licked tongue of the terrifying incarnation of Kali. She let out a ghastly bellow with the ferocity of Bhadrakali, and kicked her father on his chest and sent him sprawling. Then she bent down and took a handful of the soil mixed with vermillion and with her left hand loosened her sari. She flung the variola seeds bestowed by *Nallachchan* at her father's body.

The next afternoon was rainy and wet. The red flowers lay unwilted in the dung-coated yard; withered neem leaves fluttered down from the trees; rain sprinkled water; sunshine broke out in buds; drenched nettles fell to the ground like ice needles and broke their points. The air was suffused with the smell of the divine vermillion. Kamala lay in her bed, pasty-faced, with beads of sweat above her sallow upper lip. Her cheek bore bluish welts from her father's slap. The smell of roasted cashew nuts rose from an earthen pot in the room.

She suddenly remembered Kali with her hair loose, walking near the river bank. Kali's ruddy, tender feet, with their copper anklets, felt cold in the water when she stood on the moss-covered stone steps as blue fish swam past them. The fish swam close and gently nipped at her golden toes. The variola seeds given as dowry by *Nallachchan*, pulsating with variola germs, were lying squeezed inside her sari pouch. Kali smiled brightly, exposing her wily, feminine teeth, at the fisherboy who had brought his boat to the jetty.

'Where does the lady want to go?'

'To the thekkae mana. Kodungallur's thekkae mana.' Kali smiled again. The wavelets in the river leapt up and glinted.

'Kamala, wake up. Baby, giddy up.' The rough fingers of her grandmother slithered over her forehead. Her grandmother's aged lips had been reddened and plumped up by betel juice.

Kali was back. A bloodthirsty Kali. Kamala felt that she too was inside the rocking boat, in the middle of the river. Retribution throbbed on her fire-red lips, reddened by constant chewing of betel leaves. When the fisherboy began to repeatedly demand his ferry fare even before they had reached Kodungallur, Kali laughed.

'There's no money, boy.' Kali laughed some more, setting off wavelets in the river.

The boy lost his temper: 'Stop your tomfoolery and pay up.'

'I'll have to undo my sari, boy.'

'Undo it and pay, lady.'

'Should I really ...?' There was a meaningful smile on her lips.

'Of course.'

'So be it.' Kali undid her sari. Along with a one-rupee coin, Kali's variola seeds also fell out into the boat. Kali laughed boisterously, seeing cowrie-like blisters appearing on the Muslim boy's body.

Kamala thought she would go mad. She looked at the clouded lenses of the cataract-affected eyes of her grandmother. She looked at the thousands of furrows on her shrivelled face, at her sagging veins which resembled loosely hung clotheslines. She smelled the smoky scent of the sacrificial *kuruthi* offering, and the odour of rooster blood wafting in through the open window. In the yard, wild geranium bushes swayed in the breeze, waving their ripe, red nipple-shaped berries.

In the next room, on a cot lined with neem leaves, lay Kamala's father Karunan, his body burning. His sins rose inside him as fear and on his body as pustules.

'Be warned, Karuna. Whether you are a Christian or you wear a crucifix, be warned. What you smashed was Kali's temple.' His brother's words shook him up again.

'Your eldest met with a horribly, unnatural death; the younger one has been possessed by Kali; and you have chickenpox. Karuna, you had better do something in reparation or else Kali will destroy your family.'

A terrified Karunan tried to open his eyes. Karunan had water-bubble-like blisters even inside his eyelids. When he looked at the baroque-style wall clock, he saw three hands in it.

When he thought of Kamala, he felt a terror—the terror of seeing the Goddess of Kodungallur incarnate. When she had spat, her saliva had scalded his skin like boiling oil. Her kick had the power of a thousand horses. The first blister appeared on his face. And it became scorched and blackened from the saliva that fell on it. The sight of it in the mirror had unnerved him. Then, some popping sounds, and the smell of mustard being sautéed. Five new blisters popped up on his left cheek. And, within five minutes, there were sixty blisters.

'My holy Ammachchiyyo, my Goddess Kali,' Kamala's father cried out plaintively to the deity of Kodungallur.

'Ammachchiyyo, my dear Ammachchiyyo, don't curse us by throwing your seeds at us.' Karunan's rattling, splintered voice filled the house with wails. Hearing his piteous cries, Kamala, and Kamala alone, howled with laughter.

That evening, Brother Susheelan came to pray for the amelioration of Karunan's disease. A group of evangelical acolytes in pure white clothes accompanied him. Kamala was in the bathroom. Her hair soaked in oil, her body covered in herbal beauty paste, she was trying to see Bhadrakali in her honey-complexioned, supple form reflected in the blue-tinged mirror. Her proud breasts; her slender, goddess-like neck; the silver girdle that writhed around her waist like Lord Shiva's silvery snakes. That was when she heard Brother Susheelan's voice.

'He is hoodwinking our Achchachye, Kamala,' she heard Mallika say.

While still in wet clothes, Kali appeared at the entrance of the house. A light breeze crawled over the yard, as if coming from Kali's groves. The pastor and his acolytes, who had come to pray for mitigation, were nonplussed by the sounds of the tinkling anklets. Oil mixed with water dripped down from her underskirt. Grabbing the ochre soil from the yard, and impregnating it with imprecations, Kamala flung it at Brother Susheelan.

'You and your family must rot to death' or something similar was what Brother Susheelan heard. He sat down in the yard as if he had lost all strength, as if his body had become weightless. He felt a piercing pain in his temples, and the shock of fever entering his body. The same day, at exactly midnight, twenty-one pus-filled blisters rose up in Brother Susheelan's body like buds. They laughed within themselves, like the holy water-filled prayer beads the pastor had brought from Paris. Brother Susheelan screamed loudly at the sight of them.

Three long years went by after that. To evacuate Kali and her dead sister from Kamala's mind, the doctor had prescribed tablets. In her very remote memory, Kamala recalled the sight of a laughing girl who had untied her curly hair that resembled the bloom of palmyra trees. Even in her oblivion,

Kamala heard the faint tinkle of mercury-bead ankle bells. She had completely forgotten the smell of the seeds, though.

She had stopped the pills the day the psychiatrist had told her, 'You are perfectly all right, Kamala.' Which was the day before her wedding. Within twenty-four hours of that, the swishing and clanging of the Goddess incarnate's divine sword were heard by her. Resplendent in the sunlight, the dazzling waves of the sea near Rajendra Maidan reminded her of the flashing blade of Kali's sword. Her husband's leering eyes reminded her of the desperate cries of her sister. A shiver ran down Kamala's spine as Kali took possession of her.

'What happened, Kamala?' Her husband emerged from the bathroom blinking his wet eyelashes. Water droplets rolled off his head and made his temple and hirsute torso wet. Lost in her memories, Kamala laughed again. He shook his head at speed and drops of water splashed on her face.

'What?'

Kamala shook her head to indicate it was nothing.

He perceived a miasma of many smells—of concentrated honey, roasted cashew nuts, and many unknown scents from the inside of her red-bordered Pochampally silk sari.

'The scent of a woman.'

'*Mmm … mmm …*' Kamala nodded her head to acknowledge it. He leaned close to her.

'I always get this smell, even if I have a cold. Long ago, there was a girl who was my student. From Kannur. I forget her name …' He held Kamala's face in his hands.

'When she used to come near me, I got the same smell.'

There was a suggestion of fire in Kamala's eyes. The seeds Kali had scooped up from *Nallachchan's* basket for sowing around.

'Her eyes were like yours—fiery.'

He ran his fingers along her neck. He rubbed them gently against her protruding bones. He felt her breasts getting engorged and their unyielding strength. As he bent down to kiss her, she covered his mouth with her hand and said, 'What happened after that, tell me …'

'Oh, what after that? One day she was found dead and abandoned on the maidan.' Irritated, and in an unholy hurry, he pulled at her sari; it came loose where it had been tucked in at the waist.

'Seeds, my seeds … seeds I have to sow …' Kamala murmured. Her ears were filled with the blood-spattered anklets' sounds, blood from the animal sacrifice. Kamala searched in her waist pouch for the seeds to sow in the fields, yards, hillocks and forests as she went along the south mana of Kodungallur.

'What's the matter, Kamala?'

Her eyes became bloodshot. The fine capillaries in them stood out and pulsated. She had bitten her tongue, and now, crimson blood dropped from between her lips. Her body felt as if the clothes on it had caught fire.

'You have forgotten her, haven't you? Her name was Mallika. She was raped by you and your friends.' Her voice quavered. 'Then you hacked her and threw her into the sea.'

He was bewildered. He grabbed her by the shoulders and shook her, shouting her name.

'It was the college's annual day. Dressed as Rakta Kali, she was getting ready for the play, wasn't she?' Kamala lunged forward. Her voice was rasping; it sounded like coconut husk being rubbed against a copper pot.

'You, you are the one who laid hands on her first.'

'Kamala …' He looked at her fearfully.

Kamala's hair had come loose and tumbled about her. Her lips were scarlet from anger and the blood from her bitten tongue. The swollen mole on her nose gleamed red, the big vermillion bindi on her forehead was smudged. Her eyes, rolling up, had disappeared into her skull. Kamala stretched out and sunk her fingers into his cheeks.

'And now you want to disrobe me too, you bastard? *Phththooo* …' she snapped.

Kamala lifted her right leg and kicked his chest hard. He fell back with a big groan. Before he lost consciousness, he saw it—Rakta Kali, the incarnation of blood lust, flinging the seeds. Along with the blisters that were springing up on his body, he got the whiff … the reek of Kali … the reek of blooming variola—of festering, of suppuration—a rousing, intoxicating smell.

Kamala paused. Her crimson sari fluttered in the breeze.

It was dark in the graveyard. Darkness had come like a cool blanket and enveloped daylight. Darkness filled her eyes, body, and her sari. Her ears were filled with the hissing sound of the divine sword flashing through the air, even as her cheeks were fatigued from endless laughing. The wild sounds of Rakta Kali's anklets filled the air. The loud howling of stray mongrels exploded. Her eyes started to emit flames. Squatting on the ground, she started to dig up her husband's grave like a rabid dog. Her waist pouch came loose, and a breeze reeking of variola blew over the graveyard.

Dedicated to Mani and other frolickers who had come to Rajendra Maidan to gambol, and sung beautifully and drummed strongly without missing a beat, though drunk and unable to walk.

Daddy, You Bastard

Within three minutes of being woken up into a state of disorientation by the singularly beastly sound emitted by the wolf-shaped alarm clock at 7:30 p.m., the doorbell which mimicked the shriek of a wild animal, aggravated Balachandran's consternation. After getting over the initial confusion, he glided into the slightly slippery, wet floor of the bathroom inattentively. He rolled his yet-not-frowzy blue-striped Allen Solly shirt—bearing the smells of his air-conditioned car, his professor's cabin and the ICCU; his grey pants—worn the whole day and carrying the distinct smell of the rexine and leather seat covers of the chairs occupied by him; his metal-coloured briefs; and his soft-cotton singlet into a ball, bundled it all in an old newspaper, and shoved it between the steel bars of the bathroom's tiny ventilator.

The calling bell rang, this time in stereo, mimicking the shriek of a prehistoric bird. Though it wasn't unexpected, Balachandran was in a lather, as if it had come out of the blue. He looked at his reflection in the mirror—a face that showed the ravages of his fifty-three years. Light bounced off the silvery shade of his grey hairs. In between his undisciplined eyebrows, on his sandal-coloured forehead, amidst the frown-lines was a red shadow of melancholy, giving him the semblance of a saintly sanyasi. However, the pair of eyes looking back at him from the mirror belied the placidity of his face and mocked him like a riddle. Like a cruel and cunning man's eyes, they seemed to reveal his true treachery and the lies hidden within the darkness of his heart.

'Sir, your eyes do not suit your nature.'

'Your gaze is a sharp harpoon.'

'Will it cut?'

'Don't scare me, staring at me like a fox, Baletta.'[7]

He understood partly the reason for Head Superintendent Karunakaran, his colleague Ammu, and Saraswathi, respectively ribbing him about his eyes. He had started to wear tinted glasses to hide his eyes.

The doorbell rang again. The sound it emitted was yet another unfamiliar animal's call, more an agonised scream than anything else. He had experienced this before on his previous visit. The sixteen different sounds of shrieking prehistoric animals programmed in the calling bell, chosen appropriately for the resort named Jurassic Park, lent the remote property near the seashore a beastly and ominous aura.

Coconut palms that appeared to be bowed down by heavy coconut bunches stood at the vast sandy property's northern end. Near the eastern boundary wall stood rows

---

[7] Etta is a suffix used to show respect (literally, elder brother), though here it is said by his wife.

of casuarina trees, waving their tiny arms and acting as windbreakers. To the south, beyond the tall boundary wall, lay a desolate grave. To the west, the Arabian beauty, the sea of silvery tinkling bells. Ah, the sea. The sea that for ages has hidden and dissolved all secrets.

Before the doorbell could ring again, he bounded down the stairs, forgetting his years—with self-confidence and the masculine smell of the Axe Wood deodorant sprayed into his armpits—and cut his hand on the recalcitrant tower bolt of the front door. He opened the door.

As expected, it was her. Agie—Agnes Fernandes was her full name. She was a member of the Pentecostal denomination. Though his enthusiasm was riding high like tidal waves, though he knew how to crush her in his arms with the laughter of a lover whose interminable wait had ended with his beloved's arrival, though he had the expertise of biting plum lips in a French kiss, he, like a gentleman, only took her tender right hand in his and pressed it with a long sigh.

'When it got late, I thought you won't come, baby.' He ushered her in and shut the door, ignoring the stare of the watchman at the gate.

'You know how the auto drivers get after sundown. Their lecherous stares … It's not easy getting an auto-rickshaw, Dad.'

Though her calling him dad destroyed him inside, to keep his face pleasant, he forced a laughter.

'Come,' he beckoned her to move upstairs.

'Who's that watchman, Dad?'

'Is there a problem?' He felt uneasy.

'Nah … lech, ugh!' She scowled with revulsion.

'You didn't kick up a fuss, did you?'

'No, Dad!'

This was a long anticipated tryst. More than anticipated—desired. He wouldn't allow anything untoward to spoil it.

He was the head of the Thoracic Department in the Medical College, and a cardiac surgeon; a specialist in open-heart surgery and in mending diseased hearts; a strict professor in the post-graduate classes; the husband of Saraswathi, the only daughter of Prabhakaran Nair, the city's glass merchant and moneybag; the darling father of seventeen-year-old Vinaya Balachandran alias Ammu; and currently, the paramour of Ammu's friend, one who kept fluttering her long eyelashes and smiling all the time.

She, who answered to the pet name of Agie, who flitted like a butterfly through happy scenes of her own making. The only daughter of an America-based couple. The beauty who came to study in Kerala after completing fifth grade from a school in Wisconsin. The best friend of Ammu.

When he saw her first, he felt an ineffable, irreducible happiness. In a sea-blue skirt that had undulating green petals, she was a prancing peacock displaying its feathers. It was as if he was seeing a vision. He couldn't take his eyes off her.

It was a whimpering rainy season. Agnes was playing amidst the orchids in the yard, drenched in the light rain. Agnes wore the traditional-style silk skirt that he had picked for his own daughter after spending many hours in a textile shop, but his daughter hadn't liked it in the least. The prancing

Agnes resembled an Ottapalam lass of his adolescent dreams, or his ex-lover, Ammu, whom he had forsaken.

Agnes, who had touched his forehead with her long, soft fingers for the first time, saying, 'How shiny is this daddy's forehead! And so smooth! Like a mirror!' when he had least expected it. Agnes, who had presented him her heartbeat through his stethoscope on the feverish first day of her menarche.

'Agnes … Agnes … Agnes…'

Agnes, smiling with her jasmine-like teeth and in her deep sea-blue skirt, used to sashay into his mind while he would be falling asleep; while he would be dreaming his rare black-and-white dreams; during the dreary, perfunctory, prosaic love-making with his wife; sometimes when the breeze blew in; sometimes while driving; and even when he was staring at the echocardiogram monitor, trying to suss out the problem in the beating heart in front of him. However, for a middle-aged man like him, she was a fool's dream or a desire which had no chance of realisation. Until six days ago.

That Saturday evening, he was headed home, tired from doing three surgeries and carrying inside his nostrils the nauseating, cloying smell of human blood that would stick like thick wine to his once-white surgical gloves. The overcast sky and evening twilight had reduced visibility. Piercing the gloom, his platinum Honda City flew over the road like a silver-winged metal bird. The excitement of speeding at over 100 kmph along the deserted road by the sea, unaffected yet by the city's crowds, raised his spirits. When it started to rain, speeding raindrops through the open window tickled his face, caressing it like tiny needles. But when through the moist windscreen, Agnes' face flashed as the car raced ahead at 100 kmph, he braked hard, with the tyres squealing on the wet road and the car coming to a shuddering halt. As the car was reversed, the white, flowery dress and the sad, anxious look—as the hour was late—on her face cut through his heart gently like a scalpel and sent his blood spurting.

He opened the car door in a hurry. She slid into the seat and wiped wearily the tiny beads of sweat above her upper lip with her hand within the time he took to smile at her. A feminine body odour, mixed with scents of Blue Lady and Lakmé lotion, filled the cool interior of the car. All the while, he kept looking at her through the mirror, hungrily, like a frustrated and perplexed lover.

'This, how do I …?' Agnes tried to pull the seat belt.

'Let me do it for you.'

He took the car to the side and parked over a carpet of flame-of-the-forest flowers. The red petal tongues that came down with the rainwater fell on top of the car, and held a conversation.

As he leaned over to the left to help pull the seat belt, like a gentleman he consciously ensured that he didn't brush against her body. Yet when he pulled the belt across, his arm brushed her body.

'Sorry.' He said, as if he had done it unintentionally. Though he wasn't looking at her, the realisation that his touch had caused her body to break out in goose pimples with arousal was a shock to him. He stepped on the accelerator and swerved into the bridge jutting out into the sea, and drove till its end. She was leaning back on the seat, eyes closed. He felt terribly anxious.

'Agie, I am really sorry …'

She opened her eyes, as if waking up from a nap. Her black eyes shone as if she had been watching pleasurable dreams. Her long eyelashes opened and closed exquisitely. Her irises glinted like new stars on the firmament. He thought he saw a flash of affection in them. Inspired, he gathered her in his arms. He pressed his lips against her flushed, full lips and kissed hard. The sea was roaring below and around them. The waves were screaming in the darkness. The rain drummed softly on the car. He relived his childhood on her lips—the same feeling as biting on the rain-speckled ripe eugenia berries. He bit her lips hard without marking them. He pressed the front of the white flowery dress, and fondled her tenderly.

'*Mmmm* …' she cooed like a dove. That one moment was enough for his first indiscretion. He parted his lips. Second indiscretion … the forehead, eyelids, collarbone, lifting the dress up around the neck … like a young man, he kept kissing everywhere. Her hand slithered through his hair like a serpent.

'You … you … will you come?'

'When?' Her chest rose and fell, like a bird panting after a long flight.

'Next Friday.' He stopped kissing and touched her lips with his fingers. 'Will you come?'

'*Mmm* …' she whispered drowsily.

'Daddy, this is a lovely place, isn't it?' Agnes stood in one corner of the balcony, bathed in moonlight. She extended her hands, as if to caress the sea breeze. 'The sea breeze, it's so cold …' She crossed her arms, hugging herself.

'It's the chill from the rain. You'll catch a fever. Let's go inside.'

He tried to persuade her to go inside. The watchman on the ground floor was looking up at them all this while. His eyes resembled magnifying glasses. They were making him uncomfortable.

'When I didn't get your reply, I was worried. That you may have said yes in that evening's excitement.' He let out a long sigh.

'Oh! It isn't that. I had to read and delete the message without Ammu seeing it. When the message came, seeing my jitters, Ammu got suspicious.'

A couple of her freshly shampooed hairs, fluttering friskily in the wind, stretched towards him. He pressed them aside gently, and kept looking at her to his heart's content. She kept on chattering about how she hid the phone out of Ammu's sight, how his name was saved as D-Devil, how Ammu had searched the phone to find out if she had a lover.

'She can't imagine in her wildest dreams that this handsome old man is my lover, no, Daddy?'

He shook his head in annoyance.

'Please, Agnes, for God's sake, don't call me daddy.'

Plaited hair on either side tied up in bow ribbons. Blue box-pleated uniform skirt, reaching below the knee. White shirt with the neck button fastened.

'*Sheesh.*' He has been seeing this uniform for the last twelve years. Ammu's school uniform. Suddenly, he remembered his daughter. A shiver ran through him.

'Please change that uniform, Agnes.'

Agnes patted down her skirt.

'Oh sorry, Daddy. I have sweated so much, I must be stinking. I am not even carrying a deo.'

'It's not that, Agnes. When I see this uniform …'

'*Mmm* … I understand. You are reminded of Ammoose, aren't you?'

'Daddy, Daddy …' Agnes teased him.

'Agnes!' He was angry and hurt at the same time.

'Oh, sorry, Daddy. Sorry, sorry. It's a habit now. Weren't you the one who had said that though you are only my friend's father, I must call you Daddy? I shall try, I promise. Let me take a bath. Ah, one more thing: Ammu has her suspicions about us.'

Agnes pulled and undid the ribbons. Her hair tumbled down like black rain over her back. It gave off the fragrance of imported water lily shampoo. Balachandran felt intoxicated. She undid the top buttons of her shirt, and her chest loosened up a bit.

Every pore of his body was waking up; every atom in it was throbbing. Each cell of his body was opening its eyes like a newborn child. Thereafter, there was a strange pulsation in each of them.

She was inside the bathroom … he tried to listen. Soft steps … she was tip-toeing. The sounds of buttons coming loose. Bucket being dragged across the floor. Water flowing down from the tap.

'*Uff* …' he bit down on his tongue.

'Daddy, can you please hold this? What kind of bathroom is this, without even hanger hooks?'

The door was ajar. Her wet forearm held out the skirt and shirt. His hands shook when he took them. She closed the door and then opened it again.

'Please take this, too.'

Balachandran felt woozy, as if he was drunk. He saw the water drops on her fair forearm. Gleaming like gold, her hand held out her green undergarments.

He took them from her and smelled them. Bala, no, don't rush it. Women like to take it slow. He knew that. The two other women he had made love to, his lover Ammu and his wife Saraswathi, both were like that. Start from the top and move slowly down. From behind the tender, flower-like ears, to the eyelids, to under the chin, to the soft skin where the neck begins, the clavicle … the more he thought of Agnes, the more aroused he became.

When Agnes emerged from the bathroom, he was seated in the portico facing the sea and sipping vodka, denser than seawater. His eyes were a little bloodshot. The capillaries in his eyes were suffused with blood.

'For me, too,' Agnes slapped his head with the wet towel. Droplets flew and hit his face. He looked at her in disbelief.

'Why, can't I?' She grabbed his glass and drained it in one swig. She took the bottle and poured another drink.

'But Ammu never told me all this …'

'Whaaaa …? That Agnes Fernandes drinks? Does Daddy think that Ammu will tell him everything?'

As she laughed, mocking him, her cheeks flushed.

'My darling Daddy … forget Ammu, will *anyone* share such things with their father? By the way, there's another thing. Ammu also likes all these …'

'Please stop it, Agnes.'

'Oh yeah? That day, if Siddhi wasn't there, it would've been a mess. The ruckus Ammu had created, oh!'

'Please, Agie …' he pleaded and raised his hands in supplication. He entered the house, walking slowly.

'Don't stress. I was joking. Come to me, let no one come between us— not even Ammu.'

'What's that poem … *tonight's the night when we'll sing the saddest songs* … No, let it not be that.'

Balachandran put his arm around her shoulder. He buried his face in the curve of her neck. The fragrance of an unknown floral perfume hit him.

'Have you brought it?'

'What?'

'That … that …'

She laughed.

'Did you get it?'

'*Chee … chee …*' Agnes shook her head in denial.

'I bought the pill. I had a feeling that you won't bring it. I must take it within one hour of the act. Do remind me.' Agnes smiled amorously.

'The uncle at the medical shop from where I bought it will die of worry today. It's the shop from which I regularly buy sanitary napkins.' Agnes laughed riotously.

Balachandran closed the door to the portico and drew the curtains.

'Let the watchman at least watch the shadow play, sir.'

'*Naah …*' Balachandran shook his head, objecting to the idea. 'You are mine, mine alone. No one else should see even your shadow.'

She saw agitation on his face. His lips trembled with adoration for her.

'Agnes, you had so many other options. Yet you chose this old man …'

Agnes pushed him down onto the bed.

'True, there are boys in my class itself, shiny and bursting like rose apples. I have noticed many of them looking at me longingly … but …'

Agnes lay on top of him, lifted her head and rubbed her nose on his.

'I saw something in these eyes that I didn't see in theirs. This love … its warmth … its pleasure.'

Agnes kissed him on the lips. Her wet hair tickled his face.

'Yes, man, I will give it—my virginity—only to a man who loves me madly. And that is you.'

Balachandran's hands went berserk. He pushed her down on the bed, tore off the buttons of her frock greedily, and pressed her against his chest. A night of waves and tempests on the sea. The wild sounds of whirlpools and stormy winds resounded. Agnes' breath came out ragged, and she panted. Murmurs of love writhed on her lips.

'Please accept this … liberate me. I can't bear this burden any longer. I am the only virgin left in my class.'

Hearing that, Balachandran started. 'What, what did you say?'

'I am the lone virgin in my class,' her voice trembled with love.

'So, isn't Ammu in your class?' Balachandran was enraged.

'Yes, 12 B,' her words slurred.

'You … you want to prove that everyone is like you, don't you?' He gripped her face roughly by the cheeks.

'What do you mean, like me?' Agnes broke free. Her eyes were burning with anger. 'That I am a slut, eh?' She grabbed his shoulders and shook him.

'Tell me … is it that I am a slut? After loving you and coming here for you, I am a slut? Then you better listen carefully. Your daughter Ammu, she's a bitch. She'd do anything for pleasure. Her nude video's still there in Siddhi's mobile. I have seen it.'

'No!' Balachandran slapped Agnes hard.

'I must go. I have committed a mistake.' He leapt up from the bed.

There was a knock on the door, followed by someone thumping it hard. Balachandran was surprised. The moment he opened the door, a silver-coloured torch came down in an arc and hit his head. Blood from the gash in his head hit the khaki-clad watchman's face. Balachandran fell forward on his face. The watchman dropped the torch on the floor and smiled at Agnes. Then he started narrating in his grating voice.

'Baby, have you heard the story of the wolf? Uncle will tell you. Once a hungry and weary wolf, while foraying, heard a mother tell her child, "If you do mischief, I will throw you to the wolf." The poor wolf. It waited in front of the house the whole night, salivating. When it was morning, the occupants of the house drove it away. It was a fool, no, baby? This uncle can't be such a fool.'

With a wicked laugh, he leapt onto the bed. He tore away the sheet Agnes was clinging to. As she looked on, terrified, he grew fangs, sprouted vicious claws, and saliva was dripping off his tongue. As she backed away, he grabbed her. She was conscious of her head hitting the corner of the bed post and the wetness of blood spreading on her scalp. She screamed at the sight of the fanged wolf approaching to feast on her. As she slipped into unconsciousness, she saw her daddy as if in a dream.

'Daddy … Daddy …' she murmured.

The Autobiography of a Movie Extra

It was very late in the night that Janaki, an extra, came to know of her daughter, Gitanjali, getting the lead actress's role in a movie. It was after she had torn open the Women's Horlicks sachet bought with her daily allowance of rupees 150, deposited that in a glass of boiling milk, added two teaspoonfuls of sugar, and poured it into a shallow bowl to cool it, that her daughter walked in and, without any show of emotion, gave her the news.

The bowl slipped in her hand and, scalding her finger on its way down, some of the Horlicks spilled onto the floor with a hissing sound. She pulled her finger out of its way, and put it in her mouth, sucking it to cool it with her saliva. She stood gaping, as if she had heard a barely credible, fantastical tale.

Janaki was thirty-six years old. She had the looks and assets to be an extra. Fair, buxom, and a generously endowed body; fleshy arms; slabs of fat on her tummy and love handles on her flanks; comely face; a moderate neck; a bubbly personality that bounced invitingly in dance scenes.

When she entered the movies for the first time, she was a slim girl. The scriptwriter—adamant that the supporting actress should be lean, tall, have dimples and straight hair—had discovered her. She had caught his eye during a ballet performance at the Ambalapuzha Temple. The coloured spotlights bounced off her cheap, shocking-pink dress. She arrived on the stage, dancing to the accompaniment of a rousing riff on the harmonium.

The ballet was of poor quality, but Janaki sparkled on the stage. Her eyes weren't big, but they flashed like diamond-dust. The make-up lent a brightness to her face. Once he realised that the sharp glances from her narrow eyes were that of the melancholic girl in his story, the scriptwriter was breathless.

He took the help of the temple festival committee president to meet her father at their house to sign her up. A fan of dramatics and plays, her father was only happy to send her off to Madras to act in the movies.

The atmosphere in Madras was unlike that of Ambalapuzha, which was redolent with the smells of paddy and marshes. It was a place where broken Tamil was spoken, with a mixture of Malayalam and Telugu, and a smattering of English. It was a place where Tamil women clad in bright sarees smelled of chrysanthemum and sesame oil.

In Kodambakkam, the tiny yards in front of the huts—encroaching on the roads filled bounteously with cattle dung and even more human excreta—were swept clean and marked with rice powder rangoli. Rows of narrow huts like fishermen's shanties, and as squalid. Pimps walking about with eternally cold eyes and burning beedis on their lips, coughing all the while. Film shooting sets which reeked of oodles of money. Large, long star caravans. Fresh-faced, strikingly beautiful actresses and moth-eaten, old actresses. Actors with trimmed moustaches and cheeks shiny with moisturisers and aftershave balms. In contrast, snot-nosed, dysentery-ravaged kids, looking like emaciated consumptives with exposed ribs and matchstick limbs. On top of all this, the piercing lights of the studio in which interminable hours were spent, the incessant growl of diesel generators, the constant gossiping by extra actresses, the gunshot-like sputter of auto rickshaws run on kerosene instead of petrol—all together made Madras a wondrous, fantasy land for Janaki.

Unaccustomed to seeing even five people at the same time on the main road of Ambalapuzha, she was met by a stream of people of all colours and shapes in Madras. She knew nothing about life or acting. She was only a country girl who had joined Brains Parallel College as a freshman for a graduate course in Commerce.

Mohanlal was the hero of the movie she was acting in. Her role was that of a village belle with a bewitching smile. In the first shot itself, she made an impact. It was a scene in which she had to weep. When biting down on her lip, touching her trembling chin with her fingers, and shedding copious glycerine-aided tears down her cheeks, she stole the scene. Even Mohanlal joined in the applause and clapped hard. Murugayya, her make-up man, made an offering of a milk pot to be carried as *kavadi* to Lord Muruga. Character actor Manjuladevi wept. When the director shook the scriptwriter's hand to congratulate him for discovering her, the latter felt considerable pride. When everyone congratulated Janaki, she stood smiling and displayed no emotion.

'Amma, Amma …' Gitanjali shook Janaki. 'Why are you standing there, grinning like that?' She snapped her fingers, 'Are you dreaming? You don't believe me, do you? It's true. It's a heroine-oriented story—a love story. Shall I narrate the one-line?'

Gitanjali took the bowl of Horlicks from her hand and sipped from it.

'It's gone cold, Amma. Let it be. Just you wait for this movie to be shot. Then I will have my own ayah.'

Janaki looked at her face, which still resembled a child's. Long unibrow; suspicious eyes; long, straightened hair; fairer than Janaki was at sixteen, and taller. Not much else was different.

What could have been the first difficulty she would have faced? As she thought about it, Janaki felt nervous. It was a question, a big one. A big question with a simple answer. Janaki was first asked this question by a hanger-on of the producer's younger brother: 'Did you sleep with Mohanlal?'

'*Huh*?'

The prurience of his question, the leer on his face, the wretched specks of saliva on his lips—Janaki found it nauseating. She wanted to cry from the humiliation. Janaki was sixteen years old then. Though the heroine, Rebecca, had told her that it was one of the questions that should be ignored by an actress, Janaki still cried. The rouge on her cheeks ran, mascara congealed on her eyelashes like black glue. And when the kohl in the eyes spread on her face, she looked as if she had turned blue with fear.

'Silly girl,' Rebecca bit down on her lipstick-smeared, plump lips. 'This is usual for actresses. Don't take it to heart. The public needs something to gossip about. When I first came into movies, they even foisted an illicit pregnancy on me. Actresses shouldn't shed tears over such stuff.'

After that, an assistant cameraman repeated the same question with a cinema gossip magazine held open. A light boy, a driver, a production controller followed—the same question. The question was repeated after each of her first three movies. Mamootty, Mohanlal, Kamalahaasan, Rajanikanth—only the lead actor's name kept changing.

After the initial fear and revulsion wore off, Janaki started to ignore such questions. She dealt with them with a sardonic smile on her painted lips, or by turning away her face in derision, or by walking away as if she hadn't heard the question. This would make Rebecca smile secretly. Catching Janaki's eyes in the mirror, she would nod in appreciation. Kumariamma, the character actress from Palakkad, laughed, covering her mouth. The ingenuous pout on Janaki's face had the innocence and rusticity of her native Kuttanad. With an indulgent smile on her face, Kumariamma applied dye on her grey hairs.

'Isn't all this a kind of transaction? Business. Cinema is truly a business of exhibition. We exhibit ourselves. How does the value of new actresses go up? Depends on whom our names are linked up with.'

Kumariamma seemed to be pondering over something. Then her face took on a conspiratorial look. 'Ah, in my young age, I also had to listen to this load of rubbish. Prem Nazir, Jayan, Sathyan, Madhu, Ummer, and when I did a

Tamil film, MGR, Sivaji—those days, these were the names. The actresses of those days were no less. Whether they had slept with them or not, whether one was the lover of the extra actor or the concubine of the stuntman, as far as possible, they would take the names of the superstars of the time.' Kumariamma sighed deeply and added, 'You have just started. Wait a bit, and then you too can name names.'

'Amma ...' Gitanjali prodded her. 'What are you thinking about?' She tried to prise Janaki away from her reminiscences. Janaki shook her head. She switched off the light in the kitchen.

'Come, let's go inside. I was just remembering the past.'

Janaki shut the kitchen door. She took her nightdress off the clothesline and flung it over her shoulder. She tied her hair in a top knot.

'Amma was recalling her entry into this field, nothing else. I had come from a village. In those days, too, the film industry was a strange world—a world of women and money. My first movie was a superhit. But what's the use? I got just one decent movie after that; a lot of others never got made. The standard question of the production controllers was, "You'll compromise, won't you; you'll adjust, right?" That made me see red. Then the questions got bolder. The heroes seen on the screens taking on hoodlums for wolf-whistling at women were ready to gobble up women if they could get them alone. What adversities! Your Amma had to face every trade-off and temptation all alone. And survive every one of them.'

Janaki wiped her face nervously.

'Every door opened only in one direction. Many of them had no locks and latches. Yet, your Amma survived. By keeping the bed flush against the door, by balancing steel vessels and glasses on the edge of the door so that the slightest push would bring them down clattering ... it was like walking a tightrope. But because of that, I was able to eventually marry the man I loved.'

When she heard that, Gitanjali looked into her mother's eyes. A whole ocean was heaving inside them. Her eyelashes were moist. But her eyes stayed dry like a desert. Gitanjali knew that however hurt she was, her mother would never tear up. It was the fate of all actresses—tear glands that dried up. Eyes that wouldn't produce tears without the aid of glycerine, even in their worst sorrows.

But for Janaki, he was important. One who could be only remembered with a heart full of love and pain, whose name could be taken only with a smile and affection. He was already past fifty when she first saw him. While he didn't have a handsome face, his energetic and muscular body had impressed Janaki. He had a head full of thick, greyed yet undyed hair, parted on the left side. He controlled the unit with the self-assurance of a rebel. Scolding the feet-draggers and mocking the ham actors, he would stomp around the unit.

It was Janaki's tenth movie. When she saw him for the first time, he was looking at the rain through the camera's viewfinder. Different scenes; strange characters. A drizzle that enhanced the verdancy of Kuttanad. The waterlogged paddies with mirror-like surfaces, full of honey-rich flowers and pink, fragrant water lilies. His smiles that made vestigial marks from his vanished dimples linger … for her to fall in love with him, these were more than enough.

The beauty of her sesame flower-coloured ankles treading the wet terracotta mud in the smoke-filled field; the tiny mulberry-like scar on her forearm that invited kisses; a taciturn, sad, but ever smiling face; eyelashes that fluttered like butterfly wings; childlike movements; eyes that filled with love as they looked at him … he also didn't need many more reasons to fall in love with her.

Yet they slept together only once. That too happened in Kuttanad, on a wet afternoon. The bent-over rice stalks lent a heavy greenness to the paddies flooded to the brim. Over that, the water lily buds sprouting from their oily vines lay like floral explosions. She was the girl whose eyes turned wider than the blue water lilies that grew amidst the paddies. If Janaki's memory served her right, he had smiled briefly and taken his glasses off his fox-like sharp eyes before kissing her for the first time.

It had become dark before sunset. She could hear the croaking of frogs, the lapping of water against stones, and the high-pitched, chirpy whine of cicadas. As they lay in the inner courtyard of an old laterite-stone house, they watched the sky through the narrow slit in its roof. Their bodies gleamed under the star-spangled cotton sheet to the accompaniment of the pattering rain, the coolness it brought in, and the rustling sound of the bamboo leaves rubbing against one another from the rear of the house.

The memory of that gave Janaki goose pimples once more.

Thereafter, whenever they met, apart from giving her loving and indulgent kisses, he didn't touch her body.

Whenever he recited the lines from Tagore's *Gitanjali*, she didn't, on purpose, tell him about the Gitanjali who was growing inside her. When his wife came and fought with him and he left Janaki, she managed to remain detached.

'Amma, enough of your memories. Let's talk about something else,' Gitanjali said, fastening the hooks of Janaki's nightdress.

'Baby, you know the temptations that Amma had to fight and the difficulties she had to face, don't you?'

Gitanjali nodded.

'Though many tried, no one could take advantage of me. Even your father could lay hands on me only because he had tied the mangalsutra on my neck. I faced every challenge without yielding. My daughter should do the same. You must keep my life in mind. Then you'll be able to remain chaste, as you should.'

When she stopped talking, Gitanjali laughed aloud.

'True, true. Amma's life is an example. Despite your good acting skills, beauty, and many chances, your life amounted to nothing. When others who came in at the same time as you got lead roles and became stars, you pontificated about principles, married an aged lover, and remained an extra. Honestly, your life is a model for me—for how a movie actress shouldn't live her life. What did you think?' Gitanjali stood in front of Janaki.

'Did you think this extra's daughter got the lead role because of her fair skin?' She contorted her lips. 'All the five days that you were in Hyderabad, I went and saw the producer and director. No one lured me, no one tempted me. No one spoiled me. I cooperated heartily. Listen to this, too: how did I get through plus two when I used to fail regularly in Chemistry? The Chemistry teacher gave me plenty of marks in the internals and I got through. All it took was a study tour, Amma.'

Gitanjali paused and looked at her mother closely.

'I'll never forget the lessons you taught me. Whatever shouldn't happen to an actress, whatever an actress shouldn't do in her life—that's the sum total of your life in the movies.'

Janaki felt dizzy. The anguish she had felt when she had heard the lewd questions returned. A scream escaped from the heart. A sadness rose in her throat when she realised how her daughter had surpassed her and was now towering over her. Her throat burned. In the absence of glycerine, not even a single tear came out of her eyes.

Secret of the Soul

The fifty-year-old Kalyani was hundredth on the list. The beautiful wife of the former Revenue Divisional Officer of Ernakulam. There were a few signs of the ravages of time, clambering over her like the parasitic loranthus plant: deposits of fat that had escaped her belly and bulged beneath her blouse on her back; the grey strands of curly hair that fell over her forehead, the colour of mustard oil; wide eyes in which sadness had bled and turned bluish-black; extra-long, well-aligned eyelashes; a ruby nose stud that resembled a spot of blood on the aquiline nose; and light brown, butterfly-shaped melasma spots, from the slow secretion of melanin by her body, to put in shade the extraordinary lustre of her youthful skin. Save for these, a smile that reminded one of the shiny whiteness of the Arabian jasmine that blooms during moonlit nights, plump lips whose natural tone put applied colours to shame, stylishly pleated and smartly-worn cotton sarees, and a placid face with latent sadness, combined to give her the look of a forty-year-old.

In that waiting room, every woman except her was pregnant. With difficulty, they put up their swollen legs on the chairs placed in front of them, surveyed piteously the scene around them with their narrowed eyes in their papaya-like, puffed-up faces, and muttered their irritation for having to put up with shortness of breath, lower backache and wheezing.

'What's yours? Key-hole for you, too?' At first, she didn't understand the question put to her in patois Malayalam by the Muslim lady seated next to her. She smiled and nodded.

'We're coming from Perambra. We were set on this doctor. He was previously working in the Medical College. He delivered my first child. Faultlessly. When the child was three, I felt a kind of hypertonia in my abdomen. My husband, as ever, could think only about the next child.'

She lowered her tone. 'After all, chechi, our men are like that, though I am no less. A look from him is enough for me to get pregnant. During my second delivery, along with the child, they snipped and took out two lumps after they cut my tummy open. Then I had seven deliveries without a hitch. Now again I have hypertonia. When I came last week, the doctor said key-hole is enough. And that the lump will have to be tested. These are the days of cancer and afflictions like that ...'

Kalyani's start and the lady's sigh were simultaneous. Kalyani looked at her husband seated next to her. A fear fluttered inside her and cooed like an orphaned dove. Initially, Kalyani's complaint was of only a little white discharge. It started as white thread-like emissions and then gradually turned light yellow. Bleeding with clots followed thereafter, first intermittently and then like the menstrual flow. One rainy evening, five years after her menopause, the blood kept flowing and soaking her undergarments, as if she was a fourteen-year-old. By the second day, changing the rolled-up white cloth every fifteen minutes, and seeing small flowers bloom as the blood fell and splattered on the floor wherever she walked in the house, she felt faint. Her face had become pale and eyes white from the constant loss of blood. When she felt her thighs shiver as she walked and, like a girl having her menarche, her lower abdomen began to twist and churn, she told her husband she needed to consult a doctor.

'Barren women have higher chances of getting cancer.' The detachment on his face when he uttered those words surprised her.

'The worst curse a woman can have is to be barren.' Her sister Bhama, who had died from uterine cancer fifteen years ago, had said this. She was his first wife, and used to tell Kalyani this often during her last days in the hospital.

'Kallu baby, I got this because it remained fallow. It's the womb … whatever seed falls into it, it lets it sprout and makes it ten-fold.'

Memories of Bhamedathi always left a bitter taste in her mouth. She would then recall her hair, which always smelt of hibiscus leaves. Rich black curly hair, which fell below her knees, tumbling over her buttocks. The hair that fell out in clumps in Kalyani's hands when she poured water on it and towelled it in the hospital's bathroom in Thiruvananthapuram. The hair danced about in the ceiling fan's breeze like angry, emaciated black serpents. The room looked like a barber's saloon, with the floor covered with fallen hair. The hair hid the steel mesh of the bathroom drain, and deposited in clumps inside the WC, on the towel, the pillow cover, and in the waste basket. Kalyani had wailed looking at Bhamedathi's bald head.

She was injected with morphine twice a day so that she would sleep without pain. That night, as Kalyani watched Bhamedathi's golden eggshell head gleam in the zero-watt lamp's light, she couldn't hold back her tears. The surgery to remove Bhamedathi's uterus, ovaries, ovarian tubes and a part of her large intestine was to happen the next day.

'Kallu baby, don't cry. Keep your hand on my forehead.' There was a quaver in Bhamedathi's voice. 'Are you angry with me? Will you forgive me?'

Kalyani's throat was on fire. The picture rose in her mind of Bhamedathi embracing and holding her close to her chest in the east room of their ancestral home as she wept on the evening Kalyani's parents had died.

'No need to be worried about her. What if she's my uncle's daughter? She's like my own sister; I will take her with me to Ernakulam. I'll give her an education there.'

Kalyani caressed Bhama's bald head. A teardrop from her eye fell on Bhama's lip and splattered.

'*Shush*! Bhamedathi. Don't say anything, lie quietly,' she admonished her.

'Quietly? I have so much to say, Kallu baby. All this is punishment for the wrongs I have done to you.'

Kalyani wanted to cry again. 'I am the one who should be asking for forgiveness, isn't it? Please rest.'

'I can't, Kallu baby. If I remain silent, my heart hurts. Especially, here, this left breast. That pains more.'

Her left breast, which had undergone mastectomy, was hurting. The pain was seeping out like breast milk and spreading. Bhamedathi felt the pain in each pore on her head from where thousands of strands of her hair had got detached and which Kalyani had had to bury.

The pain festered in her intestines, in her womb, in the withered innards of her internal organs, in her heart—especially in her slow-beating heart—and on the back of her left hand, infected and inflamed from needle punctures, and inside her right thigh, swollen from the morphine shots. She was in great agony.

'Kallu baby, I was in the know of things—that Unnietten wanted you. Everything happened with my knowledge.'

Kalyani thought she had heard a thunderclap outside. Like the sound of a skull being split open. 'Lies, lies,' Kalyani kept murmuring.

'No, Kallu baby, I swear it's the truth … it's the truth …' Then Bhamedathi smoothly slipped into a stupor. She kept bobbing up and down in her troubled sleep, and moaning, as the heat of the strong chemotherapy drugs and the rasping fingers of pain met her halfway into her somnolent state.

As soon as Kalyani lay down to sleep, Unnietten switched off the light. He slinked and approached her like a crawling snake. When she heard his feet feeling for the selvedge of the palmyra mat, she pretended to be asleep.

'*Shhhh* … Kallu baby…' He tried to wake her up in hushed tones. 'Please … it's been so many days …' he pleaded.

'Kallu baby, wake up …' He shook her awake.

'No! My sister …' she objected. Even if Bhamedathi was dozing, and even if she was aware of it all, she was, after all, her sister and present in the room. Bhamedathi was moaning and whimpering as she seesawed between the peaks and troughs of pain.

'NO!' Kalyani shook him off with a vengeance. His hands too gained strength, and his eyes turned fiery with lust and anger. His face became drawn, and his lips contorted, frightening her. It was a fire that Kalyani knew only too well—the fire of a man's raw lust. She also knew how badly one could get burnt in its heat. By the scalding touch of his fingers and the lecherous smile that lingered on his lips bordered by the brush of his moustache.

Still, she tried to push him away. 'No,' she snarled, 'go away.'

He stared at her, perplexed. 'What's your problem?'

'Leave me alone, Bhamedathi will …'

'Oh, it's not something she's not aware of. After all, she started the tease. It was her idea.' He hugged Kalyani tightly and growled softly like a wolf in her ear, 'Don't make any sound. And don't resist. You know me, don't you …? She will wake up. And she will have to lie there watching us do it.'

Kalyani was close to tears. What a fate! She stared at Bhamedathi in the blue light that streamed through the window, disregarding the assault by lips that smelt of rancid cigarette tobacco and dirty talk that breached the border between amorous words and vile abuses. Mumbles of pain, signs of hurt from the soul-deadening affliction, distressed breaks in her sleep, a breathless convulsion … and then total silence.

'Edathi[8] …' letting out an apathetic shriek, blinking her welling eyes repeatedly, Kalyani lay supine and unmoving, like a sex doll he had procured. It was a replay of the night he had used her body for the first time, many years ago.

It was a pleasant night. A cool June night in which blew a breeze that smelled of monsoon. A beautiful night bathed in pale moonlight, and clear skies free of darkness. A night in which stars bloomed in clusters like bunches of night-flowering jasmine in the sky's monsoon garden. The night on which Kalyani had worn the red silk sari gifted by Bhamedathi to show her how she looked in it. It was her birthday the next day.

Dr Bhama had received a telephone call. A lady who had delivered twin girls the previous evening had begun to bleed suddenly. Bhamedathi had had to leave even before the car from her hospital got to her house to pick her up.

'Lock the gate and go to sleep, Kallu baby. And here, take this coral necklace. Wear it when you go to the temple tomorrow. You'll look lovely.'

Thin threads of rain were falling. Kalyani locked the gate as soon as her sister left. The pleasant coolness of rain. '*Ahhhh* …' she spread her arms. After she had come to Ernakulam from Cherpulassery, she hadn't felt the touch of rain on her body. In her ancestral home, every rainy season, in the mornings she used to swim like a golden mermaid, breaking the crystal surface of the pond filled with water lilies. Tickled by the crystal raindrops falling on her face, she used to squirm and dive deep into the pond, among the

[8] Elder sister.

half-open water lily leaves and their buds in half-bloom and grazing the vines at the bottom. At other times, her buttocks would brush against the weak trunk of the Spanish cherry tree with its rowel-shaped flowers, and drench herself in the ersatz rain of her own creation, as it fell from the shivering leaves and branches.

'What's this, Kallu baby? Come, come, get in ... I will be roasted if I let you stand in the rain so late in the night. Get in. *Sheesh* ... you shouldn't have let your birthday sari get wet.' He came out, held Kalyani by her hand, and pulled her towards the house.

'Go and change your sari.'

Kalyani smiled. Unnietten was a good man. He didn't have the uncouthness of her cousin brother, who would lurk in the dark corridors of their ancestral home and grab her hand and make passes, or the deviousness of her elder uncle, who, as dusk fell, invariably felt thirsty and demanded water from her. Yet when the very next moment, Bhamedathi called on the phone and he told her, 'Bhama is calling you,' she thought she saw something lurking in his eyes, which caused a nameless fear in her.

Later that night—a night when both her body and psyche were scored like a fish being readied for grilling with a sharp knife— he came to her like a wild dog, tearing her birthday sari into shreds and shattering Bhamedathi's coral necklace. He silenced her screams by slapping her viciously across her face. He bit and scratched her all over, and subjected her to brutal rape.

'Number 100,' a nurse called out loudly.

The woman sitting next to Kalyani nudged her.'Number 100, you go. It's your turn.'

The gynaecologist's room smelled of antiseptic lotion. A foetus, with its eyes closed, lay upside down inside a sectional rendering of the human womb made in plaster of Paris. The doctor's green eyes, long nose, and thin, long, red-nailed fingers drumming on the table, made her look like an evil witch.

Bhamedathi's examination room was so unlike this one. Walls hung with pictures of toothless tiny tots beaming, their tender gums on display; a blue ruler and some neatly arranged books on a glass-top table; a paperweight with glitters and a viscous fluid inside. An ever smiling beautiful Bhamedathi, with the serenity of a sannyasin; her knee-length braided hair resting on the table like a coiled black serpent; her nails neatly trimmed; and the pallu of her Mangalagiri cotton sari, redolent with the fragrance of poinciana flowers, trailing on the floor. Latex gloves delicately pulled on to her hands ... Bhamedathi carefully spread on her fingers the thick, brown disinfectant poured out by the nurse.

'Didn't you loosen the string of your skirt, Kallu baby?

Kalyani turned her face away in shyness.

'It's I who have a problem?'

'*Ha-ha* ...' Her sister laughed aloud. White pearls tumbled down from her laughter; they rolled on the floor, knocking one another. Bhamedathi's eyes glittered like diamond dust.

'*Duh* ... The problem's not with us, baby. It's him, he's the problem.' A silvery weapon flashed in her eyes and a scimitar-sharp smile played on her lips.

'Wretched lowlife, he betrayed both of us,' Bhamedathi gnashed her teeth.

'How many children do you have, Mrs Menon?'

Kalyani raised her head at this question.

The doctor was applying germicide on her latex gloves. Her long hand would dive into her body like a white octopus.

'Children? None.'

The only resemblance to Bhamedathi was in the vermillion bindi on her forehead, marked with lines of suspicion and doubt.

'Why, who has the problem? You?' The doctor stared at Kalyani.

'No. My husband.'

'What's his problem?'

'That … his count … his count is less.'

The doctor's long hand was searching for the uterine forceps in the tray of instruments.

'How long have you been married?'

'Marriage … marriage …' Kalyani had to laugh. A seventeen-year-old girl. The Cherpulassery girl, who liked to stretch her hands to touch and savour the drizzle. Slim, bony, lanky, and tender like a water lily stem. A girl who was raped by her own sister's husband. Where did she get married? Where was the brief accompaniment of nadaswaram and the jasmine-bedecked pandal? When was Kalyani's wedding? Who tied the mangalsutra retrieved from the corpse of her sister on Kalyani's neck after changing its hook?

'Were you using protection?' The doctor's face twisted with suspicion.

The same girl … lying on the cold, stainless surgical table with dried blood on her legs and blood oozing from her internal wounds … the girl who suppressed a scream within her throat. The sutures that dissolved in the needle plunging into the soft flesh.

'Dr Bhama, stop stitching. She hasn't been anaesthetised.'

Kalyani squirmed in the memory of the pain.

'Mrs Menon, were you using any protection?'

'No … No …' Kalyani shook her head.

'Then what is this?' The doctor pulled the forceps with force. Kalyani felt as if a piece of her womb was being pulled out by its roots. She yanked out a T-shaped metal piece. Covered in delicate capillaries, veins and tissues, it gleamed red in her hand.

'What's this, Mrs Kalyani? Look, this is a copper T. When it's inside you, how can you conceive?'

Suddenly, Kalyani heard Bhamedathi laughing hysterically. When, on which day? During which examination—this treachery?

'Kallu baby, let me tell you this, too …' Bhamedathi had said.

'No, enough, it's enough …' Kalyani had covered her mouth to stop her from speaking.

'Kallu baby …' her words had come to an abrupt end.

Now suddenly, Kalyani realised what she was trying to tell her before she died.

It was the tale of two girls who, clad only in petticoats, ran along the country paths of Cherpulassery—caressed by the winds from the Western Ghats, fragrant with the smells of forests and wild flowers—to enjoy the rain. A girl who had everyone … and a girl who had nobody.

The old grandaunt, wet-grinding chillies near the stove, asked, 'Who broke this lantern?'

'Who else but Kallu baby?'

'Who tore this Ramayana?'

'Also, Kallu baby.'

'Who's done all this mischief, who?'

'Kallu baby.'

'What then about mischievous Bhama?'

'Me? I was sitting here and reciting the hymns, Muthassi.'

Bhamedathi's laughter rang out. She laughed with the sharp timbre of one weapon meeting the other.

'You'll cop it now …' Bhamedathi terrorised her. In the inky blackness of the en suite urinal, Kallu baby buried her face in the niche in the wall. To prevent the scream—a helpless, piercing scream that could rend her heart and scatter—from escaping her, Kalyani covered her mouth with both her hands.

The Lexicon of Kisses

The room. Newly constructed in the Civil Station building, following the principles of vastu shastra and having all the latest amenities, and fitted with semi-circular windows. Designed and purpose-built to hold conferences. The drowsy hum of the air-conditioner. The milky light of the star-like ceiling lamps. The foreign Scottish fragrance of the air-freshener—the Collector's favourite.

With a cheery, energetic smile, the Collector patted his hair in place, and went around making solicitous enquiries: 'Is the decoction of the 11 a.m. coffee a little thin?'; 'Is the Kozhikode-style pineapple halwa served to the secretaries too sticky?'; 'Is the halwa's extra sweetness making the coffee less sweet?'; 'Has only a suspicion of being a diabetic made the Principal Secretary avoid the halwa?'; and so on.

Despite his avowed sweet tooth, he drank a mouthful of his unsweetened green tea—described by his latest Italian lover as 'a bitter green concoction sprinkled with date-rape drug or sublimated iron powder or suchlike substance for seducing women'—with obvious relish. A look of satisfaction, provided by the tea, spread on his face.

In between all this, he couldn't recollect who had left a scrap of paper with a message on his saucer.

As soon as he read the message, his face flushed, as if he had received a very gladdening piece of news. Along with the green tinge on his closely-shaven, handsome face, an involuntary and inscrutable smile also appeared. But in order to convince the person, who had placed the note, of his indifference, he regained his composure immediately, swabbed his face with a Kashmiri kerchief bearing the printed image of a polar bear, and reverted to his normal melancholy-tinged look.

He then stood up, and excused himself. With a sad smile on his face, he added meekly that one of his close relatives had died, that he would go and return in an hour, and that everyone present was a valued guest of the city of Kozhikode, and no one should leave without having the food just because he wasn't there. Wishing everyone with folded hands and nodding formally to all, he entered his cabin.

A careful scrutiny will reveal that on his rosy and soft face—on which a melancholic look acted like a beauty cream—thick, dark eyebrows gave him a cruel look, and his marble-like eyes, the guilelessness of a child. In his transparent irises, the pupils were like two black dots made with a pen. When dressed in blue clothes, either a rollicking ocean became visible in these irises, or a sky turned azure from sadness having congealed and fused with blackish-blue ink. When wearing a yellow shirt, his irises took on a yellow hue, like a patient of jaundice. In green clothes, they took the verdancy of a field filled with rice seedlings during the planting season; in purple, they turned into tongues of flame; in black, they attained an officious look.

He wanted to laugh aloud. In the coolness of the air-conditioned room, he shifted his weight fully onto the seat of his swivel chair and leaned back. He dialled his wife from the contact list on his mobile and gave her the news of the death. Before the shout of 'Ayyo!' could reach him from the other end, he switched off the mobile phone and tossed it aside.

He had never imagined anyone could feel so happy on being informed of someone's demise. From his quickening heartbeat, he recognised the blackguard cavorting around inside him in an evil rapture and chortling with a wicked pleasure.

He used a facewash on his face, scrubbed it, dried it and applied some Johnson's baby powder that he had bought for his younger daughter. His shiny face took on a baby-like glow. He wetted his comb and brushed his hair back neatly. He opened his briefcase, rummaged through it, and found the Vaseline petroleum jelly tube, and applied it on his lips softly with his index finger. He polished the lips as if he was getting them ready to kiss.

He looked at himself in the mirror: Krishnakumar, IAS officer, five feet nine inches, sixty-six kilos. Once, despite the dirty thoughts in his mind, he had innocently claimed 66 to be his weight before an elderly lover with a kinky sense of humour, and she had corrected him, saying, *No it's 69, it should be 69*, and he had kept laughing till it fatigued his cheeks. The most handsome king of the jungle. The husband of Hema Shenoy. The owner of a long, beak-shaped nose. A libidinous, lascivious, hirsute lady killer—with bluish-black hair on his chest and arms—who from his thirteenth year was the lover of many beautiful and homely women, drawn to him like a queen bee drawing drones to herself.

As he and his wife approached the dead man's house, looking at the tears welling up in his wife's eyes, he felt pity for her. She was a simple-minded woman who thought her husband was the embodiment of divinity. She was a professor of Physics at the University College. One who, in vain, misconstrued making favourite foods of her husband; feeding him his much-loved dosa dipped in green chilli chutney; pressing his clothes flawlessly; decking up in ruby necklaces, lotus-shaped earrings and emerald bangles for IAS officers' wives' party nights; lording it over the household with all the arrogance and vanity of a Shenoy woman from Kozhikode; and, at nights, in the dim-lit bedroom—also his preference—lying in bed with her long hair spread all around her, with a coyness that reminded one of a burgeoning bud, as the sum and substance of love and life.

She was aware of his philandering ways, his straying, from the flirtatious smiles and feminine voices on the calls he received; and on the nights when he returned home late, having smelled herb-infused oil, costly shampoos, Arabian jasmine, and many other unknown feminine fragrances on him, she would suffer a panic attack. As he would take off his shirt, being unable to pin down if the red mark near his left nipple was from lipstick, vermillion, or a love-bite, all she could do at times was fight with him like a roaring tempest, and on other occasions, having cried for days together and run out of tears, fight with the weapon of a stony silence. Only to lose in the end, as ever. She didn't know any better.

'Hema. She is your true antagonist, your real competition ... one who has always caused me unease and disquiet, challenging my masculinity,' he murmured to himself.

Here … the one who lies like a withered night-flowering jasmine bud near the corpse …

She whose fan-like wide eyes were filled with screams and tears …

One who rejected my love when I had been betrayed by my own friend ...

One who, in a state of unconsciousness, half-forgot her torments in the shooting pain of the injection the doctor gave three hours ago …

Here she is: Priya … my Priyamvada …

Priya, the widow.

The first time he saw Priya was in Guruvayurappan College, where he was a student. The college environs, the lucky bean tree and the peepal tree with its zillions of loony leaves that whistled in the breeze lay soaked in the late monsoon rain. All the lebbeck tree's butterfly-like petals, of a deeper yellow shade than Indian laburnum flowers, had come down with the rain. He saw her for the first time at the right end of the college playground, which lay in the shade of an ancient tree.

The earth had woken up at the first touch of rain. The Communist aura of the Siam weed—locally known as 'communist green', and which grew in a dark-green superabundance—suffused the rain.

Swathes of touch-me-not plants—their purplish-pink flowers mimicking dwarf suns in disguise—lay in wait for the children with their prickly needles. Lantanas, tickled by the rain, let go off the bunches of orange ear-studs they held. Raindrops slid down the oily surface of the leaves, like small children on garden slides. The underside of the golden leaf tree's leaves resembled the bulbous earrings of grannies as they glinted and swayed in the sliver of light that fell on them from among the dark clouds.

He was in the final year of his MA course in English language and literature. A fair-skinned, lovesick student, in whom love had flowered and was corroding his soul like some cardiac cancer, though he had irrigated it with potent anodynes of lines from Keats, Shelley and Byron. It was a time when the thirst of his soul remained unquenched, though he had diligently studied love's primary lessons in female anatomy with women of varied nature and with differently-endowed bodies such as Sanat, who used to come to light the lamp in the grove and was fair and soft like halwa; his neighbour, a bank officer who had the gait and bulk of a Red Sindhi breed cow; an elder cousin, whose marriage was getting delayed because of her buck teeth and sarpadosha[9] *in her horoscope. Whichever female form he came across, estimates of the dimensions of her beauty and her undergarments got registered in his heart instinctively. He used to read every woman as a little book, which admitted of no mathematical equations, despite his adding, subtracting, multiplying and dividing her.*

From under the narrow protection of the concrete umbrella he had sought refuge in, he noticed a girl getting drenched and shivering.

[9] An unfavourable planetary alignment which delays marriage.

Her wet clothes stuck to her body like a second, newly-grown skin. He had covered his mouth which had opened involuntarily at the sight of her curves, her generous delta-shaped breasts that bounced like fluffy rabbit kittens, and the plumpness of her pink lips.

As he stood staring at her in the torrential rain, she seemed like a marble statue to him. A statue with wet strands of long hair, bloodshot eyes, moist eyelashes, diamond raindrops dripping off the tip of its nose into the narrow crevice between its breasts, and honeyed, red lips shivering in the chill of the rain.

That statue showed no recognition of a strange, callow youth standing and staring at her. She had the look of someone troubled by something. When she remained motionless like a rock even after the rain got over, he felt an irritation.

'Don't you want to leave?' He turned towards her. A sudden, chilly breeze shook the trees near them and caused a brief shower.

The only sound that could be heard was that of teeth chattering. Ktat ktakt ktktat.

'Okay, if you don't want to leave, then don't.' He started to walk.

Her face contorted as if she was starting to cry. Was she going to cry? A little girl with a mole as dark as kohl on her right cheek, waiting to be kissed by a man. He went back.

'Is something the matter?'

She was looking at her feet. Her right leg was swollen, as though it had a ligament tear.

'Oh-o, is that all? Here, sit down,' he helped her to sit down on the steps. Assuming that she was cramping, he rubbed her feet. When he gently touched the swollen leg, she screamed.

The chill from her legs spread onto his hands. As he rubbed the feet, his hands felt as if they were burning him.

'Come, hold on to me and walk.' He offered his hand.

She tried to transfer her weight onto her injured leg. 'Argh … *I can't.'*

'Looks like a fracture. This, now …' He thought for a moment. The next moment, he laughed teasingly. 'How many kilos?'

'Forty-five.' She also laughed.

'All right. There's no other way.' He lifted her up as if he was picking a flower with its stalk, and flung her over his shoulder. He could feel her heart pressed against his own, ticking like a clock over the sound of the drizzle.

This was her … that same Priya. She was lying on the floor. Where Venu's corpse had lain, only the outline of the corpse drawn with rice powder remained. The stench of body fat melting in cow ghee wafted from the pyre burning in the yard into the midst of the intermingled fumes from smouldering oil-less wicks and Cycle brand agarbattis. The nauseating smell of burnt human flesh pervaded the air.

This was that Priya who had spurned his love, kicking it away disdainfully. Your tears. A woman's tears … that tether the vanity of every libidinous man. Through the magnifying glass of her teardrop, her kohl-black mole seemed to have grown bigger. A tiny mole which had swelled and shrunk from the many kisses Venu had planted on it.

He felt envious of Venu who was turning into ashes on the pyre. And he felt hatred. Yet he sat on his haunches and whispered words of consolation to Priya without any affectation.

'We have to bear the loss, endure … we have no other option.' He thought his duplicity was roasting his own tongue. 'Do not hesitate to call me if you need any help.'

He pressed on her a visiting card with the dual elephant emblem of the state government.

Her wide eyes closed for a second. A few drops of anguish spilled out. He held her eyes with his amorous marble eyes. In a flash, he forced his eyes back from her chest, where they had instinctively gravitated to. Then, in a voice which carried only to her, he said with a serenity only someone selfless and virtuous could have, 'Those who have left us are no more ... your daughter is crying, Priya ... go feed her.'

Despite Hema trying to spirit him away, he spent nearly another two hours there. All that time, his ears were tuned to the sounds from the funeral pyre. Malice and vendetta were smouldering inside him like a half-burnt corpse. Now, like the other woman, flames were embracing Venu's torso. The torso Priya had touched with love and affection was burning down. Lust was turning into embers. Like a voyeur, he enjoyed the wild, sibilant sounds of the raging fire. With bated breath, he waited for that last sound that had taken in all the fumes of the burning flesh. Eventually, he heard the popping sound of the skull exploding. Then, with his heart full of hatred, and eyes streaming from the fumes, he got into his car along with his wife. Before he rolled the window up, he looked once more at Priya. Except for some fat and glow gained during her pregnancy, and despite her white sari, she was the same old Priya. As he wondered why the old love that had been turned into ashes by his animus was rekindling suddenly, he recalled the smells of those rainy days.

A long corridor with innumerable pillars. Giving off their distinct smell, bunches of lilac and lavender-coloured garlic flowers and buds and their vines formed a green canopy that extended to its sides. The tiled, Greek-style, long corridor in front of the Zoology laboratory remained bright.

Behind the last pillar, a twenty-one-year-old lingered with a bad case of lovesickness and an afflicted heart. At the other end of the corridor, Priya appeared to the accompaniment of her anklets and resplendent like a bunch of violet flowers. In her hands were two glass jars with two baby snakes soaking in formalin. The reflection of the silvery rings of the common krait seemed to bounce off her face and body. Her earrings were swinging to her gait. She wore a red round bindi. An inviting smile lingered on her lips which seemed undecided on whether to remain pink or go pale violet.

He looked at his own hands. The hands which had broken out in goose pimples while massaging her feet. He recalled the scent of her body that refused to slough off his shoulders and chest even after so many days. His body was burning from a frizzling energy generated by the blood flowing through her veins and arteries.

His head was numb and his legs were smarting from the first 'female brand of intoxicant' he had imbibed. The words that Venu and Shahnavaz had injected into him as they sat in the dim-lit bar.

'Saale, there's no fun in writhing like a fish placed on land … have this one, it's the best … the tops.'

The liquor felt piping hot. His throat burned, his tongue was numb. As if liquid lightning had scalded his food pipe. It was sheer agony. Krishnakumar's eyes welled with tears, and his tongue was lolling out of his mouth.

'Da ...' Shahnavaz poked Krishnakumar.

'Take a bit of that pickle and rub on his tongue. This Konkani pattar[10] *be damned.'*

The comfort of chilli and the tempered sourness of lime was smeared on his burnt tongue.

'Who the fuck does she think she is ... Da, look here. This is Bloody Mary, but for Trichurians—it's Menstruating Maria, ha ha ha.' Shahnavaz cackled.

'I am the one who gave a couple of bottles to the attenders in the Zoology lab ... they won't bother you. You go ... I had done this in that Padmini's case too.'

Venu, his old roommate, suddenly became fresh in his memory.

Krishnakumar clung to the pillar like a snake. His tongue was paralysed. His eyes were rolling up. Though Venu was envious of his looks, he cared for him.

She was approaching.

'Briiiyaaaa ... You are a full woman in the sari. Gorgeous!'

Her eyes were growing sharp and scored his heart when their points touched him.

'Are you drunk, Krishna?'

'Nah...' He vigorously shook his head in denial. 'So, what Venu says is true—you are a drunkard. *Chee* ...'

What was that expression on Priya's face?

---

[10] A corruption of bhattar, a titular name given to a brahmin; a colloquialism for Tamil brahmin, and by extension any brahmin.

The very same face ... the same Priya ... the one who stood in the rain with a fractured bone and a slim, wet belly with a conch-shaped navel, her golden sagittal gleaming like one of the Singaporean longitudinal ornaments. Above them, the firmness of her breasts with the expanse of the ocean ... and their pink, lippy nipples.

Krishnakumar stretched his hand. With the Dutch courage provided by Menstruating Maria, and encouraged by Venu's exhortations, he laid his hands on her breasts.

'*Argh*!' Krishnakumar shook his head.

'What's the matter, Krishnetta? You're sweating ... please turn up the AC, Narayanetta.'

Hema used her sari pallu to dab the sweat off him. To this day, KK was afraid of recalling the fallout of that incident.

He was one of the smartest students in the college, and the only son of the teacher couple in the same college. More than the complaint filed by Priya, it was the witness account given by Venu that had him in tears. Bearing the dismissal order, which meant he wouldn't be able to sit for the examinations, Priya came to him and snapped, '*Phthoo*!'

'*Saale*, you are so handsome. You will get as many Priyas as you want. This was the only way I could take her away from you,' the words were skidding off Venu's treacherous tongue.

'I don't want Priya to even look at you. I am very set on that,' were Venu's parting words.

'*Argh, humph*.' He was feeling uneasy again.

'What's this, Krishnetta? When our time comes, all of us have to go. Isn't that inevitable? Don't torture yourself thinking about it.'

Hema, as much as you try, those embers aren't going to die. This is a vendetta, honed and polished over the years, every day, every night, with every breath forged in a smithy's furnace. You can't even begin to imagine it, Hema—the humiliation and anguish of a twenty-one-year-old who was forced to run away, was spurned in love, and betrayed by the keepers of the secrets of his soul. You can't even begin to understand how it feels to be rejected and banished by one's own father. You will not comprehend the agony of a son who was denied the right to perform his father's last rites … Hema, you know nothing.

You don't know the young man who fainted on the streets of Calcutta, his skin blistered from sunstroke. You don't know the youth who quenched his thirst with the rust-coloured water from roadside pipes and scrounged for leftovers in restaurants and cafeterias. You don't know the boy who polished shoes seated by the side of a drain in Sonagachi, teeming with pimps and prostitutes.

In the next four months, every move he made was well thought out: two trips in his official car to Priya's house in the company of his wife; using his influence to speed up the release of Venu's life insurance payout and to get her a job on 'died-in-harness' grounds; when buying stuff for his own third child, buying extra quantities of Lactogen, Johnson's baby soap, dresses, etc., and gifting them to Priya's child; disconnecting the calls when Priya phoned him; the first three months were used up in these and similar time-tested strategies to tug at the heart strings of a widow.

Then, convincing her of his ex-roommate's treachery; showing her the burn marks that two summers of Calcutta had gifted him; filling his marble eyes with melancholia and love in equal measure and fazing her by reciting a couple of stanzas of poetry like lovelorn Malayali film heroes—gradually he succeeded in engendering love in her. The next month, to be precise, on the 17th hour of the 128th day.

The day he was leaving Kozhikode, following the acceptance of his transfer request. On the evening he was to bid adieu to the city, amidst the many send-offs, seated in his chamber before a cup of green tea, she burst into tears. He kept a long face but kept grinning inside.

'Will you take me along to Kottayam with you?'

He chortled inside. Women are such imbeciles. She has no escape from the man who has witnessed the nakedness of her soul. Once they are in love, these foolish women shadow men like stray dogs, wagging their tails.

'Will you come?'

'I will.' Her tears were making her mole wet. 'I will, I will.' She was like a dove.

He couldn't stop laughing inside.

'I knew. That is why I sent Hema and the children yesterday itself.' Each move was brilliantly plotted.

'I have reserved two tickets. Train No. 6347, A-1 bogie, berths 28 and 29. You will come, won't you? I will be waiting.'

He knew she would come. Forget Kottayam, she would follow him to the end of the earth. Venu and her daughter were no longer in her heart. Only he, Krishnakumar, dwelled there.

The train journey was like no other. An urgent trip to collect Venu's provident fund dues.

'Is that what you told folks at home, Priya?'

She nodded.

'That means you've to go back?'

'*Mmmhm*,' she said coyly.

'What if I don't let you?'

'I won't go.'

You bloody fool … you are not even a pastime for me. I have to settle some scores, that's it.

'Come, let us stand in the corridor.' He opened the doors of the bogie. The clouds were golden in the setting sun. And there was a light drizzle …

Two drenched people under the concrete umbrella of the college—a young man and a girl. The first kiss that was lost between the two lips on that day …

The first kiss. He gently pressed his lips on hers. As if a needle plunged into his heart. As if blood was being sucked out of him.

Invoking the power of an entire universe, tidal waves were rising in vast oceans; high winds were roaring and whirling about.

Her mouth was like a pink half-open bud. Sweet as figs, luscious and wide lips. Mischievous teeth that tickled the tongue. He felt the delight when his tongue touched the soft flesh inside her cheeks. He touched everything—the tender delicacies of her mouth, the mystifying and unexplored caverns of a strange, secret world, its magnitude, its shape—he sucked it all in a frenzy.

She stood with her face resting on his left palm. He again remembered that evening when heavy rains had cooled the earth. When she got over her initial disbelief, she touched his cheeks and ears.

In clothes that stuck to the skin … trying to hide the well-defined outlines of her undergarments with her wet hair … like a golden mermaid shivering in the damp cold … the sodden girl stood with her damp books held in an embrace.

The crimson hues of vermillion rivulets on her forehead. The cool murmur that was on par with the musical rustle of the peepal tree.

One of his wayward, out-of-line, upper incisors cut her inner lip. '*Ssho* …' Her eyes slowly closed in arousal. The acrid taste of blood spread in their mouths.

He extricated his lips from hers, the way two mating serpents uncoil their knotted bodies, and looked deep into her eyes. Love was slumbering under a strange intoxication. Her large eyes were staring at him, her long eyelashes fluttering in anticipation of a butterfly kiss.

Priya was laughing loudly … love's old ledger.

'Comrade, this lexicon is called the lexicon of kisses …'

Krishnakumar mocked, 'Go, girl, what does a girl know of kissing? Should I teach you?'

'Get lost, all that I know is in this lexicon. Lickey kiss, Flying kiss, Nip kiss, Butterfly kiss, Pinch kiss, Tickle kiss, Chocolate-Lickey kiss …'

'In that case, add Halwa-lickey kiss, Lalwa-hickey kiss and so on, too … Are there any hot kisses in this lexicon? Such as French kiss, Tunisian kiss, etc.?'

'There could be.' Why was her face flushed?

'Don't blush, girl! … What is the name of the lexicon again?'

'The Lexicon of Kisses.' Her voice was vibrant with love.

Are the two Priyas the same? Is she that Priya? He stared at her face again. She was wearing the same old violet sari with golden zari.

Like tiny hands, strands were reaching out to him from her neatly braided hair. Bunches of garlic flowers were hanging from the pillars, canopy and parapet walls of the corridor in front of the laboratory, spreading their distinctive smell despite the unseasonal rains. A young man stood behind the pillar at one end of the corridor. He was, in looks—and at heart—a pale-faced child, perhaps because his moustache was still incipient or because of the childlike innocence in his eyes. Only one thing dominated his mind, blood and flesh—love. Menstrual Maria coursing in a froth through his veins and the sourness and bitterness from his first experience at the bar had broiled his brain. He lurched ahead on unsteady legs.

She was wearing a large locket set with five stones, which accentuated her ample bosom … love for him shone in her eyes.

'I am madly in love with you …' words that flitted across his lips. His marble eyes had the yellow tinge of love and the inscrutable language of the heart.

'You are mine.' He stretched his hands towards the two large white doves. Why were they fluttering in his hands? Why were they trying to wriggle out and fly away?

'Priya, O my darling …'

The formalin-filled glass jars crashed to the ground and splintered. Though dead, the animate fangless snakes fell to the floor.

Why is she not hollering like she did on that day? Why is she not slapping me hard across my face with her formalin-tinged hand that smelled of death? As they stood in the narrow corridor of the train, he squeezed her breasts with a vengeance, his heart and face brimming with hatred.

With a terrible indifference that only a man who has kissed and loved can have, he pushed her out of the compartment with both hands.

She fell onto the parallel rail tracks like a water lily torn off its stalk in the rain. Her wounded lips were still moving, as if continuing with the unfinished kiss. Her heart was shredded by the last vengeful look in his eyes.

In that instant, a train sped across those tracks with a screeching sound. He heard clearly the sound of her skull getting crushed by the iron wheels like a coconut being cracked open.

At the zenith of an evil pleasure, with his eyes bloodshot from love and a maniacal heart torn off its moorings by blind hatred, he put his hands—now white from the milk that had seeped from her breasts—under the tap. The milk dripped down along the washbasin's rusted drain pipe and fell to the ballast between the rails. He heard the shrieks of a hungry six-month-old baby girl somewhere in the bogie. The narrow corridor was awash with the smell of breast milk.

The Red Seeds of Papaya

He was dark-complexioned. His black skin was his curse. Blackness that rivalled basalt. Neither the pulayas[11] who worked in the fields nor the Tamilians from Salem who used to come to the tile factory to unload clay, nor the kohl that his mother regularly applied in her eyes had the inky blackness of his skin. Like a raven on which oil had been smeared, with every minute spent in the afternoon sun, his dark skin got darker and blacker. As the gloomy umbra of the sense of inferiority that ceaselessly haunted his heart spread, his face darkened even more, like the path to darkness.

He walked through the dark alley of Pallikkal Bazaar with his head bowed.

With its parasol-style top, a single papaya plant stood by the side of the mossy, slippery laterite wall that ran along the length of the alley. When they saw him, the Muslim girls standing beneath the papaya plant laughed, covering their

[11] One of the lower castes of Kerala.

mouths. Along with saliva, coquettishness appeared on their lips, which were pursed to hold their shaylas.[12]

Moosa saw that where the girls had poked the tree with a long pole, the broken skin had turned purplish; he thought they resembled nipples. The overripe papaya fruits dripping white sap like milk from the full, heavy-with-milk breasts of near-term pregnant women embarrassed him.

Annoyed by his looks, an irate Saifunissa gathered her sarong-like cloth, flipped it up, tucked it in at the waist, climbed on the stone placed against the wall, and knocked down one papaya with the pole onto the alley.

'Piyathoo, do you want this kari moosa?' she asked her companion, with a wordplay on the vernacular for papaya—karmoos—which, when enunciated with a break, sounded like black Moosa. Her many-ringed, tinkling earring made wry faces at him.

'What, my dear ... there's a black Moosa in the alley?'

The gratuitously insulting question from Piyathoo left a bitter taste in his mouth. Humiliation tastes bitter. The colour of abasement is black.

Moosa was his name. 'Kari Moosa' or black Moosa was the nickname used by all the residents of Pengatt Market—its children, women, and even women of his own faith—to taunt and make fun of him.

Moosa's skin was the colour of black rosewood. His body appeared to be sculpted, with muscles and sinews taut against his ribs, and a six-pack below it. He had the strength of a warrior. Curly hair grew on his chest and iron-rod-like arms. The springy hair of his head fell over his broad

[12] Head veils worn by Muslim women.

forehead and, swinging in the breeze like black beetles, enhanced the beauty of his dark skin. Two perfect rows of flawless teeth gleamed in his mouth like white pearls. The beauty of his teeth gave his face a childlike mien, but only when he smiled. The resemblance to Lord Krishna's bearing—unseen on Shri Krishna Jayanti in the countless children painted blue and bluish-black and forced to walk in a procession, a flute thrust into one hand and a blob of butter in the other—lent his precise and restrained movements a certain handsomeness. Notwithstanding this, the reddish-golden complexion, plummy lips and robust health of the other Muslim youth of Pallikkal Bazaar, Pengatt Market, Neddirppu, Aykkarappadi and Pulikkal made Moosa look even darker than he was.

Enough blackness to be the wages of sin. The first of those wages came from God to his mother, the fair-skinned Ramlabiyumma whose golden complexion matched the zari of her blouse, for giving birth to an illegitimate child.

That was many years ago; twenty-five, to be precise. The sin expressed itself as a baby's wail, exposing her ten-month subterfuge. On hearing his first cry, Aysumma, Moosa's father's mother, stood rather perplexed, as she might at sight of an unseasonal shower. It was the month of Ramzan. For the ritual *wudu*, she poured water from the granite trough on her feet. Moosa cried again. Aysumma strained her ears: it was the cry of a newborn. It was the raucous wail of a child fazed by the miracle of life being revealed, blinded by the light of the cool earth into which it had been delivered, and shocked at the inflation of his two translucent lungs like balloons of flesh as fresh air rushed into them.

The satans and djinns come into the chamber as cats, and cry like babies … They will sink their canine teeth into the blue veins on the necks of those who come running out of anxiety, and drink the blood … Aysumma was reminded of the old wives' tales of yore when she heard Moosa's wails. The wail was coming from one of the inner rooms of the house, actually the granary where the paddy had been stored. She switched on the slim torch brought from Dubai, which threw light sharp as laser when switched on. It was a house made for secret liaisons, with eighteen rooms, numerous en-suite urinals, paved corridors, three prayer rooms, a huge granary, and an attic, built in the *ettukettu*[13] style. Darkness lurked inside the house. It was an assiduous keeper of men's philandering secrets.

The baby's wail rose again from the granary, where the dried paddy had been spread on the floor. Aysumma's heart trembled in the terrifying memory of the ghouls that assumed the form of black cats and drank blood and ate flesh.

'Ramlaoooo … Ramlaa … Ramla'aaaa …'

'Misbegotten …' Aysumma cursed her daughter-in-law. She had always been afraid of the granary. The spot where the dreams of all the kitchen maids brought from Coorg and Mangalore were despoiled. Aysumma had been rendered craven from the time she had heard the first scream from the granary, the day after her marriage.

'Don't go there, Bappa won't like it,' her husband of one day had warned her. Yet every morning, before the call for

---

[13] A traditional Kerala construction style with two connected quadrangles in the middle.

the *fajr* prayer was given by the muezzin, she stole into the granary, shivering with fear. A naked form was often found either on one corner of the heaped paddy or in the chill of the en-suite urinal, shivering in anticipation of a febrile span of time ahead. With mixed emotions of mercy tinged greatly with fear, she used to cover these trembling forms with the sheet she used to carry with her. The memories of the bestial teeth and nail marks on their tender thighs and breasts were fears that she would carry to her grave ...

The granary reeked of the strong smell of drying paddy today. Since it was summer time and parboiled rice was under production, its pleasantly-appetising smell filled the granary. But when a particular smell so familiar only to women reached her nostrils, surpassing the other smells, Aysumma was stunned. It was a strange, feminine odour made up of a medley of smells—of amniotic fluid, of placental blood with as strong a stench as menstrual blood and of bits of internal tissues and lining borne by a newborn child. A mother of ten, Aysumma recognised it immediately. With a shout, she switched on the torch. The scene that met her eyes shocked her out of her wits.

In a corner of the granary, her daughter-in-law, Ramlathbi, was lying on her side. Her white nightie with a coppery flower pattern looked as if it had been dipped in red paint from the waist down, resembling the holy red cloth seen in Bhagwathy temples. Next to her was a black creature that was wailing from the primary and never-satisfied need of human beings. Resembling a wet black cat, it wailed with its mouth wide open, slapping its hands and feet on the blood-soaked floor.

'Somebody come quickly …' Aysumma screamed as she lost control. After that scream—loud enough to consign Moosa's life to eternal darkness and to be heard all over the bazaar—she herself scooped him up with revulsion and bathed him vigorously in the cold water that the granite trough had been filled with the day before by the maidservants.

How did Blockhead Mohammad's fair-skinned wife, Ramlathbi, come to bear an illegitimate child? How did she hide her pregnancy and how did it go unnoticed for ten months? How did Aysumma, a mother of ten, mistake the swelling in her legs, plump cheeks and the yellowness in her eyes for jaundice? After hiding all the infirmities of her pregnancy under loose nighties or black burqas, did Ramlathbi plan to chain her child to the granary wall to maintain her subterfuge? Or did she plan to tie a stone to its feet and drown it in the Kundankulam pond or the mosque pond, or flush it down the toilet?

The public's questions turned into a deluge. Some made guesses and issued statements; others indulged in wanton gossip.

'Blockhead has been in Sharjah for a year-and-a-half, no?'

'Uh-uh, who doesn't know that? Ramlathbi's first affair, and it's a mess.'

'When your hand's covered in cow ghee, however much you wash, it won't get washed off. Isn't it the same when you get a bad name?'

'Haven't you seen her dalliance with Mohammad's younger brother Ali Koya, *phthoo* …'

'Yes, by God! Have you seen that kid's looks—its double chin, and the black skin? A spitting image of our Ali Koya.'

'Blockhead and others all know it … After all, Aysumma's leading the charge.'

The story spread in the market, carried by the breeze. People talked in whispers, breaking into goose pimples on certain occasions and laughing loudly and biting their lips on others. They kept ridiculing the birth of Moosa everywhere—by the roadside, in Surangani Hotel, at Vappoo's chicken shop, in Vavaji's areca nut plantation, and beneath the cashew trees, the ground beneath which was littered with its flowers. When people saw him, a lip and an ear came into proximity with the most lubricious and lurid effect. Not only in the mosque yard and amidst the hisses and grunts at Alukka ghat as people washed clothes and in the crowds on Prophet Muhammad's birthday, but also on every path that Moosa trod, the dark secrets of his sinful birth chased his footsteps. Thus his bastardy sprouted beside him like a papaya seed, grew roots, and luxuriantly spread its green arms like a parasol, with the rapidity of sin.

The knowledge that a father's love for his wife's lovechild was only charity—extended as half-eaten, leftover food—made Moosa's world shrink into his own soul. That first searing wound in his heart never healed; it lingered in him and mocked him.

He realised that the colour of bastardy too was black.

His complexion was his penalty.

He was accursed.

When he was eight years old, on a rainy day, when he felt that the sum total of his sins was boring a hole in his soul and tunnelling through it, he rolled up the map of his life, and kept it back in his heart.

It rained through the day, each drop a potful. He was in the madrasa. In light of the knowledge that no one had anything to discuss about the secret wounds of the heart, sitting in the poorly-lit classroom, they allowed the letters of the Arabic alphabet float on their slates like paper boats launched on rainy days.

Moosa went and stood by the door to watch the rain. The eared watermoss, bluish water lilies, common water hyacinth with their oily leaves and peacock-feather-like violet petals, gave the Kundankulam pond—smack in the middle of the verdant, satin-like expanse of the rice field—the image of a Kathakali actor, his face made up with a paste of orpiment and double indigo. No one could believe that 'lady rain'—who kept weeping, adamant that she should add colour to the flowers before the onset of Onam—had more tears in stock.

At first, a smattering of rain descended to the earth like thin vines. Then it thickened like a glass rod. Torrential rain followed. In the plantain orchard in front of the madrasa, at least a hundred plants bearing unripe fruit were uprooted. In Asharikkavu, the broken salacia drupe fruit bunches hung low, clinging to the tree like vines. The branches of the Indian butter tree swung from the broken trunk like swings. Young areca nut plants, buffeted and harried by the wind, lay uprooted too. The silvery electric cables, torn from the insulators, hung loose between the concrete poles. The muddy water washed over everything like a brown sheet with wavelets, rendering everything—fields, ponds, ridges, the path to the market—indistinguishable.

'Ustad, may I go?' Moosa stretched his hands and touched the rain.

'Ikka, don't go.' Kaulath tugged at his shirt. 'Ustad, is this the day of *qiyamat*, the day the world ends?'

Her voice was tremulous with fear.

'No, child, no.' Ustad touched her cheek reassuringly.

'You continue the recitation, let it rain.'

'Umma will be scared at home, ustad,' said Moosa.

'What a specimen you are, Moosa … sit down. I'll let you go when the rain subsides.'

In the light of a small lantern, the white, scraggly beard of the ustad shone like a burning haystack. Reflecting the faint light, his silver ring, set with a large moonstone, smiled.

The madrasa roof started to leak. Without spilling water, the ustad periodically took out the steel vessels the students had placed beneath the broken, leaking tiles and emptied them.

'The sky looks wonderful now that the rain has stopped … what brilliance! Allah …' The ustad looked up at the sky.

'I'm leaving, ustad.' Moosa clutched the slate and the Quran close to his chest.

'Let the rain go away fully, boy.'

'*Mhhhum*,' shaking his head, Moosa went out. The damp sky looked bright after the rain. Moosa stood there, staring at it.

Even on this soggy evening do we espy the stars? From in between the cool blue valleys amidst the tender, fluffy cloud-filled sky, did they shine like the dark sparking eyes of the unseen maidens, celestial nymphs, djinns and houris who trailed the heady fragrance of attar. Rainy teardrops spilled over from those eyes and came down. Moosa was getting wet …

'Don't go, *nah* … don't go,' Kaulath simpered. 'Don't run, boy,' the ustad called from behind. Yet he ran. As he sped, crashing through the waters, he sent the water flying in all directions. His legs trembled as the water dashed against his ankles.

Though they were tiny, the chilly fingers of the rain were reaching inside his shirt and tickling his dark nipples—a feminine rain that stroked his face with multiple fingers, caressed the oiled parting of his hair and the wrinkles on his forehead, touched the tip of his nose and his eyelids and kissed his lips and chin.

He knew where the ridges of the fields lay. Though the pond and streams had covered the earth and the torrential rains had muddied the waters and the approaching darkness had spread its silken veil and dimmed the light, he ran along the ridge unerringly.

The young bullfrogs croaked, their *pekrom-pekrom* rasps resounding. The stridulating crickets, with their incessant *cheekri-cheekri* chirps, pierced the ears. The old, checkered keelback snakes raised their tiny heads, flicked their tongues, and dived back into the water. The cat fish, the striped murrel and the pickerel fish that had escaped from the pond flashed about. Snails rose up in a clutch and, with licks from their slimy tongues, planted their gunk on Moosa's kneecaps.

'Oh, my holy mother …' Moosa trembled.

'Ummaaaaa … Ummachcheeeyoooo …' his shout skimmed over the water and echoed from the distance.

Moosa then fell into a deep pit that had opened up from subsidence at the spot where Kundankulam met the Neeli stream. The Quran flew off his hand, as if it had been flung away. The slate broke into smithereens with a *tik* sound. A sharp stone cut a deep gash on his calf.

'Immaaaaa …'

He tried to push himself up with his hands. With a primal muddy taste and the murky bitterness of the swirling pit, the water entered his mouth and nose, choking him.

'Immaaaa … Ummichchiiyo …' he sobbed breathlessly. After the first surge, he slipped into another pit and was now neck-deep in water. His shirt got caught in the roots of a dwarf coconut tree, which had got exposed in the rushing water.

With only his head above, like one self-immolating in water, Moosa tried to rise up by holding his breath. The sight of two shadowy forms approaching him from the direction of his house scared him at first.

Moosa was scared of shadows, especially dark ones. 'Why, will shadows swallow you up?' Kaulath used to taunt him. His eyes were bulging with fear. The forms were walking towards him. They seemed to know the location of the submerged ridges, and, walking along them, they were shining a flashlight into the water on either side, as if searching for something.

'Merciful God, my Bappa!' Moosa raised his hand in glee.

'Vaapichchi, vaappichchi,' his shouts were drowned by the swishing, bubbling sound of the waters.

The forms were by the side of Kundankulam with the flashlight swinging side to side; what were they looking for?

'Moosaaaa …'That was his uncle's voice.

Summoning all his strength, Moosa tried to rise above the water level. The watery vines had caught him in undoable knots, and were pulling him to the bottom like an octopus that had caught its prey in its myriad tentacles.

'He knows how to swim, doesn't he, ikka?' Moosa could again recognise his father's younger brother's voice.

'Shine the torch towards the pond,' he said.

His father was squatting on his haunches. He was shining the torch, trying to fathom the depths of the pond.

'Vaaappaa …' Moosa continued to wail.

'Gimme the torch.' His uncle grabbed the torch. He then smashed it on Moosa's father's head.

'Allah …' Moosa screamed.

A scuffle followed. His uncle had grabbed his father's neck and was throttling him. His father's legs were thrashing about in the water like a giant fish. Water splashed in all directions. It was like a nightmare.

'Vaappichchi … my vaappichchi …'

Fear and distress had rendered Moosa mute; his voice got congealed within him. The busy rain arrived again, panting and pushing.

Peeping through a break in the clouds, the moon shone with a wicked smile. The water was a torrent now and flowed over his head.The muddied water and his tears were blurring his vision.

His uncle was pushing down his father head first into the depths of the pond filled with tangled water lily vines.

His father's body was convulsing, with the beastly sounds of an epileptic bouncing off the water. Amidst the tumult of the muddied waters being abraded by the sleeting rain and the cries of water creatures, frogs and reptiles, Moosa heard the death throes of his epileptic father gurgling in the water.

His uncle stood up and pulled his brother's legs. Straining, and with considerable effort, he planted Moosa's father's body upright into the soft patch where budding water lilies were bunched together. Moosa saw the pinkness of a lotus through the web of ten open fingers ... He peed and shat in his trousers. His howls and shrieks were more maniacal than the rain's sound now. His tears flowed into the torrential rain.

Kaulath's father, Razak the mussels-vendor, found him in a deep unconscious state, his legs caught in the vines and roots, and lying prone in the pit prepared for planting plantains beneath the coconut tree and its broken fronds. The pages from a Triveni brand notebook, bearing Arabic letters written in neat rows, were floating around him. The blue ink from them had run like blue kohl dissolved in tears.

'Merciful Allah, you saved him.' Razak gathered Moosa up. Though the water he had been swamped by for hours was cold, his body was burning with fever.

The skin of his arms and legs had blanched and bloated. Razak tore off his trousers and shirt. He took off the towel wrapped around his own head and towelled down Moosa's naked and shivering body. As he lay on Razak's shoulder, with only the red talismanic thread and amulets on his waist and chest, Moosa saw his father's rubber sandals floating on the water, upside down. When he saw the foams of frogs' eggs, he was reminded of the frothy epileptic mouth of his father. He broke into wails.

Kaulath sat by his bed on her knees, consoling him, 'Don't cry, my dear Moosakka.'

She kissed his cheeks repeatedly with lips stained by the violet colour of jamun from the curry of the previous night.

'Why are you crying, ikka? Kaulath has hugged and kissed you … now *shush*!' She wiped the tears from his cheek.

It was the same Kaulath, the girl with the mole above her upper lip, the girl whose nose curved like a parrot's beak. Her love was his remedy forever; her love was his disease forever.

As he stood with a feebly beating heart on the school verandah, watching other children play football and gulli danda, she came up behind him. With her anklets tinkling, and with a toothless, gummy smile on her face. That sowed the seeds of love in a seventh-grader's heart. That and the coyness on her lips as she sucked on a tiny plastic sachet of the five-paise tamarind pickle hidden in her mouth.

'Aren't you going to play with them, Moosakka?'

He turned around and smiled at her.

'Tamarind pickle, would you like some?' She spat out the tamarind seeds onto her palm.

'It's full of worms, girl. Don't eat it.'

'What worms?' They didn't matter to her. She used to keep each seed on the floor, smash it with a rock, and eat the kernel inside. Sometimes it was the Indian almond fruits, which their Vinod master famously called 'bitter almond' and compared its smell with the fumes let off by Mavoor Rayons factory occasionally in the evenings.

'There you go again … Vinod master, *pitter almand* and stuff … get lost, this is badam.'

The husky skin of the badam fruits would turn a dark shade of purple. The bats that flew in from Thamarasseri in the night would suck the fruits and drop them to the ground. Without any squeamishness, Kaulath would take them all and suck them.

'You're going to catch bird flu,' Moosa warned her.

'I will escape the homework at least,' she would pout at him, then stick out her tongue, dark pink from the almond sap. In the evenings, it fell to Moosa to smash open the shells of the almond fruit.

'My darling,' she used to say coquettishly, 'a kiss for my Moosa.' Her springy hair, stretching in the wind, wanting to tickle, would caress his cheeks.

'Mother of God, what kind of a glutton!' Moosa used to tease her.

'You'll gobble down everything that comes your way and will become like your mother.' Moosa dusted off the badam kernels and offered them to her.

'You won't find someone to marry you. Here, eat this.'

'*Nah*!' she declined with hurt pride.

'Don't eat … Are you worried that you won't find a groom? If so, don't be worried. I am there for you. Here, eat this also.'

'Moosakka.' He knew that the coquetry and coyness were her way of making peace. Its reason may be the ripe green gooseberries that hung aplenty from the trees in Kanjirakkunnu, or the blue lotus tubers in Aralipradevan's temple pond, or the spotted sterculia berries by the roadside, or the jungle geranium berries or jackal jujubes of Ashaarikkunnu.

'What else do you need?'

'For me? *Mmm* ...' Placing her index finger under her chin, Kaulath tilted her head and looked at the sky.

'*Ah*, then listen ... cashew fruits, sage-leaved alangium, jambu ... then, immature paddy—the milky rice.'

'What about the other thing?'

'*Eh*? What?' Kaulath scratched her head.

'That fruit which only you and the crows eat ... kakkapazham.'

'I don't want that.' It was amusing to watch Kaulath get annoyed.

For Kaulath, Moosa was not merely for accompanying her to see the Munimada on Nellikkunu, or pick bladderwort flowers from the Ambalppoo field and fling them into the air, or pluck the soap nuts standing proudly in the field and work them into a lather on the evenings they were let off early from school ...

He was a pal. A friend to kiss and to be kissed by. One who carried her school bag. One who carried her when her legs felt fatigued. One who opened her tightly-closed lunch box by knocking it gently against the desk or window sill. One who loved her and her alone. Their love grew as they grew up. It grew enough for them to imagine themselves as Laila-Majnu, featured in the bawdy lyrics scratched on the rear walls of the market rooms, it grew enough for her to rest her head against Moosa's black granite chest while they sat in the graveyard at Mayyaparambu, reeking of rosy periwinkle flowers.

The degree holder in him couldn't get himself to console her, 'Don't cry, Kaulath …' Neither could he bring himself to say, 'I'll take you with me, my love.' But the inside of his black granite chest was boiling like heated tar.

Everything was being repeated.

The same story as his father's and his uncle's. The story of two young brothers who fell in love with the fair Ramlathbi. The tale of the dark-skinned Ali Koya and the Blockhead Mohammad who married her.

How time had flown. Moosa was now amused seeing his epileptic older brother resplendent in a white silk kurta, the garb of a bridegroom. He swallowed the bitter taste of self-loathing.

'*Ehh … me, I ennahi hoohoohi.*'

Moosa didn't respond to his gibberish.

'*Ssssay … dellll …*'

'I shall. Such a beauty. So comely. Good … good match,' his voice was breaking.

'*Haaaw haow ishhh her?*'

'Hmmm … she's my friend, all right,' Moosa murmured.

'*Donnn sssay Kauhahaa … sssauy ihhaaahaa.*'

'All right, I shan't call her Kaulath, I shall call her iththaththa,'[14] Moosa said, applying perfumed talcum powder on his brother's face. He made tiny cotton balls, dipped them in attar, and then pushed them into the concha of his brother's ears.

Many more rainy seasons came and went. In the fields where rice cultivation had been given up, a type of dominant

---

[14] Elder sister.

weeds outgrew the flowery plants. Rainwater was thwarted by widening the ridges and cementing them. Many more papaya plants sprang up by the side of the pathways. Their ripe, full-blooded, fleshy fruits hung down and swayed in the breeze. Countless leaves lay on the ground underneath the cashew trees in whose shade Kaulath and Moosa used to hug, smooch and make out.

As their cores decayed, trees hollowed out and were turned into wood dust and then into ash.

So many wet monsoons …

Water filled the fields, yards, compounds and small pits, and drained away.

Many scorching summers sweltered and burst through Kanjirakunnu that lay like a cancerous woman who had undergone a single mastectomy, the excavator having dug up more than half of its spread, ploughing through the cracked earth of the fields and the fissured ridges, as the fiery heat made bitumen evaporate from the roads caught in the blaze.

How many more tranquil autumns …

The sky thronged with floating pappus flapping their wings …

And how many more honey-sweet springtimes …

They frolicked among the bright red of the pagoda flower, the festival of violet hues of the bladderwort, the azure gleam of the blue snakeweed flower, the innocent pink of balsam and jungle geranium, and the trembling petals of pristine, white snowy orchid, and kissed the poisonous-smelling happy button of the Indian snakeroot flower …

Moosa, only Kaulath's darling *karmoosa*—her papaya—meandered about in the absence of the queen bee which had built her nest in his heart. He rambled on like a lunatic.

In the corridors of the house, when he heard her anklets tinkle as beautifully as the sound of Spanish cherry flowers tumbling down, he felt the desire to caress those feet once more.

On the rear verandah, the contours of her body seen through wet, clinging clothes, the sensual smell of the soap brought from Sharjah, the sunrays reflected off the coppery hairs on her arms, on which gold bangles jangled; all of these aroused him and drove him crazy.

Every night, despite shutting his door, the swishing of her sari being removed reached him from his brother's room. He heard the click of the bra being unhooked. Her lust-filled moans and sighs, the sounds of bodies slamming into each other and their groans in pain drove him mad.

'*Arrrghhh … ahhh …*' In his agony, he smashed his fist into the wall; pulled out his hairs by their roots. He bit his tongue hard, gashing it for the sin of merely chanting 'Kaulath'. He scratched his thighs maniacally. It was in that trance that Kaulath found him and wiped his cheeks with her long fingers. She was pained by the sight of his derangement.

'My Moosakka …' Her tears spilled on top of his tears.

Kaulath broke the agreement that the final kisses shared between them would be the ones in their secret meeting place amidst the rose periwinkle flowers.

It was when he came up for air after reciprocating with a prolonged kiss that he opened his eyes and saw his brother's shadow through the door which was ajar.

His eyes welled over in alarm.

'Merciful God!' Moosa lost his mind. This is my fate, my ultimate destiny. A sin that I had witnessed one rainy evening, almost drowning in water.

Moosa felt as if his head was on fire. Revenge was burning his insides. He gathered Kaulath up and hugged her.

Moosa looked spitefully at his brother who stood leaning against the doorpost like a man defeated. His lips that kissed her, his face that nuzzled her … Moosa caught his brother by his hair and smashed his face against the doorframe.

His arms turned into long, ghostly vines and wrapped themselves around his brother's neck. He felt the throb of a vein, as if he had touched the belly of a fluttering bird. His brother's eyes watered and bulged out like grapes. Moosa kept laughing maniacally. His brother's fingers dug into his forearms.

'*Ahhhhhh* …' Moosa shut his eyes and let out a scream. His brother's legs lifted off the floor and flailed noisily against the doorpost. The throbbing on his warm throat ceased. Moosa slowly flung his brother's body away with the nonchalance of throwing out offal.

His frenzied fingers grabbed Kaulath with lust and malice. He comforted her trembling lips, ran his fingers over her palpitating heart, and gently took strands of her hair and tucked them behind her ears. He kissed her teary cheeks repeatedly. His own tears mixed with hers.

Then, with unbridled love, he pushed her onto the gently warm heaps of paddy in the granary to sprout sin's sizzling red seeds.

The Lament of the Eunuch

The stench of a common vine snake—the female that died immediately after mating in the scorching sun. The snake that got burnt and writhed on the floor of the manure shed heaped with bone meal and urea.

He smelled the stethoscope. He smelled the smooth, long fingers that resembled tender okra. He smelled the surgeon's apron. He smelled the exposed reptilian breasts of Ayesha, scrubbed and readied for surgery. *Ahhh* ... the snake-like smell ... the very same odour. The hand of the clock is a serpent tongue. In seconds, minutes, hours, it will spit the poison of memories and bite. It will coil around a branch of the cluster fig tree, heavy with fruits, where he had mislaid his heart, and do the mating dance.

It was 4.30 p.m.

After six long years, he had an erection.

'Exactly four-thirty.' Ill at ease, he touched the zip of his trousers, distractedly.

Six years ago, it was four-thirty in the evening when he had opened the jute sack. The radium dial of his watch shone with a ghostly light.

Four-thirty to the dot.

In Dr Charulakshmi's dimly lit garden shed lay a heap of bone meal, another heap of stinking chicken shit, and one of corrosive urea. Like a cat trying to hide its shit, he first scratched frantically at the chicken shit heap, then turned upside down the manure and urea heaps and stomped down on the mounds. Eventually, from the midst of the bone meal, he pulled out that sack—a small plastic sack the colour of a ripening banana, with 'Factomfos 20:20 Fertiliser' written on it in red block letters. Though the mouth of the sack had been sewn with yellowed jute string, her tiny, red glass-bangled hand stuck out, as if screaming 'Daddy' to him, solitary and helpless.

Rajeev tugged at the jute strings. For those he could not tear with his hands, he used his teeth. Starting to scorch in the heat of the bone meal, Charu's skin had got stuck to the mouth of the sack like scraps of flattened pooris. Putrefaction made the sack stink worse than bone meal. Charulakshmi lay curled up in it like a dead foetus. Anguished, he tried to scrape away the rheum from her battered left eye. He broke down when he realised it wasn't rheum but a congregation of worms that had covered Charu's body entirely.

'*Aiyyooo, aiyyoooo*, my baby ...'

He touched different parts of her body, and the dampness of her double-plaited hair tied up with a bow ribbon. The hair was covered in her tears, blood, body fluids and bone meal dust, so much so that he couldn't recognise its colour. The white chemise that Charu used to wear usually had been bunched up and shoved into her mouth. Her thighs had scores of slashes as if drawn with a red-ink pen. The talisman, amulets and *panchaloha* bells hung down from her girdle—a gift from Rajeev's mother for Charu's twenty-eighth day ceremony—like a broken hangman's knot. A bouquet made with orchids and ferns lay withered in her right hand. He scooped her up.

'No … no … no, Doctor,' the police inspector grabbed him from behind. 'Should I be telling you this? Doctor … this is a crime scene … there could be evidence …' He gestured to the constable to gently try and take away the body from Rajeev's hands.

'*Aiyyoooo, aiyyyayyooo* …' Rajeev smashed his head against the wall like a demented man.

He clutched Charu close to his body. From the outside, the wild colours of the flowers that had bloomed in the rain hurt his eyes. The leaves were trembling in the rain as if in fright. The monstrous jasmines on the meadow flinched as they got wet. Humungous hibiscus flowers reminded him of blood. As red-tinged darkness entered his bloodshot eyes, he keeled over and his head hit the floor. Bone-meal dust floated up, resembling white morning mist. From Charu's body that had fallen onto his chest, bits of rotten flesh fell off onto the withered body of the common vine snake.

The smell of Indian snakeroot flower was overpowering. The flower that convulsed and survived in turmeric, lime and milk. Violetish veins of the tender leaves throbbed. Along with its berries, the flowers swayed in the monsoon breeze, grazing the rear of the nagayakshi. He smelled the mythical snake pearl in her navel. He smelled the lukewarm heartbeats between her breasts. He smelled the olive-coloured downy hairs on her body. Ah, the serpent smell! She was a nude yakshi, a serpent deity. The evening twilight straining through the peach curtains made her curves resplendent.

As he pressed his cheeks against the ripe berries of this serpentine nymph, he was certain that Charulakshmi transcended a mere human female form in bed. She was a nagayakshi who did the mating dance, coiling and uncoiling, uniting and disengaging, squeezing and releasing, and moulting. Occasionally using a sibilant voice, she would moan and display her amorous, lotus-like vulva. At other times, she used to clutch the pillow case deliriously and beg him, 'Here, here …' He felt nervous when she touched her nether lip.

'Here … this way … bite, bite hard.' She touched the bite mark on her breast and squirmed in pain.

'That day, when you came to know I was married, how did you feel, Raju?'

He lifted his face off her chest. A bitter feeling of self-loathing arose in his mouth.

'Wanted to kill you … strangle you …' Rajeev hugged her hard. A sharp pain shot through his body as if a crab's pincers had pinched him. His throat felt as if it was on fire.

'And then? Did you hate me terribly?' Cobra saffron flowers sought reasons to bloom or wither in her eyes.

The primal smell of childbirth—the odours of amniotic fluid and uterine blood mixed with the odour of the human body—spread. He sensed the smells of the umbilical cord and breasts filled with cream-coloured milk too. He felt the labour pangs between the feminine legs spread guilelessly. He could smell the tiny heads that bloomed between them like black flowers. Standing in the maternity ward, he dissolved in tears.

It was four-thirty.

'I am sorry, Raju.' Dr Mridula took his hands in hers. 'But it's true. Charulakshmi has had abortions thrice. With her husband's consent.'

'Husband?' His eyes started to bulge.

'Yes. He's her husband. Unlike what we all had thought, he's not her father.' She extended fresh copies of the hospital records towards him.

An old Mercedes that reminded one of a hoary cat. The vision of Charulakshmi slamming its door shut. The pale-eyed colonel reminded him of a Siamese cat.

'He's my father.' When Charulakshmi said it *sotto voce*, there was no shiftiness in her eyes.

Some orchids grow only on trees, with their roots embracing the trunk. Did Charulakshmi shoot her roots into his heart like one such flower? Charulakshmi, for whom one cross word was enough to get cut up and wilt? For whom one gaze from him was enough to bloom like a garden of love?

'Hell, I don't know, Raju, everything's not okay with her.' Ramakrishna Pai pulled the green curtain of the ward close for some privacy, and told him conspiratorially, 'She's a bit of a mystery.'

The inscrutable Charulakshmi. Flowers were an intoxicant for her. She wore rare orchids in her hair every day, like some sorceress who held dark secrets. Young men hovered around her like strange beetles. They were perplexed by her mysteriousness which no beetle-like buzz and joviality could pierce. Massed lavender turned violet in the flowerbeds stretching across many acres. The purple of orchids turned ruddy. Yellow tulips bloomed. Trucks from outside the state came in search of her gardens that hid all the floral secrets of the universe. Oblivious of the malodours of death in the post-mortem room, she looked at Rajeev, her cheeks flushed, as if painted by chrysanthemums. He loved her to bits; his heart felt as if it had been set aflame.

'No, I never hated you, I promise.'

Rajeev rubbed and spread the vermillion on her forehead.

'Liar …' she rubbed her nose against his, like a bird rubbing beaks with its mate.

'It's the truth. Otherwise, would I ever name my daughter Charulakshmi?'

'I was a mere collateral, Raju. A mere ornament to pawn.' She let out a deep sigh.

That was true. She was a living collateral, a pledge piece. Rajeev nodded his head. In their last meeting, she had sat with her head bowed behind her husband who was older than her father. More than guilt or mortification from being found out, her face reflected the paleness of anguish. The truckers from Tamil Nadu who were loading the flowers looked at him as if he was a freak. Unnerved and pale, he stood in front of the clock-shaped house amidst the acres of flower beds surrounding it.

Smells can converse. Smells can presage, portend. He received many intimations of danger from the primal body odour of the profusely sweating Tamilian truckers. From the kiss that Charulakshmi had bestowed on him in the radiotherapy room, his life force was still burning up. The teeth marks left on his lips stung him. They were trembling like tender leaves charred by acid.

Charulakshmi was trembling too. She was terrified by the thought of the punishment that awaited her at the end of her trial of passion. The yellowed buckteeth of the giant, pan-chewing gardener, Alavi—standing about twelve feet behind Rajeev—seemed to stare at her and taunt her. Before she was to turn into manure for the orchid plants, she looked at Rajeev with trepidation. She had heard from her father that many people had become one with the bone-meal heap in the garden shed. Between the sounds of rattling bones, she was assailed by the death wail of invisible souls; their screams were battering her ears.

'*Ra … ra …*' words fell to the ground like petals dropping off flowers. Her mouth was in a churn; words and syllables tumbled out in a jumble. When the colonel left to fetch his phone, she tried again to say something.

'My price is four-and-a-half lakh rupees. I am a mere collateral for that value …' Fear for her life made her voice break.

It all happened two weeks after her father, the colonel's clerk, was found hanging in the garden.

'My mother was forty years old but still youthful. I had three sisters. I thought this was better than all five of us dying or becoming whores. When the colonel proposed this, I agreed …' she said with the helplessness of a sixteen-year-old. Her eyes flashed like a pickerel fish.

'I became the fifth official wife of the colonel.'

Erecting an invisible wall around her, sixteen-year-old Charulakshmi lay in the old man's love chamber like an anachronistic doll. Swinging between avarice and lust, seeing the childlike helplessness on her face, the colonel stroked her cheek, repeating, 'Poor thing ... you, poor, poor thing.'

'He has lakhs, no, crores ... no woman will refuse to have his child ...' Charulakshmi hugged Rajeev.

'If I hadn't met you, Rajeev ...'

As she sighed, her tender, maple-leaf-like belly undulated. Love burned in her body like a fire.

'Those days, my love for you, Raju, was like a bitch that survives on leftovers. One who gnaws at bones secretly. Yet the colonel found out.'

Bathed in moonlight, with her shoulders gleaming, Charulakshmi looked like a yakshi, her chest damp with sweat, as if swollen and sodden with rainwater.

'He knew everything. Before he died, he had gathered my hands in his with fatherly affection and gripped them tightly. "You must forgive me. I made you my own, not to blight your life, but because I loved you, more than anyone else did."' A red-tinged sadness flitted across her lips.

'I used to hate him. Yet at times, I felt a deep love for him.'

Rajeev felt that men were fools to believe that women kept their eyes closed while making love because of a surfeit of affection. What all would have been hiding in the darkness under her eyelids then—hatred, self-loathing, contempt, pain? Three daughters, sacrificed to the yakshi, flowed down the drain pipes of the maternity ward silently like aborted thoughts.

Rajeev tried to recall the innocence in the eyes of twenty-year-old Charulakshmi, who, in denial and wearing the armour of her inner defences, had buried motherhood in one half of her heart and from the other half, given him unbounded love.

The clock struck the half hour—chimes of the deaf Beethoven's *Fifth Symphony*. The sound convulsed like a snapped lizard tail.

Four-thirty.

'Raju, he knew it all … he knew everything about you. My secret affair, your sense of loss, your marrying Mridula, having a baby girl, naming her after me … He even comforted me on the day of your wedding.' Charulakshmi buried her face between her knees. 'Enough with the old tales. Isn't it only the third day after your wedding?'

Rajeev used his lips both as bait and the fishing rod. He showed Charulakshmi the secret trick of locking lips that, once hooked, stayed locked lifelong.

'*Dum … dum …*' The sound of a tiny hand knocking on the door was heard.

'Daddy, it's Charu … open the door,' she lisped.

'Just five minutes, baby,' he was panting and huffing like a steam engine. 'Go and play in the yard; there's a new ball there.'

'No, your baby will make a bouquet for you. A wedding bouquet. For the bride and the groom. A bouquet …' Her anklets tinkled and laughed into the distance. Charu was leaving. She was departing to the land of flowers.

'Ayesha, do you know my daughter?' Rajeev slapped her hard across her face with the hand that had Betadine spilled on it. He tore off the white rubber gloves. The right hand of a man with five penises was exposed. He squeezed her breasts with hands that oozed wickedness. His eyes overflowed with vindictiveness. In the room that smelled of a thousand dying or dead reptiles and had a piercing yellow light bright enough to set off a migraine attack, anaesthetics were deadening the nerves and senses. He yanked the pulsometer's sensor—that bellowed like a tiger who had forgotten its station—off her finger. Tears welled up in her eyes. Her breasts that cancer had turned livid, rose in indignant pride.

'You know everything, don't you, Ayesha? Only I didn't know that the gardener, Alavi, is your father, that son-of-a-bitch.'

He started to cry when he remembered Charu. His tears scattered like marbles, struck his spectacles and splashed Ayesha's body.

Six years ... how many evenings ... how many haunted four-thirties. Rajeev could never bring himself to touch Charulakshmi thereafter, not even once. When he made to lay his lips on hers, he heard his daughter Charu's anklets. Dressed in her shabby chemise with bloodstains still fresh on it, tiny Charu's ghostly mouth yawned in front of him. When he made to hug Charulakshmi, little Charu's loud laughter flashed around him like lightning. A woman's body never aroused Rajeev thereafter, come rain or shine, breeze or tempest. Swallowing aphrodisiacs and mustering up courage, whenever he tried to swim towards Charulakshmi like a seafarer, the little one laid her hand on the door and knocked …

'*Dum* … *dum* … *dum* … Daddy, it's me, your Charu …'

He stood with his head bowed. He melted down in the heat from Charulakshmi's torso. He failed utterly and mortifyingly.

'This thing that hangs down, it's not only a tube to pee from,' the heat in Charulakshmi, transmogrified as the yakshi, slapped his floppy failure with her left hand and shrieked.

'He can't forget her, I believe! *Chheee* … Did she die because you slept with me? Raju, do you believe so? Liar. You're lying. Instead of leaving it dangling between your legs, cut it off and feed it to some dog …' said the fierce hunger of a tigress. Her nakedness challenged him like a weapon.

'Eunuch … impotent!' Her spittle roared on his face like the waves of an angry sea.

Covering his howling mouth with his hand, he sat on the floor on his haunches.

'Don't cry … don't …' Ayesha gathered him onto her ailing chest.

'Doctor, wasn't the child named Charu? If she were alive, she'd be my age, no?' The words slurred on her tongue and crawled like evil spirits under the effect of anaesthesia.

'In the next half hour, these will be cut out. Doctor, you'll be doing it, no? These two lumps of flesh are to be dumped in the waste bin, aren't they? Don't cry … don't cry …' She touched her cancerous chest for one last time.

Dr Rajeev picked up the scalpel with his gloved hand.

He suddenly got the whiff of Johnson's baby powder. He could smell the starch of a cotton petticoat. He also caught the smell of the orchid bouquet Charu had made with her tiny fingers, and smelled the withered ferns in it. The tinkling of her anklets stopped suddenly. Silence. Then he was startled by her hands knocking on the door, *dum … dum … dum*.

'My darling Daddy, open the door. It's Charu … Charu is going to cry …'

He heard Charu crying. And he heard the helpless sobs of Ayesha in her stupor. Ayesha's dead breasts shivered in Dr Rajeev's hands like two chunks of meat.

He nervously plunged them into formalin solution, and they sank to the bottom of the jar, glugging. They stood upright at the bottom, with the same vanity as the bone-meal mound encompassing Charu's corpse; they stood with their heads raised. The formalin turned red with the blood from the breasts. Two nipples, tearless, and with marked indifference and scorn, kept staring at Rajeev in a beastly manner, like the eyes of God, which never blink.

Crying piteously, he kept suturing her body, like a eunuch whose nerve always failed at the sight of a woman's naked body.

A Story Posted in 1975

When I heard on Vividh Bharati that he had perished in a plane crash, I was shocked. Standing in between the tin sheet separators of the whorehouse, I tarried for a moment while carrying the red bucket containing ejaculate spillovers. The thought of resuming duty—to enter each cubicle and pick up used condoms and torn pill covers—was nauseating.

Four or five tribal girls brought in from Kerala passed me by. One of them even looked at me and smiled fondly.

The sounds of chenda and dappan koothu drums could be heard from the street outside. The staccato bursting of crackers, cheering and whistles exploded in the sky in flowery sparks, like blood spatter from an exploding skull. An old revolutionary song was being broadcast over Vividh Bharati.

I felt my calculations had gone wrong in some way. I put the bucket down. One warm evening three years ago, in my nineteenth year, that bucket had become a part of me. A gift from the government to those who had been vasectomised.

After selling fruit baskets during the day, I would make dosas on my pushcart by night. I whipped and poured the batter onto the roasting hot tawa. A company of forty soldiers had arrived in our village. They kept drumming on their gun barrels. As if a solution of darkness had been mixed and poured into it, my petromax got extinguished.

I lit two or three small wick lanterns.

'Give us dosas,' one of the soldiers ordered.

'What's your name, boy?'

'Ghulam Nabi.' I served mint chutney on his plate.

I was aware what was going to happen in my village. In the previous weeks, I had seen the soldiers, swinging their batons, making lathi charges at Bawali and Madoga, and curfew lighting street lamps of silence in the nights there.

'Gullu, don't worry. They won't come here. Indira-ji is a good-hearted woman.' Munni comforted me.

'*Phthooo* ... good-hearted!' The stinging response came from Chanku dadu. 'You know nothing of the backstories, my daughter,' he chided Munni. I watched her face turn pink and her lips turning pouty.

'What happened in the case of Birhors? Look at the Khasis problem. You are blaming the government without reason.'

'Munni, don't think that the adivasis' problems alone are India's problems. Each and every one in this country needs justice.' Chanku dadu was panting. 'Emergency can't be justified only because it has brought the adivasis' problems to the fore.'

'Chanku dadu, not so loud,' I warned him. I was afraid that the brick walls and door planks had ears. I knew that the boundary between patriotism and treason in India was very thin.

In the summer heat, the village was festering like a wound on which vinegar had been poured. A summer song meandered in between the bamboo groves, humming its tune. Our lodge was at the edge of the town. Standing in the midst of towering peepal and neem trees like a hefty obelisk, the building demarcated the boundary between the town and the village.

On some days, I was included in the groups that collected paddy seeds for Prof. Ramanatha Iyer's institute. On other days, I went to the village and collected jamuns dripping with juice that caused purple stains, rambutans that resembled the sweet drool of babies and fleshy guavas, and peddled them in town on the bamboo handcart. The Emergency interfered with my trade too. Gangs of soldiers used to take away the fruit baskets by force. Others forbade me from shouting 'rambuuuttaaan' loudly. The curfew made the women stay indoors. Even the laughter of the children who used to shout in anticipation on hearing my cart's bell had fallen silent. They peered with fearful eyes from behind the thick curtains blanketing the window panes.

Neither Chanku dadu nor I had the will or capacity to starve. Along with Munni, I went around the fields, gathering grains that had fallen on the ground.

'Do you know that India has the largest number of rice varieties in the world? More than twenty-five thousand. Would you believe it?' Munni imparted her unsolicited knowledge. The paddy grains had matured and turned yellow in the heat. Some of the pregnant stalks stood tired, with their heads bowed. In that heat, shielded by the haystacks, I had kissed Munni on her left eyelid.

We believed that by the time summer was over, our seed collection would be complete, and hoped that our village would have green paddies sprouting in all the fields. And the following summer, I would wed Munni.

I would touch her paan-reddened lips. Bells of their girdles tinkling, our children would run through the fields.

A feeble, warm but dry breeze swirled around us. Sounding horns and military whistles, a few new military jeeps entered our village, circumnavigating our paddy fields.

I saw him one late evening—a six-foot-tall young man with Parsi features. Our villagers did not believe that he was an administrator. Though he had a long nose, green-tinged cheeks and a finely honed, serene smile, his eyes spoke of a churning, roaring sea inside him.

We did not understand why the military had brought doctors with them. But by morning, the honey-gathering tribals and itinerant hunters had queued up in front of the tent. Like a line of yellow crazy ants. When they came out, each one held a bright-coloured plastic bucket in their hand.

'What's happening here? Isn't the curfew in force?' Some of the religious teachers queried one another.

Chanku dadu found out about it that evening.

'You fool, what's happening is vasectomy. Males are being sterilised. In return, five kilos of rice, a plastic bucket and a transistor are being handed out. Why should the tribals breed like pigs?'

I remember hearing snatches of film songs coming from some of the huts. After that day, whenever we went to the fields to gather seed grains, we strained our ears for Vividh Bharati playing in the nearby huts.

'Gullu, in a way, aren't music and vasectomy like life and death?'

I looked with amusement at the bright buckets placed in front of Birhors' huts.

'Gullu, do you know something?' Munni looked around. In the middle of the bamboo grove, bamboo sprouts waved their tiny ears and their thorns embraced one another tightly. Dry bamboo leaves kept fluttering down and dropping on Munni's head.

The paddy seeds we had collected were being sent abroad to Manila or Philippines or someplace like that.

'In return, their seeds are to be brought here. But what seeds are there to replace the twenty-five thousand varieties?'

I smelled the danger before Chanku dadu did. *India's seeds, Indians' rice* ... people in air-conditioned rooms were murmuring in hushed tones. Many obscure things were hidden behind Iyer's eyes, shielded by his thick glasses.

The summer hotted up. The harvested fields were parched and they cracked up in the heat. Tanker lorries used to come in the mornings and afternoons, bringing water for the soldiers. The villagers who came to be vasectomised collected water in their plastic buckets and took it home.

The flow of villagers to the vasectomy tents ceased suddenly. Only Birhor women from interior villages who were fatigued from nine deliveries or old Khasi men were left. Soldiers sat inside the tents, polishing their rifle barrels or applying polish on their dusty boots. The doctors' state was pitiful. The skin of their fingers, no longer anointed by blood from surgeries, cracked. Dust settled on their white coats hung out in the open. They got bored laying about lazily dressed in their dust-filled, shabby clothes. Their unoiled hair turned coppery and brittle. Conjectures spread in the area that they may return to their respective stations.

One Tuesday, Munni and I had a tiff with Prof. Iyer. We were out with the seed-gathering group, including five or six professors and some youngsters.

'We'll inform Indira-ji of this.'

'We won't be a party to this fraud.' The crowd that had gathered was angry. We were raising slogans in front of the institute.

The problems for the village were about to begin. In the diffused white light of that same Tuesday afternoon, with the grave suggestion of a smile on his face, that man came to our village again. The soldiers ran about among the huts like mad men. From the sterilisation tent, soldiers made public announcements that men with more than two children should come and get themselves vasectomised. They dragged out men with three children from their homes.

'Yes, a calamity is going to strike the town,' a disturbed Chanku dadu muttered. The dry wisps of his beard fluttered a little. He looked feverish. Seated at the northern edge of the lodge's terrace, under a peepal tree's shade, and scratching his rheumy eyes, he said again, ominously: 'Danger, danger.' His words were blown to smithereens by the siren of the military truck passing below.

'Gullu, don't go out, son. A big calamity is on its way.'

Though it was night, the traffic of army jeeps had not ceased. Sounds of soldiers kicking down the doors of huts and showering abuses on the occupants could be heard. I was reminded of a manic cavalry riding horses with shod hooves.

'Ya Allah! Is this really India?' Chanku dadu asked every now and then. Though he was too weak to get up and bend in prayer, his voice had a defiant ring.

We witnessed soldiers taking away men by force. Some were tied and dragged along the ground; some were kicked, yanked and taken to the tent. Bloodied stars rose in the sky and spewed flame.

'Tomorrow the sun will rise in the west. The world is ending. It's the Day of Qiyamat.'

I was confused. The neem leaves were perspiring in the heat, and the peepal tree was shedding leaves into the darkness of the night.

'Gullu, be on your guard.'

'They are men with three or four children, Dadu.'

'What—taking them away by force?' I saw protest straining in the strands of his phlegm that night; I saw its livid face. I saw the street turn blue and freeze like a snake-bitten girl. I fell asleep dreaming of dadu and me turning into rocks under the blue moonlight.

'Gullu.' I woke to the gentle voice of Munni. Ambulances were racing past the lodge.

'New doctors have arrived. They have now taken away the Birhori women?'

'What for?'

'Pregnant women. India has a population problem, they say.'

I recalled the helpless wails of the previous nights. The wails also of the embryos scraped out of mothers' wombs.

We suspected the doctors were using blood to wash their faces and brush their teeth after washing off the sins of foeticide. Their tent reminded us of a haunted castle. Its flapping faded top breathed in the early morning breeze.

'Our Iyer-saab, the asshole, is going to export the seeds. I believe Indira-ji has agreed.' I thought I saw Munni's eyes getting damp.

'The rice that we should eat; our own rice.' Her face became flushed like red tomatoes, and the muscles on it tightened with determination.

'I won't allow this. I'll write to Indira-ji.'

'No, Munni. It could be dangerous.'

'Munni, my girl,' Chanku dadu called out to her. His eyes were covered in rheum.

'Give me some warm water.' A stubborn gurgling sound could be heard from his chest.

'What you said is correct. We must stop this.' Chanku dadu tried to jump up from the charpoy.

In that moment, he seemed to have become a dying dog that had lost its teeth and hair with age.

'The letter must be written.' Chanku dadu drank the warm water. I saw saliva and phlegm forming cobweb patterns on his tongue and between his lips as he spoke.

Munni and Chanku dadu dictated; I transcribed the letter. Then I went to the post office to despatch it.

'Be careful. They are not like Indira-ji. They are devils,' Munni cautioned me.

'It'd be better if you posted it from Bawali,' Chanku dadu said. 'Act as if you are going to sell fruits.'

Loading up summer-sweetened rambutan and raisins, I walked along the tarred road under the blazing sun. While passing through the forest filled with bamboo groves and wild elephants, I thought I heard babies crying somewhere. The babies were sobbing, dropping honey on their mothers' hearts. I wetted the stamp bearing Gandhi-ji's image with my saliva and pasted it on the envelope. With great dread, I dropped it into the letter box.

It was the third day from then. I was praying. In the village where even call to prayers by the muezzin had been banned, I heard the sounds of soldiers arriving like a sounder of wild pigs.

The first to enter were the soldiers who used to eat dosas and jamun fruits that I had to give away free. Behind them was *that* man. They hit Chanku dadu, pushed him to the floor and kicked him.

'Nahi, baba, nahi!'

In that instant, I forgot my *surahs*.

'Where is that damned fellow? *Oh-ho*, are you praying?'

The first soldier to enter the room kicked me in my back viciously. I instinctively recited loudly the *surah* I had forgotten, 'Allah ...'

'You'll write letters to behen-ji, will you?'

One of the soldiers pressed his boot on my neck. My airway was blocked.

'Son-of-a-bitch!' A mailed fist formed in the air and came rushing at me. I felt as if the bridge of my nose had been shattered.

'How old are you?'

'Nineteen,' I screamed in pain. My entire face felt as if it was covered in blood.

'Righto, that's a good age.' He kicked my spine beneath my hip.

'Ya Allah …' In the suffering of a life-wrenching pain, I peed in my clothes.

'Take him to the camp.'

'Nahi baba … forgive us.' My grabbing his leg and his kneeing my face happened in the same instant. I fell back. One of my teeth fell inside my mouth like a homeopath's white globule. My children … my children who'll never be born of me … With a searing pain in my heart, I thought of Munni. How we had kissed each other passionately in the wheat fields and in the paddy fields which had started to sprout the unripe, milky rice. How we embraced tightly on the ridges filled with rambutan and morning glory trees!

They dragged me to the terrace. Chanku dadu lay curled under the charpoy like a lump of smash-kneaded dough. They yanked me down the grouted cement stairs; I could feel the skin and flesh being torn off my body.

I would have endured everything had I not seen Munni lying on the floor of the ambulance like a piece of raw flesh with flies buzzing around it. The sky crashed on my head to the accompaniment of blinding-white lightning.

Between my tears and Munni, there was only the body of a naked soldier. As every soldier got off her, Munni shouted, 'Indira Gandhi murdabad!'

One of the soldiers slapped her across the face when he heard this. Another one spat on her face. Munni and I travelled in the ambulance, its siren wailing along the fields in which we had gathered grains.

Munni didn't moan. Her voice rose again: 'Indira Gandhi murdabad.' I covered her mouth gently with my mangled palm. Her lips were trembling. Her chest was heaving like a fluttering dove.

'Indira Gandhi murdabad.' Munni called out for the last time. Her breath that was, until a moment ago, knocking against my hurting fingers—ceased. I shut my eyes tightly. I plummeted, swirling and spinning into the black abyss of a piercing scream.

When I regained consciousness, I was lying on the sandy floor of the military camp. The sight of the stitches in my lower belly made me laugh. The rice, bucket and transistor they had kept for me mocked me.

Who in India wants Ghulam Nabi's children?

Back in the lodge, Chanku dadu's sentinels were ants—fat yellow crazy ants. Blood had clotted on his grey moustache. His rheum-filled eyes had bulged out. He too was dead.

I eventually reached this red light street. With great self-loathing, I picked up and dropped the used condoms into my red bucket.

I had come to know that Emergency had ended and that Prof. Iyer had been awarded the Padma Shri. Listening to songs on Vividh Bharati and doing bonded labour for prostitutes, I continued to exist.

My life, the red bucket, the squalor, my unborn children. I felt contempt towards myself for the first time.

I got out into the yard and started to walk. I looked at the sky and the earth, at the trees and the soil, at people performing ablutions under the public tap. I saw people who were dancing with happiness and someone kicking away the transistor kept in front of the house. Then I counted the money in hand to check if it was sufficient to bid for the services of the adivasi girl who had been newly brought in, and walked back into the whorehouse.

Virgins Who Walk on Water

The night I came to know I was pregnant
I had a dream that the wife who was a virgin
Was walking on water.

Amuda had said numerous times that if Raziya had the reproductive capacity of a man, Amuda would have conceived her child, carried it to term and delivered, even suffering intense labour pain. Covered in fragrant flowers that looked like neatly arranged petals of moonlight, the devil's tree near the ladies' hostel, shivering and swaying in the breeze, was a witness to all these averments. All these had witnessed their love: the bronze Greek god statue's girdle bells; the burnt-down candles; the loose-around-the-waist, apple-coloured panties on the clothesline; Raziya's Gandhi-style round-rim spectacles, steamed up by the intimate scenes on view; the peeved Caucasian child on the poster, with the finger on her lips shushing everyone; the naughty breeze redolent of devil tree flowers that clambered up and peeped into the room occasionally ...

Yet the journalists who visited them at the hospital were told by them that their love 'was a secret'.

Amuda was asked 'What made you take this decision?' by one of the journalists dabbing the sweat off his nose with a handkerchief.

'I wanted to birth Raziya's child. That was my wish.'

Both were seated on the bed on which a green rubber sheet had been spread. When Amuda placed her hand on the rubber sheet, her palm became damp. Raziya was using a cotton sheet to cover the blood splatter from the surgery on her hospital gown.

'How is Raziya's community going to take this?'

'Has my community misinterpreted egg donation?' Raziya's eyes narrowed and became bloodshot.

'Listen, this is my personal matter. Wasn't my womb damaged from the kicks of the police? Shouldn't I have a progeny?'

'Not like that. How does Amuda's family ...?'

'Family?' Raziya was getting annoyed.

'I mean, Amuda's husband?'

Amuda laughed aloud without warning. Silver bells tinkled down from her laughter and created music.

'A *man* ...' Amuda muttered under her breath.

A revolting apparition that evoked the image of paan-stained lips, a potbelly, a wide belt over it, and a chest with dense grey hair.

Amuda recalled. She was his third wife. As a child, she used to call the elderly friend of her father's, appa—father—too. His daughters were much older to her.

On their wedding night, standing at the open window, Amuda saw Tuticorin's rice fields. In the dammed waters of the fields, falling rain formed shimmering silver plates. As moonlight spread, touching everything in front of her eyes, the glow of the stars from the sky and the fireflies lay submerged in the milky white water in the fields. The room was decorated with garlands of firecracker flowers for their first night.

'Do you all think that I received love there? Or even the consideration of being a wife?' Amuda asked the pressmen. 'I am still a virgin. His style of love-making was painful. My cries were his orgasms.'

Amuda remembered the voracity of an old yellow-fanged, grizzled wolf. She touched the welts and cuts caused by his wide belt.

'How did the news of your love reach Amuda's house?'

'Somehow it did.' Raziya took off her glasses. 'Ammu's father had taken her away by force. Dragging her by the hair.'

The corner of the granary filled with boiled paddy resurfaced in Amuda's memory. The wooden window pane was frozen in a half-open position. Darkness slithered into the room like snakes and climbed over the heaped paddy. The heat and the reek of boiled paddy made her breathless. She grieved that Yelagiri's skies hadn't delivered stars to the west. She stroked her own head. She felt as if she had run her fingers through a small bough of touch-me-nots.

She had inherited her mother's pale, coppery hair—lush and as if made with golden strands. If the hair was let down, firecracker flowers tucked near her nape slid down like spiders and fell to the ground. When plaited, it appeared to be a golden serpent, slithering down with its hood held prone. It would bite both her buttocks gently. When she walked, it would bounce up and down and lie with its hood unfurled.

The day she was caught at the railway station, it was by her hair that Chinnappa Chettiar held her.

'No, Appa,' she screamed, as if its roots were coming off her skull.

'Cut it, Silambarasa.'

Amuda lifted her eyes.

The young barber's eyes, which had long admired her with devotion from the end of the street, were brimming with tears. Silambarasan used to gather and keep the firecracker flowers and tulsi leaves that used to fall off her hair.

Amuda was weeping as her head was being shaved. The hairs fell to the floor like weightless rain. Her head was getting lighter. The finger of a breeze from the eucalyptus plantation touched her forehead. As he applied the shaving cream on her head, Silambarasan's fingers trembled. Hair snips stuck to the razor like tiny worms. Silambarasan wiped and stropped the blade on his left palm. When he recalled how he used to hide among the eucalyptus trees beside the paths Amuda used to frequent, he cut himself. He felt sad that her face showed no accusation. With his eyes bloodshot, he silently gathered the pile of hair lying on the floor, filled his cloth bag, and walked away.

Chinnappa Chettiar stood by, motionless, but still grinding his teeth. After her head was shaved, he didn't lock her up. The grey pall-like sky she saw in front of her, or Chinnappa Chettiar's menacing voice, or his oily moustache—nothing fazed or frightened Amuda.

She had run away the same week that eucalyptus started to flower. After hiding in the cold tea gardens during the day, she had taken the night bus to Kozhikode.

The city of Kozhikode felt like the interior of a fridge early the next morning. She walked through familiar streets, drenched in early morning rain. She saw the winged termites that had perished on the street lights. The blue stars of the early morning sky had dived behind dark clouds. Her heart was pumping like a kingfisher's that had dived into the water and resurfaced. Her damp dupatta stuck to her eucalyptus-oil-anointed body.

Amuda had to scale the hostel wall. Her palms and ankles got cut by the glass shards atop it. The blue embroidery on her white churidar ripped. Her dupatta's edge caught on a shard; her shorn head shone in the moonlight.

By the time she reached Raziya's door, she had lost her voice from fear. Like a bird rubbing its beak, she rested her face against the door and moaned softly.

It was the fifth time Raziya had woken up with a start. The sound of rain on grass blades, or a beetle buzzing near the window, or lightning entering the room surreptitiously through the gap in the ventilator and smiling coyly in the mirror was enough to break her sleep. The loneliness she felt under the sheet made her anxious. Now, in her sleep, she had heard a scream. Was someone scratching the door with their nails? Raziya opened her eyes.

'Razi… ya…' That cry was not a dream. She leapt up from the bed and pulled open the door. She was shocked to see Amuda—her shaved head with stubble which gave her a sickly look; tears streaming down her exhausted face; the darkness of melancholia in the eyes; a rough lividness on the lips.

'Ammootti …' Raziya hugged her. Amuda's body was holding in it the chill of Yelagiri, of the tea estates, the transport bus and the rain. She shivered occasionally, as if her muscles were cramping.

'Come!' Raziya started to gently take off her wet clothes. When she pulled at the dupatta, Amuda panicked.

'Ammoose, sit here.' She pulled out a stool. She used a sheet to dry Amuda's hair. She took off her sodden bra and brief. Water running down Amuda's body formed little pools on the stool and the floor. Droplets shone her light pubic hair like diamond dust. Raziya rubbed the soles of her feet to warm her. When she rubbed hard the muscles of her thighs that were cramping, Raziya felt the smell of eucalyptus oil leaching into her hands.

She gently massaged her chest. When she touched her nipples, Raziya felt as if tender grapes were caressing her hand. Amuda suddenly opened her eyes and stared at Raziya's face. Blood gradually returned to her shrivelled lips and pale cheeks. Her breasts … her breasts were on fire, as if in a fever. Amuda got up and stood in the narrow space between the wooden almirah and the wall, resting her cheek against the wall.

Raziya switched off the ceiling fan, which was making a racket. She lit a small candle. The rain's needle-like panes formed a curtain over the open window. The day was breaking. The sky looked soft and tender, like an infant's sole. A damp breeze had begun to blow and tickle the leaves and flowers of the devil's tree.

'Ammu.'

'Hmm …'

'Come …' Undoing the buttons of her loose night dress, Raziya called out to her. In the low candlelight, the tears on top of her breasts sparkled like raindrops.

Raziya stroked Amuda's shaved head gently. Amuda started to cry again. 'Don't cry!'

With lips that still had sleep's smell on them, Raziya held Amuda's lips in a kiss. Then, pressing her right hand against Amuda's earlobe, she kissed her on the nape of her neck.

Lightning streaked across the sky like a flashing *urumi*.[15] Raziya withdrew. Her eyelashes had shrunk from the moisture. In the next flash of lightning, they saw each other's nakedness. They were like snakes that had moulted, coiling and uncoiling.

Raziya knelt down. Her nose rubbed against Amuda's apple-shaped navel. Amuda bent down and hugged her; Raziya's cheeks were brushing against her breasts. Their caresses were warm, like the bellies of cooing doves.

They embraced each other hard. Their bodies rubbed against each other and sparks flew. They snarled and bellowed like wild animals caught in a trap.

When Amuda buried her face in the rumpled cotton sheet, she caught the smell of Raziya's sweat. It reminded her

---

[15] A type of sword with a long, flexible blade.

of the corrosive sensuality of tender mango sap. When she turned and lay face up, her wheatish breasts swayed gently.

'They look like bullseye on the frying pan.' Raziya stared at her breasts with a hungry mouth.

'Come darling, let's sleep.' Amuda yanked the sheet and it ballooned over them like a sanctuary. As they slept, both dreamed of walking on water.

Raziya woke up when sunlight fell on her face. She could not determine if the room was suffused with the smell of eucalyptus or devil's tree flowers. A sudden, demanding knock on the door was heard, and that shattered Amuda's sleep.

She opened the door. The sight of Chinnappa Chettiar's bloodshot eyes made Amuda tremble.

'Come here,' he said to Amuda with an exaggerated show of calm. Amuda hid behind Raziya. Then he leapt into the room and grabbed Amuda's forearm.

Raziya heard only one sentence. 'I won't let you go.'

The incident with Raziya happened that afternoon when she had gone to the court to meet the lawyer for filing a habeas corpus application. A Tamilian constable who had come to stop the picketing of the court came running towards Raziya who was standing alone away from the commotion. Abusing and questioning her paternity in Tamil-accented Malayalam, the constable kicked Raziya's lower abdomen savagely.

'Ammaaaa … aaa…'

A sliver of the truncated scream fell amidst the protesters. Raziya was bent double. She trembled like an aged and broken coconut tree. She felt as if her internal organs had been mashed up. Her lungs, intestines, uterus, bladder—everything felt as if it was stretched between two small metal hooks, and if she were to straighten herself, they would all tear and fall down. She kept her feeble hand between her legs as a support. Blood started to drip through her fingers.

After she left the hospital, Raziya did not think of Amuda. When she picked out Amuda's wedding invitation from the unopened pile of mail of over three months, she was not fazed. There was an instant when she felt as if someone had pierced her insides with a red-hot spike. That was all. Then she wiped that chapter of her life off her mind. She kept functioning like clockwork for the next five years.

Neither empty bottles of eucalyptus oil, nor people with shaved heads, nor the blue dupatta she had kept away among her clothes, nor the blossoming of the devil's tree on rainy nights reminded her of Amuda.

Till the day she received a rose-pink inland letter from her with many words smudged by her tears.

'Let's live together.' That sentence pained Raziya. The past flooded in and choked her. She boarded the train to Tuticorin.

When Raziya reached the weaver's street in Tuticorin, multi-coloured yarns hung from the drying lines were swaying in the breeze. The street spoke to her through the *kat-kat* sounds of the looms. Raziya had assumed she would find a dry-eyed Amuda behind one of the looms. But Amuda was found in the street behind the looms, patting and drying cow-dung cakes. Her clownish clothes—green, blue, orange and yellow in colour—mocked her youth.

A dark stain had appeared on her dry cheek. In her eyes was the last glimmer of a tiny candle. The revolting green of cow-dung had stained her broken nails. Veins that had gained strength from being wounded, becoming septic and getting healed by turns snaked across her forearms. A foul odour not unlike that of rotting jasmines hung about her.

'Ammu … Ammu …'

Raziya tearfully kissed Amuda's coarse, shrivelled skin that had once been smooth and reddish-golden, like a pomegranate. The chill of the needling December breeze enveloped them in a protective embrace. Raziya could suddenly smell Tamil all around her.

'Thus, Amuda and Raziya got together again. Now, thanks to modern medicine, a new guest has arrived in their lives. Behind the successful fertilised egg transplantation were Dr Indira S., Dr Nirmala T.Y., Dr …' The voice of the TV reporter standing close to Amuda and Raziya trailed off.

They were lying in the same bed.

That night, both of them saw the same dream. In the dream, the sky resembled a sheet of glass painted in blue. Morning stars hung from it like a devil's tree's withered buds. Under them was a shallow ocean of tears, in which blue-winged butterflies fluttered like wavelets. Raziya and Amuda were walking in that ocean.

Their anklets tinkling, they were walking on the water …

Both of them—the virgins.

The Muslim with Hindu Features

The sea was growling and roaring, like boiling water frothing and bubbling on the rim of a glass. The wind, like a goldsmith using the blowpipe on the embers, spread its aroma of kisses amidst the gold-flecked orchards.

Some lover's anklets, in the custody of God, grazed against the sky and descended on earth as forked lightning.

In her prayer whites, his mother resembled a giant butterfly, and was prattling with unknown passers-by. Disguised as mercury beads, water droplets tickled colocasia leaves and rolled off, putting on a show of their chemical wizardry. Flocks of seagulls pecked at each other above the sea, their squawking and squabbling resembling the sounds of manic waves. The dark-skinned and red-tongued aboriginal Arabs were leaping off the giant dhows in Beypore in search of fisherwomen. The handsome, hirsute djinn was lurking near the road to the madrasa, brandishing the lure of the attar bottle to seduce and inveigle. On the night of *khatna,*[16] a pair of scissors played sensual music and promised more

[16] circumcision

erotic nights through pain. The spring of sweat in her lotus bud-like navel touched the lip with an energising aroma. Memories, dreams and demented thoughts whirled around wildly in Mustafa's head, like in a centrifuge.

'Ya Allah.' No one heard his heartrending, bloodcurdling cry. Just above his forehead, one or two bulbs were burning, like the sun at high noon; their glow seared him. He recalled the story his grandma used to narrate to all and sundry about him.

'We had all thought he'd be dead as soon as he arrived. The first child was a stillborn. As soon as she delivered Muthu, Pathu lost consciousness. And this Muthu wouldn't cry.'

'Really?' Someone expressed amazement.

'Not only that, his whole body was yellow like anything. We all thought he was going to die. The midwife lifted him by his ankles and slapped him across his bums.'

'And then?'

'He let out a scream, loud enough to tear his throat. He opened his eyes only after that. Immediately we brought in that Arabi doctor for …'

'What for?'

'He had jaundice. His eyes, his pee, his shit were all bright yellow. He was placed like eggs in a heating machine. A bulb hung from its roof. This guy was blindfolded. When Pathu went to feed him, this rascal would shriek. When the blindfold was removed, he, like a retard, could not focus.'

Mustafa tried to open his eyes. Was that the muezzin calling the faithful to prayer? It must be early morning; his tired mind was trying to place the hour. All around him were glass walls. The bulbs were bright as the sun; their light bored into his eyes and pierced his brain like a pointed weapon, and swam inside it. Mustafa thought he was wallowing in a deep moat between sleep and wakefulness.

'Ahalya. Where is Ahalya?' He moaned in pain. They had brought him in seven hours ago. The policeman was tired from beating him.

'It's not enough to ask like this.' The fat, fair-skinned policeman approached him with a pair of scissors. Mustafa flinched.

'Open your eyes, you bastard.' He was laughing. Mustafa thought he was going to be blinded. But the policeman only snipped off his eyelashes that had turned thick with blood and tears. He then launched the spaceship of light.

Light … what kind of light was that! Wilder than fire, whiter than milk, more venomous than a snake. Whenever he tried to close his eyes, the stubble of his eyelashes poked his eyes and hurt him. He screamed. A thin, feeble wall of tears tried to form a film and keep out the light.

Seven hours that felt like seventy thousand torture-filled years.

'Why did you hide the arms? For whom did you do it?' He heard the voice of an unidentified policeman.

His whole body was aching. As he had been made to stand with his handcuffed arms raised all the time, he felt as if his arms were coming off their sockets. Since his index finger nail had been pulled out, blood had flowed down his arm and clotted in the forest of his armpit hair. Reading out the brand name on his underwear's elastic band, a policeman rolled his eyes.

'Ayesha. God, religion even in the choice of underwear?'

Tears appeared in Mustafa's lifeless eyes.

'We got a phone call about your mother being unwell. If you tell us the truth, we can take you to her,' one of the policemen lied.

His mother. When he heard her being spoken of, as usual, he was reminded of a doll. That was how it was with him. Whenever he heard her name, the images of beautiful dolls looking out from a showcase floated up in his imagination; full, bright-red lips and smooth, long-bean-like fingers would come to mind. He would recall the rosy dimples that bloomed on her lemon-like cheeks when she laughed.

There was a mere thirteen years' difference between mother and son. Most evenings, they built sandcastles on the beach, fortifying their walls using shells. On some days, they played hopscotch in their front yard, scratching squares into the ground with a twig. On other days, the blindman's buff. Under the tamarind tree, they fought over fallen fruits. When his mother ran, hiding figs inside her dress, he chased her with a hopping gait. They gambolled like sea horses in the foamy sea that looked like urine froth. The fishermen who came in, their nets full with the day's catch, used to chat them up.

'Are you two friends?'

However, his father was his enemy. A giant, swarthy man, whenever he got off the dhow at Beypore, his mother turned febrile. In the nights when, in addition to her delirium, he would hear her scream with fright, Mustafa used to make an offering to Thangal and curse his father. 'Damn the Arabi! Let him perish.'

When he built sandcastles alone on the beach, he created small moats to trap the black devil—with a tail, horns, and fire in his mouth—who appeared in his nightmares. He hid nests of black crazy ants under his father's bed. For him, his mother's tearful eyes, dimples flattened by sadness and sorrow-filled, trembling lips, were beyond sufferance.

However, after his mother conceived Kulsu baby, his black-skinned father never returned to Kozhikode. His mother and Kulsu baby slept next to his grandmother in her room that was filled with the rancid smell of rheumatism and Unani medicines. Kulsu baby was ten times as beautiful as his mother was, and she used to drool honey from her pink, toothless, gummy mouth.

He used to kiss the pink soles of her feet, cooing, 'Cho chweet, Kulsu baby'. Kulsu baby's blue eyes and the curiosity and mischief playing hide-and-seek in them used to fascinate him. And when, with her toothless gums, she used to bite their mother's nipple and tug at it, he used to wonder: Is this a djinn's baby?

The day Kulsu baby took her first steps on the beach on her dainty feet that wore no anklets—the day she called out *yikkaaa yikkaayi*,[17] drooling honey after eating the savoury *thenkuzhal* he had bought for her, was also the day his mother eloped with a north Indian truck driver.

He was very despondent when he got up in the morning. A moribund grandmother deader than death itself. The dreadful silence of being alone. The sounds of the sea, its waves and its breeze, compounded his loneliness. He

[17] Baby talk for ikka (brother).

searched for his mother in every woman he came across. He strained to hear Kulsu baby's delightful laughter whenever a girl laughed in his earshot. He continued the search for them till he met Ahalya.

He saw Ahalya for the first time during the flowering season of cosmos. As the bouncy cosmos bloomed in the yard, a cross magnolia tree fretted as to who had planted them in their midst.

Since Marad Road had been closed, the policemen had redirected Mustafa via Pallikkandi Road. He had gone through Kumaran Seraph's yard in order to reach Meenchantha quicker.

'Why are you standing in the compound? Come in,' Seraph's mother bade him. He looked at Ahalya. Her rainbow-eyelids, shaped like the Malayalam letter ∩, mystified him. Beneath them, dense, blue eyelashes bending backwards and staring at the sky. He was reminded of peachicks. She was wearing a loose T-shirt that looked as fleecy as a lotus petal. Though it carefully hid her curves, a rascally breeze occasionally pressed it close to her body, revealing them. He sensed lava-filled volcanoes forming inside his chest.

'Da, set this girl's hand, she has sprained it. There's no sprain that a twin-born person can't set.' Mustafa was taken aback. He had never touched the body of a grown-up girl till then. His face flushed like a gold pot kept on embers.

She moved and stood opposite to him. When he saw her right arm with the sleeves rolled up, he thought of a ripe, skinless papaya on which a honey pot had been overturned. Her arm now moved swimmingly towards him, like a live fish.

'*Ahhh … aaahhh.*'

When he rubbed her hand and manipulated the joint, she pulled it back in pain. Her thumbnail scored his chest and made a scar.

When he was cycling back home, Mustafa felt he was running a temperature. The lingering smell and slickness of camphor-infused karpooradi oil which couldn't be washed away caused his brakes to slip. It was about to rain, and the air became chilly. But torrid flowers were blooming in his bones. His head was growing heavy, his legs were losing their grip. Mustafa stopped his bicycle and panted heavily.

The next day, she was wearing a checkered lungi and a round-neck blouse. She blinked her areca nut-shaped eyes. Her nose was like a parrot's beak. Her plump tomato-red lips were moist. When she reached up to tear off a chandada leaf to put the fish in, as her blouse moved up, he saw her golden belly with its small conch-shaped belly button and the fiery glow of the coppery happy trail that ran down from it. He was hooked.

'Threadfin breams for ten rupees.'

Her lips were parched as if in great thirst. Her teeth gleamed between them like night-blooming jasmine. When he took the money after handing over the fish, once more her nail scratched him. He felt as if a high-voltage lightning had split him into pieces.

That night he dreamed of her violet-hued back, wet from water dripping down her hair. Even in his sleep, the smell of aloe vera from her hair and her navel, which resembled the eye of a tomato, aroused him.

For the next week or so, Mustafa found selling fish a struggle. He was hampered by the police, who were camping on the beach, and others with weapons tucked into their waistbands. Yet, he parked his cycle near Kumaran Seraph's compound and rang its bell. Both of them forgot to talk to each other when they met. Ahalya's heart was pounding. Mustafa was febrile and shivered. Shyness made Ahalya's body shrink back. Mustafa's face became flushed and bloomed. Only the mysterious sound of an anklet remained between them like a slice of beautiful memory. Only their eyes spoke of their love for each other.

Though they wanted to ask each other's names, a sort of unfamiliarity engendered by their love stopped it from happening.

In the fifteenth meeting, it eventually happened. The day four fishermen's huts were set ablaze and one man was killed by a mob of three, in the breeze around them that smelled of blood, concealing her nervousness, Ahalya asked, 'What's your name?'

Her tongue became fatigued, as if it had said three thousand letters. Mustafa looked closely at her. A dark blue blouse and striped lungi; vermillion on her forehead; the mole on her cheek—a droplet of bluish kohl that reminded him of gathering rain clouds; a trembling earring whispering into her ear; a dark blue sea of love in her eyes; frenzied waves running through her untied hair.

'What's *your* name?' He was emboldened by the ebb and flow of the blue ocean in her eyes.

'Ah … Ahalya …' She closed her eyes bashfully.

'I … I'm Mustafa.'

'Oh …' Her eyes widened in fear. She covered her open mouth with her right hand.

'Are you a Muslim?' she asked.

He could see darkness creeping into her pale face. He was staggered by the change in her expression.

'You don't look like a Muslim.' Her voice was cracking up. 'You deceived me.' Disappointment filled her eyes. Her kohl ran and spread.

'You could've told me at least once that you're a Muslim. You deceived me.' She flung the fish he had given her to the ground. A look of hatred replaced the disenchantment in her eyes. She turned around and walked back.

Mustafa was very upset. The humiliation and sadness tore up his heart. Tears blurred his vision. He started to pedal like a lunatic. Once he reached home, like a capsizing vessel, he collapsed onto his prayer mat. He wailed, broken-hearted.

Prohibition orders were imposed that afternoon on the beach. Police jeeps went around, announcing the collector's orders. Mustafa did not go out for three days. On the fourth day, the situation deteriorated. Battalion after battalion of policemen descended on the beach. They conducted a house-to-house search for the weapons reported to have been delivered using dhows.

That night, when he heard the knocks on the door, Mustafa went out. Ahalya was standing on the kitchen side, her eyes full of tears and face filled with sorrow.

'Mustafa!' She ran to him and hugged him tightly. A warm breeze blew in from the sea; trees let their hair down and danced wildly. The sea that was calm like a white carpet suddenly welled up. Ahalya cried loudly. Mustafa's cheeks were also wet. She kissed his damp face tenderly.

'Come.' Mustafa took her along to the beach. There was a row of lime-slaking rooms on the beach. They went into one of them.

'Mustafa, let's go and live in some other place.' She was weeping. 'I can't live without you,' she sobbed. Mustafa cupped her face with his hands. Tears were dripping onto her red blouse. He bent down and kissed her on the bones below her neck.

'Why did you get angry that day?'

'For nothing.'

'For nothing?' Holding her by the chin, he lifted her face and looked into her eyes.

'I had thought you were a Hindu. Your face has the features of a Hindu.' A fresh burst of breeze lifted Ahalya's hair and the smell of aloe vera spread. They stood in an embrace.

Suddenly, policemen's voices could be heard from the nearby slaking room. They blew their whistles loudly. 'Rabbe, my Lord!' Mustafa placed his hand on his chest.

'He's in this slaking room.' Their voices came closer.

'Open the door and don't try to hide, you bastard.'

There was a sharp knock on the door. Ahalya and Mustafa trembled with fear.

'Don't open it, Mustafa.' Ahalya held him close. Suddenly the door collapsed. Mustafa lost consciousness at the first blow itself. Ahalya's screams were not heard anymore. A despicable, inky black darkness filled the space.

In the beginning, the jail was a room with a large window for him. A window as dark as a night with eyes that opened only into darkness. Black walls. Long corridors. A green, fungus-covered gallows at the end of it, with neither the vanity nor the conceit of death. The hangman's rope hung from it like a broken neck.

The policemen came to his solitary confinement cell to take his statement. However much they tried, or whatever they did, they could not extract a confession from him.

On many mornings, when he was on the prayer mat reciting the *surah*, his concentration would be shattered by the footsteps of prisoners being taken to the gallows. The strumming of a funerary musical instrument would reach his ears.

Mustafa thought many a time that death was far better than solitary confinement—in which he had to drink salty, chlorine-infused water that smelled and looked like urine, eat uncooked wheat balls in which he found half-cooked lizards, and shit into a latrine that had all the yellowness of the world. When he lay sleepless in the musty cell, he used to forget that he was a human being and there used to be a world around him once. He doubted if he was even alive. A darkness filled with deathly pain assailed him whenever he closed his eyes.

Yet, whenever he slept, he dreamt of Ahalya. On the shells left for slaking, vineyards and orchards of exotic fruits were starting to ripen. He kissed hard many times the tender bones below her neck, on her chest that smelled of sweet wine. He was intoxicated by the wild taste of the grapes that were turning ripe.

'Show me the way, show me the way, O Rabbe, the Lord of the Whole Universe.'

Suddenly, he wanted to see Ahalya. He wanted to escape.

'I must live.' He opened his eyes in the middle of his prayers. All others had their eyes closed. Mustafa ran through the graveyard behind the mosque.

'Ahalya!' He surged into the path on the left. He ran as if his legs had been granted some supernatural power. By the time he reached Kumaran Seraph's front yard, he was panting like a wolf.

'Ahalya … Ahalya … come out.' He called out aloud.

The door opened a crack. Ahalya's emaciated face peered through it. He saw tears in her eyes. They had lost their feathery eyelashes. He smiled and opened his arms.

Then the door opened fully. Mustafa was stunned.

'Ahalya … you …' Tears blurred his sight. Through the blur he saw—Ahalya was carrying a baby on her hip—a baby girl.

'Ahalya!' Flashes went through Mustafa's head. He staggered on the sand and fell to his knees.

'This …?' He looked at her in agony.

'The policemen that day … in that slaking room.'

Ahalya covered her mouth and cried. Mustafa bawled. He hit the sand with his fist. He pulled out his hair by their roots and screamed like a mad man. He ground the sand in his palm and threw it on his head. His hands got abraded by the sand and started to bleed.

'Allah … Allah …'

Seeing the policemen running towards him, he extended his arms to be handcuffed.

'Take me now,' he cried like a little kid.

'It was me, it was me who had brought in the weapons. I am confessing. Sir, take me with you.' Weeping and wailing, he confessed to all crimes.

And then, crying aloud, he resumed the Salat al-Janazah prayer he had interrupted halfway.

The Lesbian Cow

A thin, slanted beam of sunshine, undulating like smoke, hit the floor of the bathroom through the glass in the ventilator. While taking her bath, Mehrunissa would pirouette occasionally, like a child. At such times, setting off a childlike curiosity in her, the shaft of light touched her navel like an umbilical cord. At other times, it lay submerged in the cold water in the orange bucket, like a light-filled periscope. Or it would shine like a bright ring on the broken tiles of the wall.

Sometimes, Mehrunissa would stop it in its tracks with her palm, or redirect it towards her wet, dripping hair. If none of these, she would just stand there, looking at the billions of pulsing photons within the beam. Most often, this was the reason behind her long baths.

On that day, however, Mehrunissa was taking her bath in a hurry. She had forgotten about the beam of light. But when she was taking out the last mug of water from the bucket, she realised that the sun's finger was missing and wasn't touching the water.

She raised her eyes towards the ventilator in shock. Screaming 'Ayyo', she grabbed the clothes discarded for washing, attempting to cover herself. A pair of eyes were gazing at her with an unnatural calmness. One half of a face was slowly withdrawing from the ventilator.

After wearing her clothes, as she got out of the bathroom, Mehrunissa shivered in fear. It was her—the Lesbian Cow!

When Mahmood Khan had arrived on his moped at Mehrunissa's rented house, she was washing clothes. He was shocked by the changes three years had wrought on his daughter. He realised that his daughter was a full-grown woman now with no vestiges of adolescence left in her.

It was a time when Eid Kamal, Mehrunissa's elder sister, was becoming more and more childlike as she grew older. She would surprise him with her naughtiness and her tiffs with him.

She had been married ten years, but showed no signs of becoming a mother. Since theirs was a Rowther family that followed the matrilineal system, Eid Kamal and her husband were staying in Mahmood Khan's wife's house. Though wagging tongues alleged that the only reason Raftash Junish hadn't divorced her was because he was living in his in-laws' home, the couple seemed as inseparable as fever and its temperature. Yet Mahmood Khan considered his daughter's inability to conceive a permanent curse on their family.

That said, when the news that Mehrunissa, who had eloped with her lover three years ago, was pregnant had reached him, all his anger and bad blood melted away.

She saw it when she turned around after rinsing the clothes and flinging them onto her shoulders. The sight shook her. At first glance, she thought it was the Lesbian Cow that had been coming into her compound for the last five or six days. It had been showing some guts, having found out that Srihari Venkatesh had gone on a long-distance tour.

Mehrunissa was surprised. Her father was standing next to the moped, a rock-like man, six-feet tall. She pulled down the saree which she had tucked up at the waist. Her father was beaming at her as if in a mid-noon dream. She smiled back. Widening her copper-coloured eyes, she smiled broadly, revealing her gums.

Suddenly Mahmood Khan felt hopeless and despondent. He had wanted to see her weep. He didn't know any other girl who wept with such beauty or looked so beautiful while crying.

Still smiling, Mehrunissa invited her father into her home. As he climbed the steps of the rented house, she saw her father stepping on the Lakshmi rangoli that Srihari Venkatesh had made a week ago. Sounding cross, she told her father, 'Move away, Aththa!'

The sourness of the lime in the sulaimani tea caused her father to screw up his face. When he pronounced that however she may have advanced in life, if a girl from a Rowther family couldn't make a good sulaimani, it was of no use, she started to weep.

Enjoying her weeping, Mahmood Khan looked at the rangoli on the steps and asked, 'Is he an artist?'

'No.'

'What's his name?'

'Srihari Venkatesh Pai.'

'What time will he be back?'

'By evening.'

Mahmood Khan nodded his head gravely.

'Do you have a photo of his?'

'No.'

'What about your wedding album?'

Mehrunissa cracked her knuckles nervously. 'We aren't married.'

Mahmood Khan kept nodding, as if he was listening to commonplace news.

'Have you converted?'

'No.'

Mehrunissa noticed her father's face glow red in anger. The grey hairs of his long beard slapped hard against his chest.

'You could have converted. It would be more dignified than what you are doing now.' He set down the cup on the parapet wall. 'I didn't know you had adopted such ruinous ways.'

He stood on the rangoli with his pointed shoes pressing against it. His clothes exuded the smell of concentrated starch.

'There's something called dignity, Mehru,' he said and started the moped.

Mehrunissa stood still, as if in a dream.

The unblinking and sleepless fluorescent bulb in the portico showed Srihari how the rangoli had turned into a riot. Shoe-sole marks were stamped like sin on its sugary-white powder.

Though tired from his long journey, he went to the kitchen and brewed some tea for himself. Srihari's and Mehrunissa's unwritten rules-and-regulations handbook was strict and scrupulously followed. In their studied mutual formality, there was a gravity and discipline.

As he sat drinking the tea, Srihari decided that he should ask her the question. Srihari believed in omens, and the signs he saw upon his arrival spoke of the presence of three persons.

'Who were the guests?'

'Aththa.'

'Aththa!' Srihari felt ashamed. He knew that her father was a rich diamond merchant in the city. He assumed that his father-in-law must have mocked the pitiful condition of their rented house.

There was another reason. One of his own aunts used to visit them once in a while. The tall, fair-as-a-water lily, buxom aunt with her diamond nose stud, was fond of Mehrunissa. Even Mehrunissa's religion didn't put her off. She used to present many reasons for it, one of them being Mehrunissa's fluency in Konkani, a language she used with more felicity than any Gowda Saraswat Brahmin girl; a lilting, lispy, melodious Konkani it was!

But the aunt hated and was mortally scared of the termite-eaten door frames and the rat- and spider-infested, cobweb-filled attic Srihari and Mehrunnisa lived in. So she used to often worry and quarrel with them over it.

Srihari didn't ask what Aththa had come for. The absence of any written rule notwithstanding, they used to temporise and ameliorate all civil and vulgar conversations possible between a man and woman.

Before Srihari could prompt her, Mehrunissa started to narrate her dream about snails. 'Yesterday morning around ten o'clock, I dreamt of some snails without shells. I saw their thick, gluey fluid and the eggs they had expelled along with it, floating on the water. The snails were pushing out their fleshy bodies and depositing their eggs in the water. The sticky eggs covered the water with white froth. Holding a shiny china clay pot, I was sitting on the ridge, watching with curiosity the snails laying their eggs. And from there, using a scoop made with jackfruit leaf, I scooped up the eggs and deposited them in the pot. I saw the fallen paddy stalks convulse under water like green tentacles. It was when Aththa summoned me to get back that I accidently stepped on the snails that were crossing the ridge between the fields. The crunching sound under my feet left me disturbed.'

Srihari scratched his head in surprise. After they started to live together, this was the first time that Mehrunissa had narrated a dream to him. It seemed as if she had herself experienced what she had seen.

'It's not a dream I saw while sleeping, if you are thinking that.'

'Then what was it, Mehru? A day-dream?' Srihari poured some tea into the saucer and offered it to her.

'I started to feel some discomfort two days ago, in the afternoon. I vomited. By yesterday morning, the vomiting had reduced to mere retching. As if there was nothing left in the body, only a yellowish liquid came out. When I was standing near the well and washing my face, again, accidentally I stepped on three snails and crushed them. In that instant, the cow grabbed me from the rear and held me close, and I lost consciousness. I dreamt about the snails laying eggs in that dizzy state.'

'Mehrunissa,' Srihari called with determination. He could not contain his happiness. He kissed her forehead and eyelashes.

Mehrunissa lay on the bed like a live clock. Her eyes shone like the dial of a digital watch.

Srihari felt elated, as if he was in his father's watch shop. Venkatesh Pai—who had spent his whole life peering at the innards of watches and at their wheels and cogs through his watchmaker's loupe—was his father. Srihari had always imagined his extraordinarily sharp-sighted father as having clock-hands in his eyes. He kept this clock working by moving his irises up and down all the time.

In one of the Gowda Saraswat Brahmin streets in Andhra Pradesh, Pai had installed a clock tower bearing the legend 'Donated by Pai & Sons Watch Works'. One morning, that gargantuan clock—it had till then never missed or chimed outside the hour—stopped and, with a loud ringing of its chimes, fell down in a heap without any warning.

At the same time, in Pai & Sons Watch Works, on his easy chair, Venkatesh Pai lay inert and motionless, like a clock that had stopped working. His right eye was holding a loupe tightly in place. The only sound audible came from his ticking pocket watch.

The cohabitation of Srihari and Mehrunissa upset the villagers. The public kept arguing. Some said it was not proper for two people of different persuasions to live together; others said it was the right thing to do. Srihari and Mehrunissa had left a note saying they would be living together when they moved back from the hospital into the house.

Mehrunissa was sixteen when she had first met Srihari in the arbitration committee of the ayurveda hospital. Apart from being the social welfare officer there, he was a handsome young man, with a bluish tinge on his face. This face, with its greenish-blue veins, gleamed from the liberal use of oil on it.

It was a knotty problem. Mehrunissa's gummy smile and tiny teeth created an interest in Srihari. He was thirty-six years old at the time.

The accused nurse kept staring at him like a belligerent cow. His glances at Mehrunissa were insufferable for her.

Mehrunissa had come to the hospital in search of treatment for paralysis. She was not fazed by the most rigorous methods of treatment. However, the accused nurse was stomping on her body with obvious relish as she did the standing massage. Srihari read such a line in the copy of Mehrunissa's complaint that had been given to him.

'That woman smells like a cow, sir. She has a bovine look. Tough, hard feet like hooves. She used to stare at me all the time. Do you know how much revulsion I felt towards cows in general because of that?'

As she heard the word 'revulsion', the accused's face hardened. Srihari kept observing the accused. Her eyes were like an ancient warship. Srihari noticed water spouting out of her eyes like a watery procession amidst cannon fire and smoke. It hung on her cheeks like bandoliers, like molten glass shards, like ocean waves.

'She stomped hard on my chest with oxen shoes,' said Mehrunissa, placing her hands over her chest.

'From the beginning, I had thought it strange. When my child would be sleeping, she used to kiss her. How can she behave this way with my sick child?' Mehrunissa's mother, Nihad Begum, gave witness.

'My body became more pliable than kneaded clay. After each standing massage from her, my body felt as if it was being fried in oil, and I slipped into a state of semi-consciousness. After that, various nurses have bathed me. Each of them has shown the respect and kindness that an ailing body like mine deserves. Except this repulsive cow.'

'I was loving your body, Mehru,' the nurse spoke, giving her a lovelorn look, 'like a cow loves another cow.'

Listening to her brazen confession, even Srihari paled.

The nurse hailed from the Gaumata family, and her name was Nandini Gaumata. The punishment she received from the committee was a three-month suspension and a life-long ban from Mehrunissa's ward …

'After that, she used to sneak into my room when no one was looking. Once, when I woke up, I found her kissing me wildly.'

'Srihari.' Mehrunissa opened her eyes. 'That abominable creature was propositioning me when I regained consciousness.' Srihari frowned and sat up straight. So she was the third guest.

Srihari woke up with a start when the night sky was covered in fiery stars and bright moonlight. They used to sleep with the windows open. That did not make him nervous. But he felt as if the cow's ears and battleship eyes were reflected in the night's pane. Something wrapped in a white paper flew in and fell in front of him. Someone ran into the darkness beyond the compound wall. Plaintive cries rose from the cattle in the dairy farm in the neighbourhood. The words 'Give Mehrunissa to me' were scrawled on the paper that had been weighted using a fruit.

The next day, when Mahmood Khan, Nihad Begum, Eid Kamal and Raftash Junish came to their house, an embarrassed Srihari forgot even to ask them to sit down.

'I have come to ask for something important.' When Mahmood Khan took off his glasses, the arcus senilis rings of cataract around his greying irises were revealed. A pointed pendulum of old age, swinging without timing from those eyes haunted Srihari.

Khan openly asked him to marry Mehrunissa. He reiterated that the required dowry, traditional ornaments and jewellery and landed and movable property would be given. But Srihari responded in a very unexpected fashion. He openly told them that as long as he was a feminist, there was no question of him recognising the institution of marriage.

'Women should be given the utmost freedom. Mehrunissa deserves that and more.'

A distressed Khan kept shaking his leg, and wiped the long needle of water that slid down his cheeks with his hand. Srihari remembered his father who had told him, 'Each human organ has a clock in it'. He touched Mahmood Khan's feet. 'Bappa, you should forgive me. These are my principles. Don't consider this as disregard or insubordination.'

At the same time, inside the house, a startled Nihad Begum was gathering information on the Lesbian Cow. After her arrival in their rented house, Mehrunissa had not thought of her even once. Neither the five-and-a-half-acre dairy farm in the neighbourhood nor the huge cows that sauntered in through the gate to eat the pinwheel flowers reminded her of Nandini Gaumata. But recently, the Lesbian Cow had started to appear along with other cows to feed on the pinwheel flowers and peep into her bathroom when she would be taking her bath.

'Come, let's get married. That's what she has been telling me.'

Nihad Begum was scared. She had heard of heartbroken, lonely men who stalked their married lovers like maniacs, or rolled on the ground their ex-lovers' shadows fell on. But she could not understand why a woman would pursue another woman, claiming to love her, saying that she lusted after her and similar things.

'Some nights she can be seen watching our house, sitting in the room on top of the dairy farm. While closing the window, I have noticed that her skin looks tough like a cow's—the skin on her face wrinkles like a piece of hide put out to dry.'

'My baby, maybe she is a witch!'

Eid and Mehrunissa felt scared.

'But there's no problem, Mehrunissa. Because your Aththa and I have lived for five months in a village full of this kind of people. They were called Panans. Since they used to eat cow meat, the villagers used to consider them vile and base. The cow was venerated in those villages as a sacred animal. The Panans were cowherds. If some disease killed a cow, they tied the carcass to a rope, and, with much merrymaking, dragged it to their huts. They used to roast and eat the meat. If anyone among them thought they could get away without eating the meat, the villagers whipped them. Your mother has seen this with her own eyes.'

Mehrunissa felt as if her body was going numb.

'All the divine organs of the dead cow were given to these Panans. That made them wizards and sorcerers. They have the power to vanish. My dear, the person who can vanish thus can assume any form. But they will be naked. Mostly, they vanish into the form of a cow. *Otiyans*, as such shapeshifters are called, take revenge on those who have hurt them.'

Mehrunissa felt as if her head was about to explode. Thunder and the bellowing of cattle sounded in her ears.

'*Otiyans*, in the form of cows, tail women they are in love with. They take revenge by kicking at their pregnant bellies, I am told.'

Mehrunissa tried desperately to believe that the stories about *otiyans*, made up of superstitions and hyperboles, were only a myth. She dreaded the sight of the aggressive Lesbian Cow who would come and stand, rattling the iron gate of her house once Srihari left for work. Did the top of her head have two bumps? Two bumps under which her pointed horns had been hidden?

That evening, while returning home after buying milk from the market, Srihari heard the clip-clop of hooves behind him. The Lesbian Cow. He observed her with purposeful attention.

She was wearing hide-like, coarse cotton clothes. Her dupatta's ends rose up and flapped like a cow's ears. On her feet were high heels with oxen shoes nailed on them. Her eyes were like warships. Her pink skin was softer than butter.

'You should let me have Mehrunissa. You should let her go. She's not even your wife.'

'*Chee* …' Srihari Venkatesh lost his cool. 'Don't bother Mehrunissa any more. Otherwise, I will call the police.'

'Look here, Srihari. Anger is not going to get you anywhere. Listen to me. I have a greater right on her than you. I have touched her breasts much more than you have. I recall every cell of her body getting thrilled and aroused by the touch of my fingertips,' she said, sounding overwhelmed.

'Get lost!' Srihari shouted and pushed her.

Her face underwent a transformation in a flash. Flushed from lust till then, it contorted in anger. Blood rushed to her face through her dilated veins. The smell of gunpowder rose from her. She rammed her head into Srihari's chest. She kicked him viciously with her oxen-shoed hooves as he lay on the ground. Then, pressing her foot against his face, she bellowed like a lunatic: 'I will kill you!'

As he lay like butchered meat near the abattoir in the market, reeking of cow urine and dung, Srihari Venkatesh decided that he had to marry Mehrunissa.The Lesbian Cow turned around and stomped away. Srihari Venkatesh kept looking at her cow tail-thin plaited hair as she disappeared from sight.

Srihari wed Mehrunissa twice, as per both Hindu and Muslim customs. On the same day, the Lesbian Cow broke down the boundary walls of the dairy farm. Two thousand cows descended on the village through the breach in the wall.

The rumour spread in the village that the cows had been let loose because they had contracted the mad cow disease. The anxious and confounded villagers ran helter-skelter. Children didn't attend school. A post-war-like pall of inertia descended on the village. Some of the young men roamed the village holding staves and poles with nails and spikes fixed at their tips to save their land from the calamity. They collectively attacked the cows, hit them with stones and tins, and killed many of them.

As if in revenge, that afternoon, Srihari married Mehrunissa legally, too. On their way back from the marriage registry office, they found heaped cow carcasses in many places.

Srihari feared this may lead to a communal riot between Hindus and Muslims. Like in the times of riots, no men or vehicles were seen on the roads. Half-dead, wounded, and many with their heads smashed in, cows were dragging themselves along the road, lowing in pain.

Srihari and Mehrunissa saw that a crowd had gathered at the western side of the dairy farm. Srihari stopped the vehicle and went towards the crowd. The Lesbian Cow was lying on the road, naked. The blood flowing from her chest had mixed with the bitumen on the road and was seen bubbling in the noon heat.

Srihari felt the air was filled with the smell of fresh colostrum.

'Angry at being gored by this mad cow, the mob stoned and hit her with spiked staves.'

Srihari Venkatesh felt an overwhelming sense of relief. 'Oh, it's dead.' He said that with the nonchalance of talking of a mere cow's death.

'Whose death are you talking about?' Mehrunissa enquired.

'Oh, nothing. A mad cow has been beaten to death by the mob. That's all …' Srihari pulled the car door shut.

The next morning, when a curious Mehrunissa picked up the newspaper to read the news item headlined 'Mob stones to death farm owner mistaking her for a sorceress', Srihari interjected and bade her to go to the kitchen and fetch a coffee for him, as he leaned back in his easy chair with all the sense of entitlement and egotism of a husband.

Premasutra

Dedicated to all the women in this world

Preface

I remember with joy all the women whom I have loved and who have loved me. *Kamasastra* is the authoritative book of my life. This is only a brief memoir based on it. The main narrative in this treatise comprises my thoughts about the first and the last woman I made love to.

I open my story with the backing of *kamasastra*. Some poet has written that starting to make love with the *Kamasutra* open in front of you is like driving a car looking at the driving manual. I, too, had ruminated on this in my nineteenth year, on the conflict between theory and practice—isn't that praxis? Whatever it may be, she was my first sex guru. Untrammelled by such doubts, Mrinalini Mukherjee, the initiator of *premasutra*, never gave me an occasion—forget an epistemological or doctrinaire discussion—even to think about it. If I compare to Sage Vatsyayana, I can't even begin to describe who she was. You will all wonder if such a description would fit a fourteen-year-old girl, and whether she was deserving of it. My dear people, let's proceed with my story. The saga of love and sex: my *Premasutra.*

Chapter 1

Preethimala

I was nineteen years old then. A youngster whose masculinity hadn't been sullied by any woman. I had indulged in some hack writing, not being particularly partial to prose or poetry. Having listened to a surfeit of heroic and bawdy balladeers of the yore and their conquests, my heart had developed calluses. My hero was an accomplished poet who had done stuff to a maid with her laid prone on a grinding stone. Since my attempts to get the washerwoman Parukutty—washing clothes at the stone steps of the pond redolent of the froth of the 101 brand washing soap—to be my own prone serpent maiden on a sandalwood grindstone had left the stinging imprint of her hand on my cheek, I had taken a vow that under no circumstances would I make passes at maids, my colleagues, classmates, girlfriends of friends and lady neighbours.

I am digressing. Let's come to Preethimala. Comrade Vatsyayana had named the process of listening to poetry, delving into its meanings, appreciating and rejoicing in their beauty, as 'Preethimala', right? I was a master in Preethimala. I used to pen love poems. Given a chance, I used to get them published in children's sections of magazines. I changed the name Ravi Menon Vallikkad into a pen name. As soon as a couple of poems got published in a couple of publications, I dubbed myself as a poet too.

My father was a Nair, a titled aristocrat from a very famous *tharavad,*[18] and the editor, nay, boss, of a famous newspaper. A holder of the view that boys should be given all freedoms. When I was given birth by my mother as her first-born, she was sixteen and my father was forty. Clad in white khadar kurta and dhoti, and toting a pastel shade-border veshti, he used to smile on the world like a beatific yogi. But that was what he was on the outside; he was nothing like that inside. I had heard gory tales about him from many sources. He had taken part in the Independence movement in 1943. Though he loved Gandhi, was possessed by khadar and was against ornaments, he was more romantic than any poet and artist.

Till he went to Presidency College in Madras, he was an out-and-out patrician. Once he enrolled, everything changed. He fell in love with a classmate and turned into a patriot. On this, one of his uncles not particularly fond of him had put out a story. The girl's father was a freedom fighter. He had been jailed for taking part in the Quit India movement. When he was kicked viciously in his testicles by the British, the poor fellow fell to the ground, peeing clotted blood. His eyes closed gradually, even as the raised fist was held high; the next moment, like many other Indians, he fell dead, surrounded by other Indian corpses. In his place arrived his daughter. The story goes that when that sweet-voiced girl went down the steps of Presidency College singing Tamil patriotic songs—having flung away

---

[18] Tharavad (ancestral home) is a system of joint family practised by people in Kerala, especially Nairs. Contextually, it may also mean one's lineage/ pedigree and upbringing.

her jewellery and holding a fistful of earth close to her chest—my smitten father was in tow. In his memoir we found after his death, there were only a couple of lines about that love of his.

That streak of independence in my father had been inherited by me. After my graduation, the germs of independence that teemed in my mind gifted me with the idea of going out of the state for further studies. I informed my father of my decision to go to Calcutta, now Kolkata, to study.

He was busy with *sootranjali*, devotedly spinning the khadi yarn. The white yarn, thinner than cobweb, stuck to the charkha. The only sounds in the room were the *kat-kat* of the spinning wheel.

'Why Calcutta?' My father stopped spinning the charkha and drank some water from an earthen water jug. 'For womanising or drinking?'

A saint-like smile. That was how he was. I was shocked out of my wits. His face had the expression of one querying. 'Son, are you trying to fool your own father?' That was the kind of information that someone who left early in the morning in a car for the newspaper office and returned late in the night could not have. At the next question, I found the source of his doubt. I was shaken.

Chapter 2

Panakaadiyojanam

'Where's your chain?' Achchan removed all my doubts. I was trapped. Not even in my worst nightmare had I imagined that my father would come to know of my nipping down to the den of Seethayamma akka[19] and Kallu akka, moonshine distillers of Munimata in Kanjirakkunnu. Nor did I know that Seethayamma and Kallu were Sri Vidya's paternal aunts. Sri Vidya used to sing songs for the Thiruvathira dance, and was a good-looker. Her body looked as if it was sculpted in stone; she was that firm. Curves, swerves, swells, valleys, uphill, downhill … my God, *you* are the real sculptor.

Her beauty lay in her overlapping teeth when she smiled. She was a brilliant student, a talented singer, and used to sashay when she walked. To see the beauty of her gait, she had to be watched from the rear. Her long, luxurious plaited hair was like a black serpent. Its lethal hood would be biting her buttocks in fun. As she walked, it would hit one bum and bounce off and go hit the other. We youngsters enjoyed that bounce and swing.

Femme fatale, a true femme fatale. I wonder who chose the name Sri Vidya for her and why. It was a good name to murmur, standing behind her. A name I have carried in my heart and called so many times with indulgence and love.

'You naughty girl, my Vidya, you little mischievous …'

Her slim figure was the fount of her beauty; and also her complexion, resembling golden trumpet vine flowers at sunrise. Wide eyes with tapering corners. Even the liberally applied kohl had a certain seductiveness. Long, yak hair-like eyelashes, setting off the magnetic eyes. A puffy, milky wart on her chin. Small lotus bud-like breasts. Her flat belly, a crescent that would shine through the saree—a curvy

---

[19] Elder sister in Tamil.

shape that made one feel, the Malayalam letters റ, ഢ, ഡ were discovered from her body. If only that nose also had a nose stud … Once, Karimpanpara Shreekumar Nair, the University Union Councillor of the college, felt compelled to ask, 'Swaying Vidya, does everything that you eat end up in your booty?'

I was standing by. Though I am a man, when I heard that, I blanched. What then to talk of Vidya's state? Her wide eyes brimmed with tears. My darling baby. My body turned to ice. I followed her, wanting to lay her head against my chest and wash off her wretchedness. Then came the poem:

As you lie seductively
Prone on the sandalwood grindstone
We romp, O beauteous one …

I kept walking. The verdant paddy fields lay on either side like a wet silk saree spread out to dry. Alexandrine parakeets were swinging gently on the silver lines hanging slack from the electric posts. Rose-ringed parakeets were feasting on the plentiful fallen paddy grains. The maroon berries of the soap nut plants swayed in the breeze. The water striders—named after the author of Adhyatma Ramayana—skimmed over the surface of the small streams, writing their own rustic, romantic version of the epic. It was an elevating scene, enhanced by the gentle breeze and redolent with the smell of paddy. The postman was riding along the ridge between the fields, displaying precarious balance, and ringing the cycle bell and admonishing a small herd of sassy horn-waggling cows.

'*Mmpaa …che … chee … po … po …*' Sri Vidya reprimanded the cow. Chastened, the spotted cow ran away. Vidya's blume fruit-coloured sari was billowing in the wind. Could it be that she hadn't noticed that I was trailing her?

We then turned into a dark alley that felt like a gritty, coir-carpeted nook. It turned into a slick path carpeted by slippery cashew leaves and laterite cobblestones worn from years of mist and rain. Rosary pea vines topped the spiny bamboo fence like a laurel leaf crown. I broke off a bunch of rosary pea berries from it, and they spilled down and scattered like my heart fracturing into pieces. A miracle—a rosary pea was growing on the tip of my finger too!

Then we entered a broad country road with ochre hillocks on either side. A road used by speeding tipper trucks that were transporting the red earth. One of the truck drivers thrust his head through the window and leered.

'They'll drink your milk …'

The cleaner, too, leaned out. Sri Vidya hurriedly lowered the books held against her chest. As she saw me, she gave me a friendly smile. What bloomed on her cheeks were not a couple of honeyed dimples, but two pink mulberry fruit buds.

'Where are you headed, Ravi?'

'I … I …' I was nonplussed for a moment, and then blurted out the first thing that occurred to me:

'Akka's, Kallu akka's …'

Her face clouded over.

'Why do you want to … Ravi, don't do it.'

I became an obedient lamb. I suppressed my thirst; I suppressed my hunger. Only love spilled out of my eyes.

'If Sri baby tells me not to, I won't go.'

Ah-ha … a name that hadn't been used till then: Sri baby.

'Ravi, you really are something.' She blushed. Say how, ah, like Neruda said—about what spring does with cherry trees … whatever it was, she bloomed and flowered like the spring.

As I watched her walk into the distance, a bit of Tagore's *Gitanjali* spilled over in my soul. When she disappeared, the akkas rose up in my mind. I recalled the words of Biju, a hostel inmate.

'Them akkas are smart—in distilling arrack, serving, dispensing, and making people drink.' I took the path as described to me. I walked with my fingers grazing the plentiful rose periwinkle flowers that bordered the path, and plucking and nipping into the low-hanging cashew fruits. Even when I crossed the cremation ground of the pariahs, I felt no fear. Butterflies were shoring up bunds on the bones in the ashes. Below, in the navel of the hill, lay the Sashthamkotta lake. Its girdle was the most beautiful ornament I had ever seen.

I was bewildered by the sight at the akkas' den. There was a queue, and all the deadbeats were present. As I turned around to leave, Seetha akka came running.

'Ayyo, who's this? Isn't it Ravi kunju? *Ediye* …' she called out. 'Kallu, come and see who's come.'

Kallu akka bounced out in her polka-dot blouse. 'Now who's come?'

The she-goat tethered in the compound bleated in contentment. Its bell tinkled as it leapt about.

'Kallu, come this side. Do you recognise this kid? Look at him … look at his face … it is … yes, it is … he's the spitting image of Raman sir …'

Ayyo, the drama is not in misplacing the characters. They knew the characters, all right.

Some of the arrack imbibers stared at me. Some were giving me welcoming looks. Some were puzzled: What, K.S. Ramankutty Warrier's son *in this place* …?

'*Goooshfranshsss*.'[20]

'Come, come inside, sir … young lords get special consideration here.'

The sour smell of warm arrack pervaded the room. The tables and chairs were clean. There was a charpoy; a small face mirror; a tin of Cuticura talcum powder; two combs, one nit comb; a case of kohl—it appeared to be the sisters' bedroom.

'Seethayammo, where is the pot?' Kallu akka made her entrance. The nervous look on my face gave her pause.

'What? What's bothering you? Is this your first time? You will get used to all this, don't worry. All you need is one day here with us akkas. Shall I go over to the other side?'

'Mmm,' I nodded.

I had heard of the akkas from Shreekumar, Biju and Thomas. They were the gurus of all the youngsters of Kottiyam, Pattarumukku and Umayanallur. They were the guides for both drinking and fornicating. Spend less and enjoy more. In Biju's opinion, since the akkas were twins, distinguishing between them was difficult. If five hundred rupees was paid in advance, both would come together.

---

[20] Good friends

'*Da*, Ravi, how will we match up to their prowess? We'll come up short.' Biju salivated like a hippopotamus. 'They are hardly forty.'

Forty years old. My mother was younger to them by five years. Guilt horrified me.

'Don't be silly. All women are someone's mothers and sisters,' Biju said. 'Ain't it so, Thomacha?'

'What can I say, brother?' Thomas scratched his head. 'Once they take off their clothes, even God himself can't tell them apart.'

'Absolutely,' said the wearer of soda-bottle glasses,[21] his eyes looking bulbous through the thick lenses.

'Everything will come in double doses.'

'I swear upon the Goddess of Parumala temple.'

'I can't describe it, Ravi … it's indescribable … it has to be experienced.' Biju couldn't control his excitement.

There was another popular tale about the akkas. One was known as Mangalam akka and the other as Manorama akka. They were good readers. Since they believed in socialism, they didn't discriminate between customers. They were believers in 'open to all comers' and the 'Vasudhaiva Kutumbakam' philosophy. They liked to read romantic stories, but due to their busyness at work, reading was often interrupted. Therefore, it was confined to the occasions when they were servicing plebeian customers who used to pay only a hundred rupees.

For that they didn't need a room, bed, mattress, etc. All that was needed were two old palm-leaf mats, two pillows

[21] Thick-lensed spectacles are called soda-bottle glasses in Kerala.

and a clearing under the cashew trees in the grove to the left of Munimada. A small lantern with its wick up would be kept on the side. They would lie on the mats and read in the orange light of the lantern. The flowering cashew trees would hold a parasol with their leaves over the two sisters as their screens. They would stuff the currency notes given by the men into the blouses, without even counting them. Everything was left to the customers to do.

'Get lost—what kind of a fellow are you! Have you come here to swat flies, what the hell is this?'

'Don't think of moving up after paying a measly hundred bucks. It's not done. Make do with whatever is there below, that's all you'll get.'

'What the hell, don't jerk around so much! My eyes can't focus.'

The akkas' famous dialogues, their poses, the way they lay on their sides reading books, their facial expressions, all were part of Biju's mimicry repertoire in the nights.

'Drink it up, boy,' Seetha akka poured the tear-like arrack into a glass and offered me.

'And what else, boy? Are you interested in the other thing?'

Oh, are there women like these? Such blunt questions were beyond sufferance. She moved closer and bent forward. The rim of her blouse and her cleavage were attractively damp with sweat. The gold chain on her neck resembled a slim snake. Who's she, a snake peddler? Even in that dim light, her skin shone as if anointed with coconut oil infused with wild turmeric.

'There's someone else next door, though she's been spoilt by too much *eddikashn*.[22] She's my niece. Are you interested?' I nodded my head, without considering that I was till then thinking of touching Seetha akka's neck with my fingers.

'It'll cost you five thousand rupees. She's top class, untouched by anyone. I have reduced the price because it's you.'

I checked my pockets, fully knowing there was nothing there.

'Don't worry about cash. Give me that gold chain.'

'Ayyo!' I clutched my gold chain.

'You're worried that your folks will ask you about it. Tell them you lost it.'

Akka was smart; the idea was good. The devil in my heart, in a hurry to swim in the sea of pleasure, smiled and bid me peremptorily, 'Give the chain to her.'

'Yes.'

'Then give me the chain and go to her. She might cry and protest. Don't mind it. You may have to use a little force.'

'Will there be trouble?'

'What trouble? Amn't I her mother too? Have no fear. Go!'

That was the worst day of my life; I haven't suffered as much as I did that day. My damned concupiscence led me into the next room.

I kicked the door open, like a hero ready to use force. But the sight there left me totally destroyed. With eyes bloodshot from crying, her hair dishevelled, and in rumpled

---

[22] Education

clothes, she … she fell at my feet, and, clutching them, cried. Her tears scalded me. My toenails melted in the lava.

'Save me … Ravi, save me …'

That was Sri Vidya, my dream girl. Also, Shreekumar's slut. I stood there, helpless and grief-stricken.

'Shree annan[23] is waiting at the Health Centre. Help me, Ravi, don't forsake me.'

The information that Shreekumar and Sri Vidya were lovers completely disarmed me. That brought to an end my second attempt to have sex. In that moment, I received a new insight on girls in a nirvana-like enlightenment.

After many years, when I look back, the memories of that incident still gladden me. If I had not gone there that day, I wouldn't have been able to rescue Sri Vidya. She wouldn't have married Shreekumar, become the mother of three children, or lived her life happily in the company of her grandchildren.

Nor could have Sri Vidya fallen at my feet on this day, and hugging them, shed tears of gratitude in this manner. Now tell me, am I an ordinary man?

Chapter 3

Dashanavasaangam

Mrinalini Mukherjee, my first girl, had studied *Kamasutra*. She was a twenty-year-old maiden. I saw her the first time when I went to Prof. Mukherjee's house to meet him. She was standing on the balcony, leaning against the balustrade

---

[23] Brother literally, here used to show respect.

and staring at me. She was neither fair nor dark, and had a buxom Bengali body. Her face resembled a rosebud. Her lips were plump and violet-hued, like that of a long-time smoker. She looked intently at me, like a policeman staring at a criminal.

Her chungidi design kurta made her look taller than she was. The kurta had long slits on both sides. Since she wasn't wearing a churidar or salwar below, each time the breeze blew, I saw her thick calves and shiny thighs that looked as if they had been smeared with ghee. Her beautiful, unmarked knees bore witness to the fact that she had suffered no falls in her childhood. She wore lip gloss and bright enamel on her toenails. She stood there imperiously, with one leg on the grille of the balustrade.

Her air of an arrogant princess standing on the balcony pushed me into an abyss of inferiority complex.

'*Oye, kaun*?'

'*Main*?' My voice quavered. 'Ravi. *Professorji hain*?'

'Oh, Ravi.' Two dimples appeared on her cheeks—two radiant spots filled with a titillating smile. God! Why are you blessing every girl I come across with dimples and putting me in trouble?

'Is that you? Come in, Babuji is home.'

The sweaty skin behind her knees and her voluptuousness aroused me.

That was our first meeting: the poem that sensed me as soon as I stepped on Calcutta's soil. As I walked the streets of the warm, sultry Calcutta, poetry sprouted inside and outside me like sweat. I followed the footsteps of Tagore along mustard fields. The bookshops were festooned with copies of the Bengali edition of *Gitanjali*.

Once I disembarked from the train and had a look around the city, I decided that I should do an exceptional translation of Bengali love poems. I should skin the beauty of the Bengali language, which sounded as if the speaker was holding a hot potato inside his mouth. I didn't have to make much of a pitch before Prof. Mukherjee. He said, 'Come to my place on second Saturday.'

He was a lean old man. The cottony look of his home clothes lent him more years. Long, aquiline nose; yellowed teeth covered in plaque; brown eyes; ruddy chicken pox scars on the face. His silky white hair spilled over to his forehead like silver strings. The oil from it had drawn greasy pictures on the top of his easy chair.

Chapter 4
Lathaveshtikam

We weren't even halfway through the translation of the poems when she conveyed her love to me. Our love was like the sunset in which flowers never bloomed. Yet I recalled the lines about love being full of hidden blue rays and wildly intoxicant white flowers. When seen from her room, the November chill outside was felt with double its strength. I felt wonderful in the chill, the prattling, whimpering rain, the lugubrious rays of the setting sun bouncing off the window glass, and the recondite emotions of poetry's throbbing heart.

Her bed with its pure white linen was a sight to behold. The white orchids done in silver at the foot of the bed and their falling petals lent the room the fragrance of spring. The floor was littered with paper bearing Bengali text. On the bed lay a Bengali edition of *Gitanjali*. The drizzle outside made me feel feverish inside. And somewhat nervous.

Mrinalini's return only after she had had a bath—when she had excused herself to fetch tea—amazed me. Her cheeks were shining from the wetness and towelling. The damp strands of her hair seemed to be set with watery stars. And then the defiant rotundity of the vermillion bindi. The imperious nose and breasts that rose and fell.

I had been shuffling playing cards at my hostel when her call came at 11 a.m. She said that the professor wasn't home and I needn't go over for doing the translation.

'But …' she paused as if she was thinking about something.

'But?'

'I am alone here …' she cut herself short. I could hear feebly the sound of her breathing from the other end. And the slight panting. She then let out a long sigh. She spoke after a long pause, as if after a long think.

'*Tu aa jaa.*'

That is all I needed. Though nervousness had covered my face, I smiled.

We were two kids. Two babies. Her first demand was that I should marry her.

'Uff … that's not possible, Mrinalini.' I slipped a finger into my pocket and felt for it, making sure what I had bought from the medical shop was still there.

'Ravi, will you marry me?' She hugged me from behind, full of love.

'No.'

I could have lied. But I was never one to make women empty promises.

'No, never.'

My assumption that the hands around me would loosen was wrong. She hugged me tighter.

She looked into my eyes. Her lips were shiny with spittle, and were stored with kisses. Her naked arms entwined around my neck and under my armpits, like vines embracing tree trunks. She pressed her face against my hairy chest, and honoured the bluish-black stain on it, with her plump lips.

Chapter 5

Udbhraantachumbanam

Mrinalini was my first experience of having a woman. The nervousness and the ecstasy of it had caused my body to tremble. In a few places, there were faux pas. My only experience of being kissed was receiving my mother's kisses as a baby and, after I grew up, from babies in my neighbourhood who had been bribed with lollipops, but always on my cheeks. Mrinalini kissed me full on the lips. When a woman's spittle touched my lips, I felt both a lewd irritation and shyness. It had the sweetness of unadulterated honey, a touch of sourness and the vigour of aged wine. I must have frowned at the aftertaste.

She took my face in her hands. 'Is this your first time?'

'Mmm ...'

'If you don't like it, we won't.'

I hugged her tightly, unable to reply. She kissed my forehead, the greasy softness of a new pimple and my eyelids repeatedly. She was standing behind me. I stood there like an imbecile, with the bitter aftertaste of the first kiss. She gently and lovingly tilted my head back. She lowered her lips onto mine. In reality, I was the one who was waiting for kisses like a maniac. I shamelessly begged her, crushed her in my arms, and dived between her tongue and lips like a young bee trying to discover the honey pots.

Chapter 6

Vyaaghranakham

I was like a baby. I had the face of a famished wolf cub. And she knelt down like a feral beast of prey that hunted by stealth. Her nail scored my chest and it bled. Her aggression and the fiery look in her lusty eyes woke the animal in me, born in the race of men, innate cannibals. In the intoxication of tasting human flesh and blood, I scratched her. The scratch mark, running down from the tip of her aureole, adorned her right breast like a tiger's claw. The bright red drops of blood shone on it with the brilliance of a necklace set with rubies.

Chapter 7

Varahacharvvithakam

I wasn't the first man in Mrinalini's life. The knowledge that, though unmarried, she was not a virgin didn't faze me. In certain things, she was certainly a guru to me. We created more poetry on the bed than in the translation of *Gitanjali* on which we were working together. Its language was neither Bengali nor Malayalam. In fact, it was neither poetry nor prose. Love was its tongue; lust was its form. We paired with gay abandon, like wild animals in a forest. We rolled in the grass filled with flowers; we dived into the fish-filled bed-lake and came up for air; we tasted wild grapes snapped off their vines. She had the teeth of a baby mongoose; they shone like well-honed weapons. Each of her bites hurt me and pleasured me. My chest and inner thighs were filled with livid teeth marks, as if savage pigs had bitten me.

Chapter 8
Indranikam

Mrinalini was truly a lotus-filled lake. Her knees reminded one of pink lotus petals. If her clothes had the lotus nectar smell of Bengal cotton, her body bore the intoxicating fragrance of the queen lotus in full bloom in the blue moonlight. Beyond my capabilities and inexperience, I revelled in the spring of her skin, the nectar season of her cheeks, and the rainy season of the fleshy mangoes of her chest, like the virgin soil of a deep forest soaking in the sunshine, light winter, and summer rains.

All the seasons and oceans of the universe rose in our midst with unseen fury.

Chapter 9

Roopajeeva Vysikam

In seventy years, twenty-two women came and went. I had earned the reputation of a lady killer. Especially, among some clueless, tasteless men. Sons-of-bitches, they were all envious of me. Unable to do what I did so effortlessly. Jealousy—they were overcome by its cupidity and grudge. And enraged at my family life staying intact. Get lost you dogs; scram! When I loved a woman, I tried to make her proficient in any one of the sixty-four arts. Except in my marriage, I made no obligations to any woman. But at the same time, those who came to me, I didn't disappoint. Not one woman who had shared her body with me had, at any time, an occasion to feel guilty about it.

Their bodies were the special treats they fed me. A gift from their hearts. I didn't accept any woman who didn't love me. I only relished relationships that had an equal mix of love and lust. I kept secret the identities of these woman who loved me. I never alluded to them, even in jest, before men at drunken parties. I didn't ever look at them as sluts. Each time, I accepted a woman's gift to me with due respect. I respected its confidentiality in full. That itself made many beauties willing to receive my attentions. Secrecy is key to every adulterous relationship. Discreetness is fundamental to *Premasutra*.

Whenever we ran into each other, we behaved normally, like acquaintances. At shopping malls, we exchanged formal nods. On the beach, we offered each other half-bitten peanuts. At weddings, we smiled and waved at each other, and we had our group photos taken. However, when our eyes met, old memories fluttered inside us. In honour of those memories, we applied invisible smiles on our lips and secretly exchanged glances. An unexpressed sense of triumphalism that we had duped the whole world enveloped us. I made small talk with them in the presence of my wife and remained a proper gentleman.

Didn't I make blue water lilies bloom in the lake of your navel that day? Didn't I darken the colour of the gum karaya fruits of your lips? When such erotic-poetic questions arose in me, I would hide them with a smile, and ask:

'Hope Gopal is doing well?'

'Didn't you commute your pension?'

'What's the problem with your daughter's horoscope?'

'Was your Singapore trip enjoyable?'

All of them were equally good actresses.

'Ravi, you've become a grandfather. That calls for a treat.'

'Her hysterectomy is over?'

'What's going on with Rajashekharan Nair?'

'How's the new daughter-in-law?'

They'd ask many such questions to me.

But do you know what would be on our minds? Each woman would have her own thoughts.

If it was M, she'd be thinking:

'You scoundrel … I had bitten you on your shoulder because I couldn't contain my love. And you stopped talking to me for three months!' (I've been like that since I was a child. If it hurts me, I lose it. I won't have any truck with any woman who hurts me physically, you hear that?)

J would be thinking:

'You rascal, you had me in your sights from the day of my wedding. Does anyone try to steal the bride sitting on the wedding stage? I was scared by your looks as I sat there on the stage.' (Oh hell, you were a dead ringer for actress Sumalatha. Talcum powder covering up where acne scars had fallen off. Your hair in glory, framed by jasmine. The bones of your shoulder set off by your slim neck. Your bride-like nervousness. To one who's going to be another man's wife … why am I attracted so much? What's this?)

K, the scientist, would say:

'Why, you are losing trust in me. When I met you, I was still a virgin. You are the first man even to touch me. Believe me, Ravi … I was a virgin then.' (Ayyo, what's the need for all this song and dance? Why these lies? I'm not her husband. Then why this drama and buffoonery? When I see this false modesty of Malayali girls, I get hot under the collar. Am I a fool? Didn't you come with inked tissue paper to make me believe you were a virgin? Go try your tricks on someone else.)

R, the owner of big eyes, fair complexion and long sideburns, and with coppery down on her face. Seeing me, she would do all her pouts and pranks, irrespective of who was around. She'd smile slyly and wink at me. I wonder if she still is as scorching hot as she used to be. Those days I used to really drink. I had chosen her navel for drinking rum from for the first time. As my inebriety increased, I poured it further down, and lapped it all up in one whoosh. She screamed as the alcohol burned her delicate parts.

How many more chapters should I narrate? The group orgy with S; the shower with the fat girl in Goa; escapades in Amsterdam and Paris … My body was a trap for sixty-nine years. I would go to any lengths in search of pleasure. Some clever girl, I don't remember which one she was, had nicknamed me 'The Hedonist'.

Chapter 10
Death

Now I will talk about Aparna Bhattacharya, the last woman I made love to. The public believe that I have remained a research guide in the university out of my love for the language. But that's not the truth. Beautiful women … girls … stolen glances at torsos seen above saree pleats … smart girls who look at their guide as if he's God himself—what more can Prof. Ravi Menon ask for?

Aparna entered my life on a rainy day. A small-boned girl. She came and introduced herself. Truth be told, I had no intention of seducing Aparna—she was possibly younger than my youngest daughter—nor did I make any moves. She came on her own and dropped at my feet like the petals of phototropic flowering plants. Her love rendered me helpless. More than being romantic, hers was an intense, lethal kind of love. Sometimes she trailed me like an orphan. Despite my repeatedly forbidding her entry, she used to come into my office in the evenings when I would be sitting alone. Lurking in the corridors, she used to crush me in surprise embraces. Behind the bookshelves of the library, she used to kiss me like one possessed.

Aparna was the youngest woman I made love to. A girl delicate as a tender coconut. Yet in bed, she was an empress. More beautiful to me than the twenty-one women who came before her. Like every Bengali woman's love, hers was a feral one that roared at me from her Durga-like eyes. Her cotton dresses that smelled of lotus and her vine-slim body made her my dearest. It was a very antithetical relationship, a strange play between man and daughter and father and woman. I still don't know how it all began. Yet sometimes when I was man, she turned into a daughter. When I was a father, she would be a full-blooded woman, a woman who drove me mad with desire. We revelled in that lethal state where we didn't know where the love for a daughter ended and that for a lover began. I even made speeches that Electra's was the most beautiful state of love.

One December morning, when her course was due to end, she kept crying without reason, and that made me angry. What was there between a seventy-year-old me and a thirty-four-year-old her? This was the first time a woman in a relationship with me was in so much distress.

A needless obstinacy. A defiant insolence. The self-inflicted pain of those who love intensely. That could have been Aparna's problem. I could understand it. Unlike in all my earlier affairs, an invisible string of sterling love had me connected to her. That whole night, she lay with her head on my chest, weeping silently.

'Don't cry, my precious.'

I tried to be mushy, lovingly stroking her hair that reminded me of the mustard fields of the bygone days. I brushed her teeth using my finger as the brush. I bathed her using a baby soap. When I poured water over her head, she sobbed breathlessly and hugged me.

'Let it be, don't cry, darling ...'

She left wearing a new churidar-kurta set I had bought for her.

Yet, that evening, she came to me in the company of her father and mother. I still remember the day. It was a chilly Christmas Eve. I had kept ready a translation of *Gitanjali* to gift Aparna. The scraping sound of a Bengal cotton saree's hem reached me. A familiar fragrance wafted in.

'Ravi ...'

I looked up. It was her: Mrinalini Mukherjee. The one who had taught me the A to Z of *Kamasutra*. The nineteen-year-old who had translated *Premanjali* for me instead of *Gitanjali*. My *Premasutra*.

The girl who had shared the bed with me even on the night before her wedding, and left with a smile.

The knowledge that Aparna was her daughter made me happy and sad at the same time. The thought that I had won both mother and daughter doubled my vanity. I laughed aloud. However, an unnamed fear was gradually churning my insides.

It proved to be prescient. Mrinalini re-entered my life that evening, bearing a dark night before darkness had fallen.

When she came, I was a little nervous. Somehow, the thought of Aparna also arriving at the same time frightened me. I suddenly remembered the eve of Mrinalini's wedding.

Mrinalini who had sworn she'd never marry, when she was thirty-five, informed me over the phone of her decision to get married to Debtosh Bhattacharya, a teacher and her colleague. I did go to the wedding. Held in the same house. The house of my karma. The easy chair in the sit-out had gathered dust. The professor was smiling down gently from the wall.

Mrinalini came to my room in the night. She took the pill before switching off the light.

'I don't like it.' She screwed up her face at the thought of the smell of rubber. We turned into two calves. We heard the sounds from Vrindavan—the gurgling sound of the river, the prattle of baby parakeets, and the breeze. The smell of butter warmed our hearts.

Mrinalini hugged me. I turned into a thirty-five-year-old. I hugged her tighter.

'Shall I tell you something, Ravi?'

Her voice was wrapped in love.

'A secret …'

'Mmm … tell.' I stroked her hair.

'I haven't loved any man as much as I loved you. So, Ravi … I cheated you only because of that.'

Her big eyes were filling up and turning red.

How so? Before I could ask that, she started to sob.

'Aparna is our daughter, Ravi …'

'Oh my God…. my God …' My head felt as if it was exploding. My blood vessels were bursting. I was haemorrhaging. My God. What is happening to me? What putrid flesh is getting scattered inside my brain? The blood from which of my sins is staining my hands? Why was I falling down with a plaintive cry on my lips …

Now you tell me: is my life as ordinary as I stated before? Can't you see me communicating with the world through the ventilator, five days after I was declared brain dead? The blood vessels in my brain have burst in various places. My brain has been cooked and heaped like rice for oblation to manes by someone. I lie here with both sides of my body paralysed, like an animate corpse. Yet I was fully aware of Aparna's jumping to her death from the sixth floor of the college department the very same day… Do *I* alone continue to exist after I die, my God?

'My dear child, who … who has told you this lie that I am your father?'

A great sin appeared with a searing, heartrending pain, and shut off my memories.

Annotations

Preethimala: One of the sixty-four arts in *Kamasutra*. Vatsyayana's view is that men, when they are young, and women, when they are still maidens, should learn these erotic arts. Preethimala is the art of reciting erotic shlokas and understanding their hidden meanings.

Panakaadiyojanam: The art of fermenting and distilling alcoholic drinks and essences. Drinking them before and after coitus was a common practice.

Dashanavasaangam: Nail and lip painting done by women to make themselves attractive is part of this section.

Lathaveshtikam: One of the important embraces in *Kamasutra*. The woman entwines herself around the man like a creeper around a tree.

Udbhraantachumbanam: Holding the head from the back, tilting it, and kissing while standing behind a person.

Vyaaghranakham: Scratching the woman's breasts with nails in the shape of a tiger's claw during lovemaking.

Varahacharvvithakam: Love bites that look as if one's been bitten by a pig.

Indranikam: One of the main types of sexual congress.

Roopajeeva Vysikam: The writers of kamasastras have described many ways in which courtesans can earn money. This is one of them.

Death: The sastras say that lust has ten stages. The last of these progressions of lust is known as death.

Acknowledgements

One: Jawahara Kurup.

Two: A lady friend who challenged me to write an erotic tale from a man's point of view and who, with much adventure, procured an edition of Kamasutra *for me.*

The Fantasy Fruit Orchard

Old Rudeethai's deep-lined face wore a proud look, as if she was the keeper of the autocratic Thai kings' fortress keys, their treasury and the secret maps of their borders. It went into a slight frown as the smoke from the hunted but unmangled crocodile's flanks and pork loins roasting over an open fire reached her. Her cracked, bark-like skin fractured some more. The blood that had fallen into its fissures had cut channels on her face. The orange light from the fire flashed on Rudeethai's dry cheeks a few times and vanished.

She stood there, grilling a tender, skewered crocodile heart. Smoke was swirling up from it. She looked like an evil witch with her flat nose, deep-set eyes and double-bent spine. Whenever she smiled at Airavati, she wanted to tell Rudeethai to close her mouth. The surviving stumps of her teeth, smashed by the rifle butts of Charlie Company, and her bony gums filled her smile. The blackness of those dark days lay steeped in the gaps left between the moribund stubs; the gums carried the yellow patches of dead, putrid blood. Her old age helped mask the secret that all the lines on her face were the handiwork of a soldier and his Ka-bar knife.

Behind them was the sandy outcrop where Pa Tong Sea met Kamala Sea and the rocks that had been smashed by the tsunami. A group was praying on the beach holding paper lanterns ready to be released into the sky. Once lit, they floated away into the sky like strange-looking stars, trailing orange tails filled with Buddhist prayers and good wishes.

The arrangements for the Vesak or Buddha Purnima celebrations had been completed in Bangla Street. The hedonistic lighting gave the street a ravishing look. Wearing sparkling headgear set with stones, plume garlands and pearly skirts, *kathoeys* or lady boys were out on the streets, hawking their beautiful transgender bodies to gay men, whispering 'Thai baht' in their transsexual tones, and haggling over prices.

The *grima*-like sound of glasses rubbing against one another could be heard from roadside bars; intimations of frothing beers' bubbles and sparkling wine bottles popping; the splash of whisky bouncing off ice cubes and licking them wet on the way down.

Caucasian girls sat behind the glass walls of go-go bars, displaying their bodies and waiting for their gluttonous customers. As they thrust out their melancholy-tinged breasts under the multi-coloured lights and touted themselves murmuring 'Russian, Russian' from within the restaurants' glass cages, bulbous-eyed blue lobsters—whose eyes encompassed a sea in themselves—king crabs and carrot-eating rabbits looked on bemused. The fruits stalls contained all specimens of Asian rarities. The reek of durian, the sourness of dragon fruit, the sweet-astringent taste of persimmons—all measured pedestrians' hunger.

Nopjira was a roadside vendor of fetish and necromancy items. Her basket had items that sent a shiver of revulsion down the spine. Devil masks, soaps the shape of human organs and trinkets in the shape of breasts, genitals and excreta. She tried to win Airavati's custom, showing a turd-shaped keychain. Airavati averted her eyes in disgust.

'Our people have clear, unmarked complexion. The three of us who escaped after the My Lai incident had marked bodies. Not the way *you* think of "marked", girl.'

Rudeethai spread the hot and sour Thai sauce on the smoked crocodile liver. The flames sputtered. The appetising aroma of well-done meat spread. Airavati stood by, hungry.

Till she arrived in Thailand, Airavati was a vegetarian. Rudeethai taught her to eat fish and meat. 'That's because you've never known hunger,' Rudeethai mocked her on the first day itself for not eating meat. Airavati was piqued. She couldn't imagine a street food vendor struggling for a meal.

'Hunger makes no distinction between vegetarian and non-vegetarian. Hunger has just one facet—hunger itself. During the war, they poured kerosene on our grain fields, poisoned our waterbodies, shot and slaughtered our cattle and poultry. We had nothing to eat. Most of the days, we survived on the leftovers in the garbage dump behind the military bases. We pilfered the liver, tripe and offal they kept aside for their dogs. We fought the swine, cattle and birds that came foraging to the garbage dump. To a hungry person, what does it matter if it's garbage dump or offal or scraps?'

Rudeethai offered Airavati the skewered liver on a bamboo spike.

'Those days, cooking wasn't possible most of the time. There was no fire, there was no wood. Even if we had, the moment the smoke rose up, the soldiers from Charlie Command would be upon us. It didn't matter if there were sick people, women, or babies. Every Vietnamese was an enemy to them. Every man was a guerrilla as far as they were concerned. The habits formed then for surviving on whatever came to hand: fungus-ridden grains thrown out of the military warehouses, wild button mushrooms, tender leaves … These can be seen in our foods even now.'

Rudeethai put some sticky rice into the sauce. With her chopped-off ears, thin lips, smashed and flattened nose bridge, she resembled an animated wax statue.

'Haven't you eaten Chinese food? Forget it; you must've seen at least—foods made up of insects, worms, slugs and larvae? Do you know why?'

Airavati shook her head.

'The five-hundred-year-long famine, the Great Famine. A habit born out of it. Only the Chinese overcame this famine. The fundamental philosophy of hunger is to consume anything, everything, and in any way.' She looked at Airavati.

'Haven't you still realised it, child? One's own survival is paramount. That's the truth. Nothing else. You have suffered nothing in life.'

Rudeethai took hold of Airavati's hand and placed it over her own heart. 'Throw away this life, girl. Why? It's an egg. A flutter of the wings and the egg shell will break. Then you can fly. Break out of the egg and emerge …'

Airavati was amazed by the puissance of Rudeethai's breast, hacked in half by the soldiers. Her toughness was reflected in the sweat on her face that glistened in the light of the fire. Airavati decided what needed to be done with her own life …

It was Airavati's first and last foreign tour with Balaji. And their last trip as husband and wife. It was her desire; in fact she was adamant that they should make the trip abroad—one that they had planned while they were still in love and had not separated. During the initial years of their marriage, as Balaji's litigation for his family property was going on, they had no money to spare. They survived somehow on her government job salary, scrimping and scrounging. Buying her aunt's quota of ration rice at a rupee, haggling and buying vegetables from the Palayam market, or going to the beach on their second-hand bike and eating fried mussels and roasted chickpeas with the meagre money left after paying off their educational loan instalments, were not mere exercises in economy. It was made possible by the bountiful love they had nurtured and which was now flowering like a jasmine plant inside them. But in those days, when they made do with the moringa, wild spinach and banana flowers grown in their rented house's yard and unripe jackfruits from the unoccupied neighbouring compound, spiced with their love, they couldn't have gone on a trip within the country, forget foreign jaunts.

Balaji won the case in the fifth year of their marriage. The movable properties, bank deposits, the half-acre plot on

Mavoor Road on which the Akademi building stood and the damages made them richer than anyone else. Money arrived in their home, but there was no love left by then. They rowed for days. A kind of polar similarity in their looks, words, stances, laughter and sleep set them fuming inside, and repelled them as would like poles of two magnets. At those times, troubled by migraines that refused to be alleviated by warm teas and dabs of Amrutanjan, Airavati used to revolt.

A humdrum marriage with no high points. In their flat's sea-facing balcony, the animus between them would fall silent as disappointed sunsets slipped into defeated nightfalls. That is when Airavati pronounced that a house without children was like hell ... Children made men sufferable to women and women sufferable to men. In their absence, as darkness crept into homes in the wake of twilight, it brought along discord and complaints. The sounds of rows that breached the high volume on TV sets would be drowned out only by Tamil love songs played in the neighbouring houses. From the corridor bereft of children's laughter or cries, Balaji would move on to a private call on WhatsApp, and Airavati would slink into the darkness of her room, her heart scathed by hurtful words. Her anguish for the unborn child would give her nightmares when she fell asleep.

Their aim now was a friendly trip, beyond the usual recriminations, beyond their animosity and hollering throats.

When this trip ended, Airavati would sign an unconditional mutual divorce petition that Balaji had kept ready in his file. Balaji would marry her dear friend Jayanthi in a simple ceremony. On full-moon nights, against the backdrop of the sky with a rotund, lunar bindi, they would kiss. They would hug each other into breathlessness. They would together dream a single dream. They would have children. The bed, which Airavati—broken-hearted from being called barren—had lain prone on and wetted with her tears, the children would wet copiously.

This was the last night of their trip.

It was Rudeethai who had suggested they see the ping-pong show in the Secret Bar after they had spent the day in the sun, sailing through the emerald green sea between the thigh-shaped limestone karsts of Phang Nga Bay and its tunnel-like sea caves called hongs.

'Do you know that prostitution and all that are dignified occupations here? You can't even imagine what all diseases the women who, for a few bahts, do the shows in these bars will die of …'

The girls on Bangla Street were mostly farmers' daughters coming from villages.

'The fathers and brothers of Thailand know only one work—pimping. These girls send at least 30,000 bahts, earned by dancing in bars or selling their bodies, to their homes; the men splurge that. For some women, it's their husbands who pimp them out. You shouldn't cry,' Rudeethai deprecated Airavati's brand of sorrow when she griped about Balaji's treachery.

Before they reached the show, Airavati felt a severe burning sensation in her chest. Initially, she thought it was the after-effect of flying. It was her first flight, and she had become airsick. Her ears became blocked. She had felt light, as if her body had lost its weight, and dizzy and nauseous. To add to that, her period was late.

Seeing her uneasiness, Rudeethai gave a meaningful smile and looked askance. Nopjira seemed to second her. Dicing passion fruit, Boribun the fruitseller confirmed it. They cautioned Airavati, 'You shouldn't eat papaya.'

'Why?'

'You'll have a miscarriage.'

'What?' Airavati asked again to make sure she had heard correctly.

'That's not possible. I am not pregnant. Nor will I ever be.'

But a suspicion lingered in her. She bought pregnancy test kits. When both stripes turned red, she wondered whether one alone turning red was confirmation of pregnancy. She read the instructions again. The second and the third kits also had two stripes turn red. Her body burned thinking about Jayanthi's treachery. She wept, laying her head against the lone breast of Rudeethai, whom she had met only five days ago.

'What else will the world present fools like you with? You maintain friendship with your husband's lover. And to top it, you go to her for your treatment.' Rudeethai touched her lower abdomen, pressing it upwards.

'You are pregnant, I can say that a hundred times over. This is the internet era. What is the difficulty in checking out that medicine?' Nopjira cut mushrooms and dropped them into the boiling water.

'I should have checked it out. I would have immediately come to know of this betrayal. Yesterday I checked with another doctor back home. I mailed him my reports. I believe clinically I have no problems. But I was told I had fertility issues and given medicines; they turned out to be birth control pills. Heartless cheat!' Airavati pulled at her hair as a bout of migraine hit her.

She felt as if the beach on which she had walked the previous day with Balaji had turned into quicksand and sucked only her in. She gasped, as if sand was blocking her windpipe. The nose rope of barrenness that had constrained her for so long now struck her down. Her helpless heart bellowed with vengefulness.

As children, they—Ivy, Jayanthi and Balaji—stuck together in Balaji's father, Prof. Shaktivel's magic academy, playing hide-and-seek, eating together, having tiffs. Airavati recalled that in those days, Balaji and Jayanthi often ganged up on her. When she went from one room to another, they jumped her, wearing devil's masks and scaring her with loud noises. They used to make traps by digging pits and covering them with dry leaves, then let her fall into them.

They used to shout 'Airavatam, Airavatam' pointing at her squat, dark form and laugh uproariously. 'Airavatam is a white elephant, but this is a black elephant calf,' Balaji would tease her, struggling to suppress his laughter. By swinging her thick, long plait, they used to ask, 'Can you all see the trunk?' Mortified, Airavati would begin to weep.

'Forget it, darling. Do they know who Irawati is? They have no sense, darling, ' her father would say.

The black-and-white image of Irawati Karve in her father's old album, with her posing index finger poking her cheek, and another one in her parents' wedding album, in which she was kissing her mother's forehead, remained in her memory.

'She is a big person … my professor of sociology in Pune. The teacher who conducted my marriage with your mother in Burma.'

But Balu and Jayanthi would not allow her to raise Irawati's name.

'Don't bluff. Professor … Pune … Sociology … father … mother …' they used to scoff.

Airavati would swallow what she desired to add—that Ayeyarwady was a beautiful bluish river in Burma and that there was a type of white-skinned dolphin in the Bay of Bengal that lay on its back and spouted water into the air.

'Amma, where do you have amma, *kumma*, it's *kumma* …' Jayanthi would make monkey faces at her. Balaji would laugh loudly, ridiculing her. Her confidence shot to pieces and her head bowed in shame, she would stand before them like a retard. Then she would cry like a loser.

Till Airavati came to know that Jayanthi's father had caused Balaji's father's death, she was only like a slave before them. Airavati didn't have top grades. She wasn't wheat-complexioned. She didn't win prizes in literary or art competitions. She didn't know how to recite poems. She didn't know how to sing or dance like Jayanthi. She was no child prodigy. As a plain Jane, with Dravidian features, short stature and crooked teeth, she was so nondescript that even her father may have missed her in a crowd. She was so pedestrian that she remained subservient to them.

'Rudeethai, they should have got married the first time around. I was always an outsider. As a child, Balu didn't even call me by my name. It's possible that he developed affection for me once he came to understand that my father had brought him up, only we were there for him, and that Jayanthi's father was a snake.'

'Love is a big scam. A kind of compromise designed only to achieve certain ends. Selfishness, more than sincerity, is its soul. I loved to cheat and betray. Perfidy is necessary. Selfishness is essential. Masking everything, you must act very sweet. Only then shall love have an edge. You'll feel a rush …' Rudeethai started to cackle, like a vessel filled with pebbles being shaken, and kept laughing like a loon. The breeze that had swirled above the sea turned and headed ashore. Her laughter was carried away by it.

Rudeethai remembered …

Like any Saturday morning, the light was bright and cheerfully pervasive. It had rained much the previous night. The wet paddy field of black rice looked bright green. The damp rosary pea vines entwined on top of the dried bamboo spine fence hung down like Vietnamese greater green snakes. Button mushrooms held their parasols over limestone mounds. The rain became expansive. Diamond earrings swung from its watery ears. Rivulets ran through the small paths between the rocky formations. Tiny shrimps leaped up in them. Whirlpools formed and dissipated in the channel by the ridge. The American soldiers came through the village paths, holding their long hunting guns, either to pick up girls for fun during their furloughs or to hunt the rock-black crocodiles of Son Mai village for their meals.

The appetising smell of raspberry seeds being boiled hung in the air. The rotting durian fruits in the front yards of My Lai's huts made the place smell like a community open-toilet.

After the young had risen early and left for harvest, only the elderly, women and children were left in the village. Rudeethai was suckling one of her twin babies when he walked in. His cold eyes were dead, deader than a corpse's. An officer of the 20th Infantry regiment of Charlie Company, his name was William Calley Jr. His gait and posture reminded her of a duck. With his chest and posterior jutting out, he struck a feminine pose. Like the trunk of Phra Phikanet, his effete libido became tumescent inside his army issue shorts.

'Not only the child I was suckling, but the deaf one, and the seven-month baby inside my tummy was his.'

He walked in slowly like a woman. The weapons on his waist were reminders of the cruel vendetta of war. He stood silently and gazed at the child at her breast. His crooked teeth protruded from between his pursed lips, like the tusks of a rogue elephant driven out from the herd.

'Are you an agent?'

Rudeethai became distraught for a moment. He smiled with the implacable malice of having found her out. Her heart stopped still for a while, as if the blood had stopped circulating and frozen in her arteries, veins and capillaries.

The infant stopped suckling and looked at him. His son. The child looked at him and gurgled.

'If almost all the men in the camp should have the same disease, there has to be a conspiracy, Rudee, no?'

Rudeethai was petrified. Her breasts stopped lactating in fear of him. Women's breasts are like that. During times of war, they turn into steel and are ready to attack stealthily like a wild animal. They will thrust their belligerent nipples out, like the tiger its claws. Motherliness vanishes, and the milk dries up.

'Even though they swore before they died that you are their leader, I haven't believed them yet. Rudee, you are the mother of my children. We love each other, don't we?'

There were sixty-nine women in the guerrilla group. Rudeethai was the seventieth, and the leader of the kamikaze squad. Their vengeful bodies were teeming with the germs of syphilis and gonorrhoea.

'It was known as the battle of virgins.' When Rudeethai frowned, accentuating her wrinkles, the illustrations of witches who travelled on broomsticks and were burnt at the stake came to mind.

'The farmers and small-time traders from Thailand, Laos and Cambodia brought plenty of pathogens steeped in rice and paddy across the borders. Every Vietnamese child was given these liberally.

'Survival was the issue. When that is threatened, people turn primitive; it's the same world over. We also did that during the war, that is all. We used our own bodies as a biological weapon. I kept trying for three years to get into the army base, to catch the eye of Calley Jr. who wasn't interested in women. I mixed treachery and love for those who were destroying my country. That is all.'

Those were the times when the soldiers, on the pretext of looking for guerrillas, came on a combined hunt to the villages in search of women's flesh inside the huts and crocodile meat outside in the rivers and streams.

'It's women who pay for the hubris that comes when power meets and mixes with impunity. They are the ones who have to bear the curse, privation and miseries of war. We did what had to be done when disease joined hunger and starvation. Charlie Company destroyed our village. Shouldn't that have been avenged? Shouldn't I have avenged my husband being dragged out of our bridal bed and taken away? That is why the women in my squad answered all the atrocities visited upon us with lethal pustules of syphilis.'

'Your tongue must be stuck to the roof of your mouth, right?' Calley Jr.'s scream scared the child who started to bawl.

'*You*, child of betrayal—it's *your* tongue I'm going to paste to your palate ...' Before finishing that sentence, he placed the muzzle beneath the child's head and shot him. Wisps of smoke rose from the gun like mist. Three shots rang out. Rudeethai felt the burn of the bullets that passed through the bloodied mouth of the child, bearing pieces of its tender flesh and her milk, and hit her breast.

'The first victim of the My Lai massacre was our son—Calley Jr.'s and mine. A barrage of shots followed. Shrieks from children and wails from women rent the air. I had fallen off the chair, stunned. He used a knife to slash the words "US Army" on my face and my body.'

Suddenly, an insentient night filled with dark clouds entered Rudeethai's eyes and turned the sky, seen through the window, inky black. It turned the air chilly. The sky looked like the naked, silken shoulders of a black woman. No stars, no moon, no radiation from unknown celestial bodies. A cold blindness, like a black patina, was gathering in her eyes. Rudeethai felt as if, coagulating below that, every bit of vision was getting lost in the darkness.

He kicked away the infant's body with his steel-tipped boot. Heavy-lidded eyes with dense eyelashes in the hairless, apple-smooth face of Calley Jr. In his hand was the Ka-bar knife. Rudeethai could see its razor-sharp tip. It flashed like a tiger's eye in the dark. Its edges were like a comet's tail gleaming with sulphur fumes. They smiled at her menacingly.

He plunged the knife into the side of her bullet-riddled breast with the ease of carving a mango. The magnolia-coloured birthmark on the centre of the breast he used to suck was slashed into two. He twisted the knife between the ribs below her breast. She screamed as if all the four chambers of her heart had become one.

'Don't scream, you devil. How I loved you. How much I trusted you! It's not just me you betrayed. You betrayed even the child in your womb. You are the only woman I have touched in my life. And your gift for that to me is clap? There's no cure for it. And I will be dismissed from service. You knew everything, didn't you?'

Like a frog squirming in a snake's throat, Rudeethai's organs convulsed under the point of the knife. She tried to laugh at him.

'Didn't you betray my country? Didn't you destroy our peace? Didn't you kill my husband on our wedding night? Did you think I would love you? You fool!'

'Are you justifying this?' He let out a growl, like a beast fleeing with the prey's neck in its jaws. Then, he slowly pulled the knife down towards Rudeethai's navel. He cut through the intestines and plunged the knife into her uterus. Rudeethai felt as if a thousand butterflies had burst out of their cocoons in her lower abdomen.

With the ease of using an earth rammer, Calley Jr. smashed Rudeethai's face. Her nose bridge collapsed; it tore and fluttered like a red one-winged butterfly. He squatted on his haunches then and cut off both her ears.

'You must die as a lump of raw meat.' He bent back the fingers of her right hand and broke them all. He hacked off her left thumb. As he was about to gouge her eyes out, the warning siren sounded.

The crocodile's heart held over the fire seemed to convulse and wriggle, and slipped down the skewer. Airavati kept staring at Rudeethai.

'See, it's been an hour since this heart was plucked out. There's still some life left in it. God, it's like me. It won't die even if killed; it won't die even when it dies.' Rudeethai laughed ingenuously.

'For days, I lay like a piece of rotting meat. Except for my deaf son and Nopjira, everyone in the village was dead. I am a relic of sutures and medical experimentation. I don't know who took me to the government hospital in Krabi. But from the time I was able to stand on my legs, every night I have done in at least one enemy … smothering them in their sleep, mixing poison in their medicines. That, my child, is war. An eye for an eye; a life for a life. Get even, every time. *That*, my child, is life. Not running away like you do, shedding tears. Come on … eat up now.'

Airavati tasted a half-cooked crocodile heart for the first time. The slight saltiness of blood; the saltpetre sourness of

Thai chilli; its eye-watering heat; meat's raw taste that even holy basil couldn't tame.

'This is good for healing wounds. Also of the heart.'

Airavati nodded. She didn't feel the revulsion or nausea of someone eating meat for the first time. Like the Ayeyarwady river that swallows crocodiles when in spate, she hid the turmoil inside her with a serene look on the outside. Moving ground black pepper, dried mushrooms and powdered-prawn vinegar to the side with her spoon, she ate a crocodile heart.

She wondered sadly where she had read the words 'The crocodile is my heart's deity'.

The stage light dimmed gradually; shadows moved around like ghosts. They rolled up artificial potted trees and plants in the semi-darkness. Mango trees with ripe, yellow mangoes swinging from them. The air was redolent with the smell of flowering and ripening mangoes and mangosteens. The attractive golden sheen of their skins. The heady smell of the flowering orchard, that reminded one of Gandhamaadanam.[24]

Light seeped in diffidently through the narrow paths between the plants like morning twilight. Sukhon made an entry through that glimmer with doves in her hands. Behind her were Kim Li, Mayi and Foo Wong.

All of them held birds in their hands—spotted doves, little cuckoo-doves, snow white pigeons, ashy-headed

---

[24] The flower-filled mountain residence of Hanuman, famous for its floral fragrance, and from where Lord Rama viewed Lanka for the first time.

green-pigeons, with their wild smell and oily feathers. A pale-capped pigeon let off into the air flew, cooing and displaying its dotted, coppery feathers, close to Balaji, and swung back and perched on Sukhon's dainty shoulders. She lifted the pigeon like a conjurer. The theme music of wilderness rose; the tongue tingled in the chillness of the beer. The head felt light.

Foo Wong bowed her head like a shy bride. She lifted up the dove in her hand and stroked its head. It started to coo. Then she pushed its head so that the beak was buried in its chest, spread her own legs, lowered her hand and thrust the dove into her body. The coppery tail of the dove slowly disappeared from view as it went up her vaginal passage. Airavati was stunned; she averted her eyes. Rudeethai stood by, suppressing a smile. Balaji felt singed by the spectacle, as if his eyes were stinging from the marijuana smoke in the bar.

That was a terrible night, foreboding and dark, as if wrapped in a heavy blanket. The sounds of percussion instruments, unseen pipes and other musical instruments and blue light gave the venue a moist look, as if it were washed in tears. Balaji rubbed his eyes, as if trying to shed light on some indistinct memories. An ominous sound rose from the ornaments worn by Sukhon. The lights' angles changed. That changed the colour of her skin to a Dravidian wheat-chaff brown. Her flat nose turned aquiline. Balaji saw Sumana and his mother in his mind's eye. He saw their pale faces, washed and bleached by tears. They were like twin sisters in their short dresses. The seventeen- and thirty-five-year-olds looked the same in the heat of his youth. A wave of the magic wand had their dresses dissolving like clouds. The bloody secrets of the flesh; black moles that crawled like ants; the fallow lands of pubic hair; blue eyes like deep-set crystals …

In the magical forest on the stage, Sumana stood naked. Suprabha stood behind her. Little Balu, holding Shaktivel's magic wand, was awakened with a start into that nightmarish scene.

Karuppayyan, the manager, came running, answering Balu's silent cries of 'Amma … amma …'.

'My child, you should take the medicine. Are you hungry?'

Two small fruits, a handful of salted savouries, a glass of warm milk. He added sugar to the milk that Suprabha had kept on the table.

'Get up, baby. Come here. Careful …'

Like Sukhon, Sumana and Suprabha were divested of all clothing. Only their ornaments remained on them.

In the make-believe underwear provided by light projections, magical artifices gleamed. Not only from clothes, they had been liberated from death too. Prof. Shaktivel found deliverance from accumulated debts of four lakh rupees through a death in the sky; Balaji's mother and sister were being freed from the same debts through the fantasy fruit orchard show.

Time was playing games with his mind.

Sukhon pulled out the dove from inside her body. Having been freed from the serpentine yoni, the bird cooed cheerfully and flew up, flapping its wings.

Next came Mayi's routine.

The same trick that Sumana used to play. The one with swallowing down a ball of string many metres long. Mayi opened her hands wide. One end of the string was still hanging out from her mouth. Sumana bent down. The string was being pulled out. There were gleaming silver blades on it. With her right hand, she pulled out the string with the blades strung together. Sometimes it was a string of nails.

'Amma ...' Balu thrust his tongue out that had got cut when he bit down on it in pain as he ate the savouries. The cruelly painful, sour taste of blood. The audience was heckling. He remained helpless in front of life's greatest insult. Little Balu covered his face, unable to watch the naked lust in the spectators' eyes.

Kim Li stepped up.

She had three eggs in her hand. Balaji covered his face in agony. He needn't watch the scene—it was one of his earliest recalls. The egg-eating show of the Nagakali theyyam: the magic show of swallowing six eggs in one go. Sumana swallowed upto nine eggs on stage. Prof. Shaktivel clapped along with the spectators. The eggs re-emerged from her mouth, intact.

But in the fantasy fruit orchard act, Sumana didn't take in the eggs by swallowing.

'Amma.' Balu started to weep.

'Don't cry, son, don't cry.' Karuppayyan covered his eyes.

He watched it through the small gap between his fingers. A row of ten glasses on the floor; the eggs fell, one by one, into one glass and then the next, and broke. The spectators clapped loudly. The yellow yolk spread.

Seated in the ping pong bar, he cried bitterly after many years.

He remembered the rope of his life. The funereal image of the white cotton string that tied the ten fingers into a lethal bundle came to the fore. The whiteness of the pall—as if cut from a cloud-white mull cloth torn off the sky—brightened. The acrid smell of an oil-less wick burning inside a split coconut. Swarms of greater striated bispinous ants that had arrived to lay claim to the rice outlining his father's corpse. Yellow crazy ants that had accounted for the paddy.

'Balu, Balu. Now you have forgotten everything. Your memories, thoughts that haunt you, your problems, your nightmares … Look at the stains on this yellow kerchief. I have wiped your memory clean.'

As the ten-year-old Balu lay unmoving on the cold hypnosis table, Balaji's father drew lines on his forehead. Like another trick of magic, Balaji forgot the death-like chill in his father's fingers. He forgot the electric effect of his words. He forgot his father first, then his mother, then his sister. He forgot everything. It was like diluting the colours of life by adding water till only colourlessness remained. There was only a dampness left in his mind of old memories.

'The old Balu is no more. This is a new Balu. A brave, new Balu,' said the doctor, pressing his string-bean fingers gently.

Balaji remembered the yellow pills with yellow and black dots on the rounded ends. Capsules in the shape of birds' eggs. Forgetfulness that rose up like thorns on their heads; the thorns that scratched out memories.

The amnesia of the ten-year-old rose up like an ogre in his fortieth year. Memories woke up, rubbing their eyes, like Rip Van Winkle.

The dampness was gone. The battle of white and black was over. Colours had waded in.

The playful laughter in his sister's tinkling voice.

The starchy smell from his mother's sari.

The tickle of his father's magical beard.

His indistinct thoughts started to take distinct shapes. They found light. Holding the magic rope thrown to the edge of the empty sky, Prof. Shaktivel went up. As he climbed, stepping on the invisible steps of the staircase, people clapped. He wore a zari-lined magical dress—like a potentate in Arabian tales—that flashed like lightning with his every move. As stardust fell off them on little Balaji's face, he clapped his hands loudly.

'I am a magician's son.' He stood there with a frown on his forehead and a vain look on his face.

Shaktivel looked at the crowd, smiled and waved his wand. A leaf appeared out of thin air. Intense smell of flowers pervaded the hall with an eye-stabbing display of colours.

The magic spell played on the parting of Shaktivel's lips like a gentle breeze. The flowers that blossomed saluted the sky. Seeds fell off them onto the floor with *shhray shhray* sounds, as if they weren't seeds but anklets. The fruit act was developing on the spear-like eyes of leaves.

Saplings turned into little trees. Little trees turned into big trees and kissed the sky. Magical trees grew beyond the confines of the hall and waved their branches in the sky. Balu stayed wide-eyed. The lights dimmed. Fruits appeared on the trees now. Green mangoes swayed in the green grove, pining for salt; cashew fruits dripped their warm sap; a yellow ripeness appeared on nenthran plants; juicy pineapples appeared out of nowhere. A magical fruit orchard. The spectators clapped, enraptured by the display. Little butterflies fluttered their tiny wings, hovering over the flowers. Greedy, chattering birds came after the fruits. The buzz of beetles filled the hall. The sweet lips of butterflies and bees were covered in honey. Nameless insects that lived off flowers appeared from somewhere.

Balaji looked at his father in admiration. Shaktivel's kohl-lined eyes—that resembled a Middle Eastern potentate's—brimmed with tears. He waved to Balu. Throwing Balu a flying kiss, Shaktivel threw his magic wand to him. The fruits started to fall and plop to the ground with *pdhum pdhum* sounds in the wind. Gluttonous children ran to the stage to pick them up. Little Balu chortled. The mystic smile of the magician. The secret language of the fluttering fingers. The charming wave of the wand. Balu started his wizardry.

The orchard disappeared from the stage; lightning flashed; thunder, rolling like tribal drums, made the sky tremble. Prof. Shaktivel stepped off the last rung of the staircase and entered God's palace at the end of the magic rope. Fanfare music erupted, followed by the wild music of rain. Thundery fists smashed into the unyielding heads of tribal drums; they sounded like fire crackers. Lightning flashed like incendiary bombs. The atmosphere was filled with the fumes of cordite. The spectators started to cough. It seemed as if something dangerous was about to unfold.

Now was the turn of the young magician, Balaji.

Before his incantations of *om hreem, om hreem* were over, butterflies flew out of his magician's hat. When he walked, coins fell out of his flashy shoes. His silken robes glowed and beamed flashes. Dark storm clouds gathered in his cape. Like a sultan's prince, Balu raised his left eyebrow and commenced his act. Like moths around fire, butterflies danced around him in a magical circle.

'Abracadabra … abracadabra …' Balu raised his eyes to the sky.

Where the magic rope had disappeared into space, two stars sparkled. At the first pronouncement itself, Prof. Shaktivel opened the small egress window and winked at him. Now his Appa would talk to God and call forth rain. Tiny crystal drops of water. Balu would get wet. After that rain candies would fall. A garish, gift-wrapped dear little moon would fall, too, for Balu. With them would come down red beads and rosary peas.

Balu cast his spell and waved the wand with confidence.

'Abracadabra … abracadabra …'

'Rain, open your Pandora's Box.' It was time to rain. He looked at the sky expectantly. Rain stayed away, as if the incantations had been incorrect.

'Open … open …' his voice started to become tremulous. He became nervous. The rope had disappeared into the sky. The impatient crowd heckled. Where is the rain? Balu could see the stars where the rope had ended burning up. The spectators could see it too. The short tail of a star was alight and descending as a trail of smoke. But where was the rain?

1 … 2 … 3 …

Tip.

A raindrop hit Balu's cheek. It *was* going to rain. He wiped his cheek in relief, then looked at his hands with confidence. There was blood on the back of his hand. Prof. Shaktivel appeared at the end of the rope. The people were cheering and clapping their hands. The professor had his back to them. In a magical swivel, he turned to face them directly. A sleight of exactitude. The magical rope his neck was caught in was strangulating him; his eyes were still and bulging; his spectral tongue was sticking out; his magical trousers had been scratched and torn.

The spectators went quiet, as if they had been slapped into silence. Little Balu doffed his hat ceremoniously, bowed, saluted the crowd, and turned back, and looked at the scene behind him stupefied. From the livid corner of Prof. Shaktivel's mouth, a thin thread of blood was oozing down to the floor.

Balu understood. The spectators understood. The famous magician Prof. Shaktivel Prabhu had, during his act, hung himself on the stage.

Balaji opened his eyes that he had screwed shut tightly, and looked up. Was the magic of death visible? The lungi- and singlet-wearing street magician Rustam Ali from Palghat had taught Balu and Sumana the initial lessons of the magical orchard: the street performer's magic of burying a mango seed in soil and turning it into a sapling. Once Balu had shown Rustam Ali supra-magic by swallowing lotus seeds and having a lotus vine burst through his chest and grow two buds. They could smell the lotus.

'Baba, this is magic of the heart.'

Rustam Ali stood with his mouth agape.

But there was no such thing as the magic of death.

Baba Rustam Ali wasn't there either. Only the sky filled with prayers released to Buddha was there. And the small red flower at the tip of the narrow stalk of memories. The flower that had sprouted from his heart, risen into the sky and turned around to look at him.

Suddenly he wanted to burst our crying. The memories were now strong and clear. The corpse of his father was flying down like Jatayu. A photograph had been published in newspapers' front pages the next morning. Of the junior magician Balaji Shaktivel bowing to the audience, hat in hand. In the background, the professor's still-warm corpse hung from the stage ceiling, arms extended and with a moist-with-blood half-smile on his lips, dying a slow magical death. Airavati had cut it out from the newspaper and put it away secretly. After a long time, Balaji remembered the picture with a shudder.

He recalled the helpless orphan he was, having lost three members of his family. He also recalled the cases filed by Jayanthi's father, his treachery, the frozen accounts, the endless litigation for property, the blackhole … She approached from the life-giving light at its edge. The girl with the mole on her upper lip. She walked in and took his hand in hers.

'Airavatam. Airavatam.'

She mercifully invited him who had cruelly mocked the motherless child as an elephant.

'Balu, come.' In the house bereft of a mother, she shared her father with him. What all had she given him! He turned to look back at her. On her seat was a ripe mango. She was missing. As he bounded back to their hotel room, Balaji was panting. What had *he* given in return? Using the self-confidence robbed off her, he had extinguished her dignity. For redeeming himself from his manias, he had given her manias. Wounds in return for one who had healed his wounds.

Hatred in return for love.

Then betrayal.

Then …

Nooses of death through which the necks of his parents and sister had passed.

Next to Puluang Massage Parlour, he saw Airavati's favourite star gooseberry tree, laden with fruit. The smell of durian, which only she could withstand, now enticed him too. He realised that the call girl wearing the red gown—Airavati's favourite colour—in 2Gether Bar had the attraction of a melancholic innocence. The breeze carried in a salty chill from the sea and the esoteric music of fisherfolk and mermaids.

When he touched the baby Ganesha in Poppa Palace Hotel; when he looked at the Buddha statue in its lobby …

All the while, he was sobbing like a guilty child—as he read '*onnu podaappa*'[25] scribbled with a Reynold's ball pen under the legend inside the lift, 'Bringing durian to the room is punishable', and as he opened the room.

The humid blue light inside the room welcomed him with a deathly magic. A lady magician in a red gown was

---

[25] Get lost, man.

waving the wand. Wild flowers with an alien fragrance were bursting open vigorously, with popping sounds. The bed had been turned into a stage. Airavati was letting seeds rain on the white bedsheet, like they used to as children. He waited in anticipation. The fantasy orchard. Spring made peacherine trees sprout on the bed. Butterflies with tattooed wings, dragonflies with bulbous heads—residents of the orchard manifested. Balaji recalled that, as a child, Airavati used to perform wonderful acts along with his father.

'Abracadabra … abracadabra …'

When she twirled the magic wand, her red gown turned into a large crow pheasant and flew up. She was fully exposed. A glass dish lay between her legs on the bed. The lights above her were changing colours, and were now a pumpkin yellow. She arched her body like Sukhon in the ping pong bar. As she slashed the air with a knife that jumped into her hand from nowhere, the skin that appeared out of thin air turned into scales and got attached to her body, giving it a golden sheen. Her neck, wet with sweat, squirmed, shining like newly-moulted snake skin. Her eyes sparkled as bright as the diamonds on her neck and ears. Her narrow, smooth, rounded shoulders resembled inverted ceramic bowls. He was stunned at the sight of her slightly protruding pregnant belly. A stormy sea gushed from the umbilical cord. Her navel was his primordial lotus whence his own creation could have sprung.

'Have no doubts, Bala. Once it was clear that we were going to separate, I stopped the treatment. So now I am pregnant. Don't be surprised.'

Balaji heard the disembodied words of the sorceress, echoing as if from inside a cave.

She raised her hands like the sorceress Suprabha. Like the sorceress Sumana, she started black magic with the eggs. The drug-spiked eggs from Rudeethai appeared in her hand. Airavati opened her mouth. She slowly swallowed the eggs like a nagakali, a serpent deity.

Balaji felt as if tiny dragonflies of death were flying around the bed. He saw his father, with the noose around his neck, waving the magic wand. His mother and sister were dangling from the ropes behind him.

The enticing smell of the orchard was dissolving in the atmosphere. The stupefying odour of death appeared. A bitter smell that caused a splitting headache. In the shadows that gleamed like serpents, unknown souls waved magic wands. Beyond that, the noose of Shaktivel's magic rope knotted to the fan and Airavati's neck in it. She thrust out her tongue, let her eyes bulge out, played dead, and then laughed aloud.

'What, you thought I'd tighten the noose and die? Get lost!' She eased out of the noose, showing disdain.

With a bright smile and great self-confidence on her face, Airavati pressed her hand on her navel. She laid an egg, and it fell onto the glass dish. The embryo's yellow brain shattered with the fall. Its white body spread inside the dish.

Balaji tried to cover his face using the paper lying on the table. That was their divorce petition. The mutual divorce petition that both had to sign. Airavati approached him with the raised hood and cold composure of a serpent queen. Behind her came the springtime of the orchard.

'Aivy ...'

'Shhhh ...' With a serpent-like hiss, she lifted her finger and bade him to remain silent. She snatched the divorce petition. Plucking the flower that grew out of his heart, dipping its stem in the blood oozing from her thigh, she signed the divorce petition in a viscous ink and in broad letters. His blue litmus sky turned red forever.

He saw the embryo of a mammalian bird—with a human torso and white feathers of a dove—rising from the broken egg in the glass dish and, spreading its tiny wings sticky with blood, fly off into the orange sky of Buddha Purnima.

www.ingramcontent.com/pod-product-compliance
Lightning Source LLC
La Vergne TN
LVHW010311070526
838199LV00065B/5523
9789395767972